DEPARTMENT
OF DEATH

Praise for *State University of Murder* by Lev Raphael

"The academic mystery is a long-standing and delightful sub-genre, and Raphael performs admirably.... Any reader who has had the misfortune to attend a SUM or the good luck to have a life enriched by teachers like Nick and Stefan who love to teach should thoroughly enjoy this return to the groves of academe."

—Yvonne Klein, *Reviewing the Evidence*

"Satirical, amusing, scalpel sharp, and relentless, this Nick Hoffman murder story will engage most academics, offend a few, and in the bargain, offers up a classic whodunit."

—Carl Brookins, *Buried Under Books*

"A finely-honed tale of vengeance and death, this is a satirical whodunit full of delicious plot twists, witticisms, criticism and abundant glimpses of bizarre academic behavior."

—Ray Walsh, *Lansing State Journal*

"Brilliantly talented – with a rapier wit and deep knowledge of literature – Lev is one of a kind."

—Hank Phillippi Ryan, *NYT* best-selling author

"Raphael's sharp takes on university politics, the distinctive characters and authenticity of the setting keep the story moving forward. Series fans will hope they won't have to wait years to see Nick again."

—*Publishers Weekly*

DEPARTMENT OF DEATH

A NICK HOFFMAN MYSTERY

• • •

Lev Raphael

Perseverance Press / John Daniel & Company

Palo Alto / McKinleyville, California | 2021

A Perseverance Press Book
Published by John Daniel & Company
A division of Daniel & Daniel, Publishers, Inc.
Post Office Box 2790
McKinleyville, California 95519
www.danielpublishing.com/perseverance

Distributed by SCB Distributors (800) 729-6423

Book design by Studio E Books, Santa Barbara, www.studio-e-books.com
Set in Melior

Cover photo: claudio.arnese / iStock

10 9 8 7 6 5 4 3 2 1

LIBRARY OF CONGRESS CATALOGING-IN-PUBLICATION DATA
Names: Raphael, Lev, author.
Title: Department of death : a Nick Hoffman mystery / by Lev Raphael.
Description: McKinleyville, California : John Daniel & Company, [2020] |
Summary: "Years ago Nick Hoffman was given a position in the English
    Department at the State University of Michigan because SUM wanted to hire his
    partner as writer-in-residence, but now he's been unexpectedly installed by his
    dean as chairman of that department. It's a wildly unpopular choice and he's
    suddenly the focus of more animosity from his colleagues than he's ever dealt
    with before. He can't seem to make anyone happy and can't get a handle on his
    myriad new responsibilities as an administrator, a position he never wanted.
    Then tragedy strikes again way too close to home: Someone seeking his help
    is murdered, and under the shadow of another recent murder, Nick is a prime
    suspect. Hounded by campus police, the local press, and social media, Nick
    wonders if this could finally be the end of his career-that is, if he manages to stay
    out of prison. In the spirit of David Lodge, Francine Prose, Richard Russo and
    Jane Smiley, Department of Death is Lev Raphael's most blistering satire yet of
    the current perversity of academic life" —Provided by publisher.
Identifiers: LCCN 2020027789 | ISBN 9781564746191 (trade paperback)
Subjects: GSAFD: Mystery fiction.
Classification: LCC PS3568.A5988 D47 2020 | DDC 813/.54--dc23
LC record available at https://lccn.loc.gov/2020027789

To the amazing Mary Chartier,
whose help with this book and others
has been absolutely invaluable

Life is, in fact, a battle. Evil is insolent and strong; beauty enchanting, but rare; goodness very apt to be weak; folly very apt to be defiant; wickedness to carry the day; imbeciles to be in great places, people of sense in small...

—Henry James

Part
One

· · ·

1.

WHEN I STARTED teaching at the State University of Michigan over twenty years ago, I had three strikes against me.

I was a bibliographer and had published a guide to everything ever written by or about Edith Wharton in all languages, a book that anyone studying or writing about Wharton could consult. But despite being indispensable, bibliographies are dismissed as grunt work by most people in the Ivory Tower because they're actually useful. Academics and the administrators who give them promotions prefer "monographs": abstruse, narrowly focused, jargon-filled books that nobody reads and that are way over-priced.

Worse than that, I enjoyed teaching basic composition, something my colleagues found suspicious and even perverse. I was also what academics call a "spousal hire." I got the job because the university wanted my partner, Stefan, who was making a name for himself as an author.

Topping that off, I was a New York Jew living in a provincial, WASP-y, middle-of-the-road town.

I guess that's more than three.

Things only deteriorated from there. A cloud of crime slowly formed and enveloped me on our bucolic Midwestern campus. I had been involved in more than my fair share of murders, which should have been none, zero, given that I'd never even been mugged growing up on Manhattan's Upper West Side. Was I jinxed? The victim of bad karma? Or some kind of death magnet like Jessica Fletcher in *Murder, She Wrote*? Whatever the cause, my very presence seemed to damage the State University of Michigan's "brand." University administrators invariably eyed me with suspicion and even hostility.

Despite all of that, I'd somehow risen from the very bottom of my department to the very top. I was now the new interim chair of the English and Creative Writing Department after a series of bizarre events that as usual involved—you guessed it—a murder. On campus, other faculty were calling my academic home DOD, Department of Death, due to its high mortality rate. I couldn't imagine what they were calling *me.*

But being the chair opened me up to a whole new set of pressures and new problems I could never have imagined dealing with. I'd only been elevated to my new position for a week that fall semester when the associate dean for summer programs in our College of Humanities suddenly appeared at my office without warning first thing Monday morning.

I'd met Dawn Lovelace only a few times, always in large informal gatherings, and every time, she made me feel acutely uncomfortable. Slim, short, pale, with a helmet of thick black hair and a heart-shaped face that made her look like a Roaring Twenties flapper, she typically wore severe dark gray suits and sensible black shoes, but her necklaces were big, extravagant, and sometimes bejeweled. Today she had on a heavy chain of thick interlocking gold and silver rings, and wore a black Chanel shoulder bag.

Her husband was director of SUM's fund-raising unit, the Office of Strategic Evolution, a fancy name for what most universities called "Development." Maybe his fund-raising work had rubbed off on her, because Lovelace herself had the air of a corporate Human Resources type whose job was firing people with maximum speed and minimal fuss. A kind of fixer who made problems—and the people who caused them—disappear. This was someone who spoke for the powers that be, never herself. So her friendliness—if you could call it that—wasn't exactly fake, but felt like something she'd acquired at a weekend workshop.

I was actually surprised that her secretary hadn't set up a

meeting over in Lovelace's own office since she was higher in rank than I was, and I had no idea why she wanted to see me anyway.

She entered briskly, trailing an expensive perfume that was a mix of roses, vanilla, and patchouli. This was something I recognized as Kilian because my cousin Sharon, an ex-model, sometimes wore it. Now, they say that if you live in Michigan long enough, you develop the "Michigan nose" because we're almost surrounded by the Great Lakes and all that water somehow messes up your sinuses and leaves you frequently congested. But the opposite had happened to me and my sense of smell had oddly become more refined.

Without mentioning my unexpected accession to the chairmanship, or even the lovely view of stately old maple trees from my windows, Lovelace shook my hand and sat down. "Nick, we need your help. We need you to step up."

And she smiled as if she had just offered me a wonderful gift.

I could feel my mouth going dry. There was something ominous in her request. Lovelace was going to ask me to do something I know I wouldn't want to do, I was sure of it.

"Nick, we need you in Sweden."

"*What?* Why?"

"The summer program that Viktor Dahlberg has been teaching. This coming June."

I knew what she meant, but didn't understand why she was recruiting me of all people. That four-week summer program was based in the old university town of Lund in southern Sweden and was very popular for a number of reasons. The area was green and beautiful, students were thrilled by how well Swedes spoke English, Lund was a madly scenic small college town made for biking and strolling, and Dahlberg's familial and personal connections to Sweden had made the program unique.

He had decided to retire, sick of the craziness in our department, and who could blame him.

"But Viktor taught *film* courses," I said. "And screenwriting. I've never done either one, and I've never taught abroad before."

Lovelace shrugged all that off. "There's nothing to it, and you could make over the program however you like. We'll give you carte blanche. You're a fan of Swedish crime fiction and you've been studying Swedish."

How did she know these things?

It was obvious to anyone paying attention that more and more surveillance cameras were appearing on buildings all across campus, but who was watching all this video—and was the university using facial recognition software? Could the rumors about a secret SUM surveillance committee be true? Was everyone's email being read, were we all being monitored while we worked?

And why was the faculty so supine and unconcerned?

I sometimes thought it might be more than just self-absorption in their teaching and research. There was something narcotic about SUM's enormous verdant campus. With a mix of over six hundred buildings dating from the late nineteenth century to a few years ago, it was a carefully curated ensemble spread across several thousand acres, linked by curving paths and crisscrossed with straight, businesslike streets as wide as avenues. In springtime lilacs, tulips, irises, daffodils, and forsythia bloomed in stunning profusion and in the late fall the cascade of harvest-colored leaves from towering maples was like theatrical snow. Entering this domain, no matter what was troubling you, could have a similar effect to crossing a quadrangle of a venerable European college adorned with stained glass, spires, and gargoyles. The campus had a particular kind of beauty and gravitas that perhaps inspired inertia. Why fight anything? Why not just enjoy academic privileges and pleasures?

How else could you explain the fact that none of us had challenged the provost, Merry Glinka, about the mounting assaults on our privacy? When pressed by stubborn reporters, she had only said, "If you've got nothing to hide, then you've got nothing to fear. And I would urge everyone in our university community that if you see something, say something."

See what? Say what? And to whom? What were we supposed

to be on guard against? What was the crisis? Were agents of a rival university scheming to destroy us?

My administrative assistant, Celine Robichaux, had told me that the surveillance committee was supposedly empowered to have faculty, staff, or students arrested if they posed any kind of threat to anyone on campus—and was in direct contact with the Department of Homeland Security in Washington.

But who determined what constituted a threat? What were the criteria? And why was it apparently called the Committee of Public Safety when the French namesake was responsible for the execution of thousands of people during the Reign of Terror?

"Nick," Lovelace said, snapping her fingers to get my attention, "you're the ideal candidate to take over for Viktor."

I didn't believe her. "Who else have you asked?"

She smiled and examined her beautifully manicured nails, holding her left hand flat in the palm of her right, then the reverse.

Not answering told me that she'd put the squeeze on other possible candidates already and been rebuffed. That made sense, since not everyone liked teaching abroad. The stipend wasn't that great if you took a spouse or family along, students could easily go rogue in a country where the legal drinking age was lower than it was in Michigan, and most professors treasured their long summer vacations away from the classroom even if they weren't writing or researching a book.

"It's an important program," she murmured. "A *successful* program."

In a time of collapsing enrollments for the Humanities, Viktor had foresight. He'd wisely designed his program as two weeks shorter than most of SUM's other summer programs based in Europe. Even with the high cost of living in Sweden, the program was more affordable because of the shorter length and because there was just one professor running it: himself. The traditional six-week programs taught by two professors were on their way out, despite efforts by floundering and short-sighted department chairs to keep them alive.

"But Dawn, I've *just* been made interim chair. I need time to settle in. And I'm not prepared to teach abroad next summer. There's not enough time for me to get ready. And I have to be on campus in the summer to work on the budget." I didn't know a lot about my duties as department chair yet, but I knew that much.

More than that, redesigning Viktor's program to fit my teaching interests and giving up a huge chunk of my summer vacation wasn't remotely appealing. Sure, I wanted to go to Sweden someday, but only after I felt comfortable speaking the language, which I enjoyed studying, and then only on my own timetable. I'm not gifted with languages like Mayor Pete of South Bend who taught himself Norwegian just to be able to read his favorite author in his native tongue.

"Nick, you're the one we need." Lovelace's steely blue eyes fixed me as if she wanted to put me into a trance. There was something unnerving behind her single-minded determination.

She clearly would not negotiate. Despite her surface charm, this was a *summons* from the College of Humanities, the Summer Abroad Office, and who knows, maybe even SUM's provost and president, too. Summer programs were very profitable for the university and burnished the image of SUM as a global institution. Students loved them, typically saying they were the best part of their college years.

But the programs were a lot of work for faculty, and even taking over a program that was already established would demand preparation, organizing, time spent recruiting students and holding informational meetings. I'd never been tempted before, and I certainly wasn't now, given that I had barely begun to grasp what my new position entailed.

"I really think I need to understand being department chair before taking on something that big," I said.

"You need to demonstrate flexibility and support," Lovelace brought out tersely.

"Whom am I supporting?"

"Students, first of all. Then your colleagues, your peers."

I'd never liked that word "peers" because when I first encountered it in elementary school, it was associated with the House of Lords and afterwards I always absurdly thought of eighteenth-century powdered wigs and snuffboxes. It was a kind of brain glitch.

"You're worried about enrollments," I said. A successful summer program generated buzz and made people take more classes in the department and college that housed it. If nobody offered the Swedish program, that could have a small ripple effect.

"Isn't everybody?"

Well, no. SUM was marketing itself heavily and successfully in India, charging those students three times what in-state students paid. The Indian students clustered in engineering, business, pre-med, and mathematics. Because they spoke and read English fluently, some of them might take a course or two in the humanities beyond required ones, but not many. That was never their mission.

These foreign students weren't just good for the university's general fund. They were having a huge impact on the economy in Michiganapolis. They were big spenders when it came to cars, clothes, restaurants, and real estate. Their advent had led to a construction boom, with high-rent apartment buildings with ludicrous names like Mountain Top sprouting up all over town.

"You're asking a lot," I said.

"Not really. Loyalty shouldn't be difficult."

I think that was supposed to sting, but it didn't.

Lovelace rose and surveyed my large office. Our new three-story building, Shattenkirk Hall, was white and sterile inside and out, like the grim 1960s headquarters of a small pharmaceutical company. One of the few buildings on campus that seemed out of place, it was the gift of an alumnus who'd won the Nobel Prize and had some very clear ideas about architecture. The Board of Trustees had happily taken his bequest and allowed his vision to blossom. It gave me the creeps. To counter the coldness, I'd had the walls of my office painted apricot, changed the metal blinds to cherrywood, laid down a black-and-orange kilim rug, and hung striking Matisse prints on the walls. It was an oasis of color.

"You know, Nick, you really have to move to the chair's office ASAP."

I bristled. "What's wrong with staying here?"

The whole department had been moved from another building over the previous summer and I was not interested in repeating the process so soon, even if the chair's office was just down the hall from mine. And maybe I was a little superstitious, too. Moving into the office of someone who had been murdered seemed like the opening scene of a horror movie. I assumed it had been cleared of all his personal effects, but what if something had been overlooked? That would be eerie. I had access to all his digital files—wasn't that enough?

"I like this office," I said.

Lovelace cocked her head at me as if I were a student who'd just said something utterly naïve and uninformed in her class. Then she leaned forward and spoke very slowly. "If you don't move, it sends absolutely the wrong message. It undermines administrative order. It also says you're not wholly committed to being chair."

"But I'm fine where I am." As the French say, *j'y suis, j'y reste*. I'm here, I'm staying here.

She shook her head. "You don't get to make those decisions. If you stay in this office, you set a bad example and you cast a shadow over SUM. The optics are all wrong."

So there it was, the lifeblood of every university administration: fear of bad publicity.

I wanted to tell her that not moving to the official office of the department chair could hardly create public controversy, but given SUM's low standing at the moment as a den of criminality, I might be wrong.

"What about 'People Power'?" I asked, quoting the university's new slogan.

"Don't be an idiot," Lovelace said, and left as if she'd been

insulted that anyone could possibly take "People Power" seriously—or think that *she* did.

What right did Lovelace have to lecture me about my choice of
office? She was only in charge of summer programs in the College
of Humanities. I didn't report to her. And if she wanted to get me
signed on to teaching in Sweden, lecturing me about my responsibilities didn't seem like a smart approach. Unless there was some
perverse strategy behind all this that I couldn't quite work out.

Were they trying to push me out of the way for some reason?
Isolate me far from campus for the summer? What would be the
point?

• • •

I had never even imagined being an administrator, and if the head
that wears the crown lies uneasy, well, I was miserable and felt
stuck wearing a dunce cap. When I had received the dean's text,
just a week before, about my sudden appointment as interim chair
after two murders in my department, I was stunned.

But why me?

Dean Magnus Bullerschmidt had summoned me to his palatial
office, in the heart of a suite of offices, where he presided behind a
mammoth gold-and-white marble desk like a Byzantine emperor:
fat, disdainful, paranoid.

His expensive suits and extra-long ties were always perfect,
but I bet he would have been happier in gem-encrusted brocade
robes. The story on campus was that he craved being the provost,
but had always been rebuffed because his hunger was too naked
and voracious, so he would never rise above his current rank. That
could account for the brutality he usually treated people with, and
the air of smoldering resentment. Miserable himself, he wanted
everyone around him to suffer.

Stefan, the department's writer-in-residence, thought that he
had "crazy eyes."

Years before, Bullerschmidt had always intimidated me, but
now I was in a very different place. I'd been a tenured full professor for long enough and was in charge of a writers' fellowship

set up by a former student of mine that was actually named after *me*. I even had Celine to help with the workload. And I needed the help, not just with the logistics, but fielding applications from surprisingly egocentric authors like the best-selling novelist Mara Milano who said that she would be happy to brighten our "sleepy little campus." I guess she hadn't bothered to Google SUM and discover that it had sixty thousand students.

The way she phrased her offer didn't surprise me since she was an author I considered one of the New Egomaniacs. She posted everything on Instagram from her manicures and pedicures, dog walks and morning smoothies to plumbing problems and flower arrangements at her drop-dead-gorgeous vacation villa in Dalmatia. She was a good enough writer, but her personal connections had surely boosted her career. Her first husband was a *New York Times* editor, her second a Broadway director, her third a night-time talk show host who loved having her on his show because she was "so much fun."

Exposure to arrogance like hers had toughened me.

So I sat opposite the large, imposing man aware that I wasn't quite so powerless anymore. And before we were even done with small talk about the weather, I blurted, "I don't understand why you want me to be interim chair."

He smiled, but his heavy-lidded eyes looked as cold as always. "It's very simple. You're the right person at the right time."

"I just don't see it."

He let out a mirthless chuckle. "That's because you don't have the big picture. SUM has suffered from outrageous attacks in the media, and you can be a good advocate for us."

That made no sense whatsoever, since I'd been at the center of controversy, unless he thought I could somehow reverse SUM's death spiral of bad PR because I demonstrated diversity on campus. "You want me to give *interviews*?"

Whatever bonhomie there was in the room quickly vanished, and Bullerschmidt practically barked at me: "No! Just keep your head down."

His advice seemed contradictory, so I asked, "How will that make up for all the murders on campus?"

Bullerschmidt gave me what I think he believed was a wise and fatherly look. "Leave that to us."

"Why not pick someone with administrative experience?"

"You've been here a long time, you understand the department, the college, the university. You also have an excellent administrative assistant who knows SUM inside out. And your work is...accessible."

I couldn't disagree with that last assessment, but I still wasn't convinced. None of this made any sense as reasons to appoint me, though I was tempted by the offer, which he sweetened by saying that instead of teaching just one course second semester as department chairs typically did instead of the regular two, I would be excused from all teaching duties while serving as chair unless I wanted to offer a student independent study, or had a course I was eager to teach. Time off is always precious.

"I already have adjuncts lined up to take over your fall courses," he said, "and the semester's only a few weeks old so the transition wouldn't be too awkward."

I hadn't yet bonded with the students in either of my classes (that often took a full month), and the promise of so much freedom—or time out of the classroom—was seductive, especially since Stefan was on sabbatical and maybe we could have more time together. Another incentive: last year I'd had a number of difficult students, like one who had complained that I should grade her papers higher because her mother helped her write them and her mother was a high school English teacher.

But the break from teaching and more time with Stefan wasn't the only lure. As a spousal hire, I had lived my life at SUM in Stefan's shadow, since he was more successful and obviously better known than I was, even before he wrote his best-selling memoir. I confess that the boost in status appealed to me.

More than that, however, as interim chair for just a year or two—depending on how long it actually took to conduct a national search for a permanent chair—there was a chance, however small, that I could alter the vicious, back-biting culture of my department. Or at least soften it. In Jewish mysticism, there's an idea called *tikkun olam*, which means "healing the world." Wasn't the department my world, for better or worse, so why not try?

And maybe I thought it would help heal *me*, compensate for all the years of disrespect, harassment, and prejudice—and more than that, somehow make up for my having been the target of a psychotic stalker the previous spring semester.

Big mistake.

2.

MY ASSISTANT, Celine, and I had been through enough crises together that we would have become romantically involved if we were in a movie, no matter how improbable that was in real life. Efficient, calm, well-informed, she was my anchor on campus, and sharing a Google calendar with her was especially helpful now that I was interim chair. I trusted her and trusted her judgment. So after Lovelace left, I walked through to Celine's office to ask if she thought I should move mine.

Celine shrugged. "You have an office. You're the chair. That makes it the chair's office by default, right?"

"I like the way you think."

She smiled. "They can't *make* you move."

"Good! One less thing to worry about," I said.

"I've ordered you better furniture, though, from University Purchasing. Nothing too flashy, but it's a definite upgrade."

"Thanks!"

"If you're not here when it comes, can I empty out your desk for you and transfer things over?"

"Absolutely. By the way, Lovelace didn't ask you if I was busy when she showed up, did she?"

She sighed. "No, she sailed past me like I didn't exist." She shook her head. "Do you want some tea, Nick? I just made Constant Comment."

"I know, I could smell it in my office."

"And I could smell that Lovelace woman's mendacity."

I grinned at the reference to *Cat on a Hot Tin Roof*. Celine and I shared a reverence for Tennessee Williams.

I took a mug of tea from her and I sat in the chair facing her desk, waiting eagerly to hear more because she seemed to know gossip about everyone. Perhaps people confided in her since she was so receptive and unflappable. Celine was looking very Sixties today, dressed all in purple, her newish afro crowning her round warm face.

"Nobody trusts Lovelace in her own unit," she told me. "They say she's a liar and a sociopath. She treats staff like crap and they're about ready to chip in for a hit man." She rolled her eyes, apologized silently for the reference to murder.

"How come she's still there?" Troublesome administrators weren't fired at SUM, they were moved to a position where they could do less obvious damage. It was a tactic meant to suppress any hint of scandal and avoid lawsuits.

"She's still there, Nick, because people are afraid to complain—they think she'll screw them over. You know what this university is like."

I did. It was in many ways venal, corrupt, and too often inhumane. But I stayed because I loved teaching, I loved Michigan, and after two decades here, I think I had lost the ability to imagine myself living anywhere else. Stefan and I took great vacations, from Santa Fe to Aix-en-Provence, but I never felt about any other city or town that "*This* is where I have to be."

"You heard her pitch about Sweden?" I asked.

Celine frowned. "Don't go. Viktor Dahlberg's been a workaholic since his wife died. He needed to drive himself like that. That's not your speed. I know how you're into Sweden and all, but running the whole show yourself, you'll never get enough rest."

Celine really did know me well. And like her, I had maintenance insomnia—I'd have no problem zonking out at night for a few hours, but then I'd wake up and have trouble falling back asleep. We had both tried a range of solutions from melatonin to cognitive therapy for insomnia, but the truth was that we had survived nearly being murdered last year in a campus blood bath, then there'd been two recent murders, and now our lives had totally shifted off center. Who knew how long that would last? Maybe we would never find that illusive cultural obsession of "closure."

"Just a reminder, Nick, you have a ten o'clock meeting with Ciska Balanchine."

I was already spending much of my time now in department meetings or meeting with faculty members individually. Luckily I wasn't working on a book or I'd be feeling stifled by my hectic schedule. "Thanks! Send her right in when she gets here."

I took the tea back into my office and waited at my desk. The associate chair for undergraduate studies was coming to fill me in on departmental efforts to recruit more English majors because the department had been hemorrhaging students for ten years, like many others across the country. We had fewer than five hundred, which was half what it had been only a decade ago, and our graduate program was on life support. None of the faculty wanted to be associate chair for graduate studies—it would have been like being a tourist guide at the ruined Chernobyl nuclear plant. I would have to appoint someone, and I was holding off strategizing whom to pick because I wouldn't have wanted the job myself.

I wasn't personally concerned about the decline of the graduate program, though, because given how few jobs were available in our profession, it struck me as dishonest and even cruel to groom doctoral students for life as an adjunct. But I kept my qualms to myself.

Now, Ciska wasn't like other faculty members because she lived in my neighborhood and had been to our house, and so our collegiality wasn't quite as superficial. Somewhere in her thirties, Ciska had the grace, bearing, height, and looks of a fashion model. She had curly black hair and luminous dark eyes that revealed as little as the eyes of one of those long-necked women in a Modigliani portrait. Her ancestry was both Dutch and Russian which might account for how exotic she seemed. To me, anyway. British expressions popped up now and then in her speech since she had lived in England for a while.

"Hello, Nick," she said, striding in, wearing a black linen pants suit and a pearl choker. She had a joint appointment in Women's Studies and we had occasionally chatted about my specialty, Edith Wharton. I knew Ciska somewhat better than other faculty members might, because she had told me about being assaulted by our former chair. But I sometimes wondered if she had drawn further back precisely because I knew something so intimate about her that she regretted having revealed to me.

And now that I was the interim chair, I felt her self-sufficient remoteness pitched at an even higher level, as if she had to always be on guard against me in my new role. All the same, I was feeling aloofness and suspicion from many of the faculty because they obviously resented my sudden and unexpected accession to power. And at times like this even I wondered how I had gone over to the Dark Side.

Ciska nodded as if listening to some offstage cue, sat, and opened a blue three-ring binder on her lap. "May I share what I've learned so far in assessing our efforts to grow the department?"

"Of course!" I smiled, but she didn't return it.

"Well, for two years now there's been a new mission statement on the department website to the effect that English majors qualify for the best jobs because of their skills in research, analyzing a text, and naturally their ability to write well and present their ideas."

I vaguely remembered the topic being raised at a departmental meeting some time ago, but couldn't remember who was in charge of drafting the updated statement, which was filled with buzz words to please the dean, I suppose. I had tried reading it sober but needed a shot of vodka to wade through the swamp of PR-speak and academese.

"Is it true? About the jobs?"

She looked at me blankly as if I'd asked a question in a foreign language that she knew, but was taking time to shift into. "Well, yes and no. But in any case, it hasn't helped us. We still keep losing majors every year, and five years ago we wouldn't let classes run with fewer than fifteen students. Now we're lucky if a class gets as many as ten."

The previous chair had wanted to drop Jewish-American Literature for consistently low enrollments, but that wasn't going to happen under my watch because the problem was now department-wide. Good news/bad news. It was one of my favorite courses to teach and typically brought in a very diverse group of students. Maybe next fall...

"We also have a well-catered Open House twice a year and invite students from across the College of Humanities. Students show up and even leave their emails on a contact sheet, but almost nobody selects us for their major. Our Facebook page and Twitter account are updated on a regular basis by someone hired just to handle our social media presence."

"And I assume there's no impact there, either?"

"None. Or, minimal."

"Which courses are doing well?"

She didn't have to consult her binder. "Creative Writing, Film Studies, and courses co-listed with Women's Studies. Oh, and anything offered as a summer abroad program."

The last one made me wince. "So what's the answer? *Is* there a solution?"

She leafed through her information and sighed. "We're like many university English departments because the faculty likes to teach cultural studies more than literary history. And that's basically how the curriculum is organized now."

I thought then of what the critic Harold Bloom had written in *The Western Canon*:

What are now called "Departments of English" will be renamed departments of "Cultural Studies," where Batman comics, Mormon theme parks, television, movies and rock will replace Chaucer, Shakespeare, Milton, Wordsworth and Wallace Stevens. Major, once-elitist universities and colleges will still offer a few courses in Shakespeare, Milton and their peers, but these will be

taught by departments of three or four scholars, equivalent to teachers of ancient Greek and Latin.

When I was an English major, before colleges and universities
had started talking about students as "customers" and professors
as "content providers," literary studies meant meat-and-potatoes
survey courses like The Modern American Novel or British Poetry
from Chaucer to Byron. They gave students a foundation and a
context for everything else they studied as English majors. You
could argue that multi-disciplinary cultural studies courses did
the same thing from a different angle, teaching students through
a lens of race, gender, class, and sexuality. It was trendy at the
moment, but sometimes I felt it was turning us into a sociology
department.

I asked Ciska, "What about DH?" The previous chair had
somehow gotten the dean to give us two new positions in Digital Humanities, which was a newish field in which scholars
across disciplines worked in what they called "the intersection
of humanities and computing." It was hot because there was grant
money available and people were desperate for anything new that
might attract students. The two positions in our department had
been filled by young, argumentative, German-born, identical twins
who quarreled about everything, including sharing an office, and
that would be comical if they hadn't come to blows at a departmental retreat. They had just been hired but I think most faculty
already wished they were gone.

"It's too soon to tell about DH," Ciska said glumly. "But I don't
see how anything can rescue us from the hit we took when the
dean pushed for a separate Professional Writing department a few
years ago and got it approved." Now her eyes narrowed and she
held the edges of the binder as tightly as if she was thinking of
tearing it apart or flinging it at someone. I hoped that wasn't me. "If
Bullerschmidt had just let us create Professional Writing courses
in the department, we wouldn't be in such bad shape." Her nostrils
actually flared at the chance we had lost. "I was ready!"

At the time, I hadn't understood why courses that taught writing skills to prepare people for careers in editing, publishing and beyond weren't housed in our department. With a degree in Professional Writing you could be a corporate communications specialist or find writing or editing jobs in government, technology, media, medicine—almost anywhere, in fact. Very much like the opportunities English majors might snag, but it had a sexier title, I suppose, and seemed to guarantee employment. Or so they said.

"That department is a parasite," she said, rhythmically smacking her right fist now into her left palm. "It's killing us. What the dean did to us is bloody unforgivable." Her eyes were wider now and seemed focused on some scene of carnage or revenge. I had looked up her unusual first name once and it was supposedly connected to the kind of axe used by the medieval Franks. Right now she looked like she could happily wield one. "He is such an evil *bastard*."

I had no argument with her on that score, but stoking Ciska's anger wasn't a good idea. I didn't know how to cool things down, though, so I pretended to check my Apple watch and said, "I'm sorry, but I have a meeting with the financial officer to prepare for. How about we have a departmental meeting to address recruiting more students?" Someone had to have fresh ideas.

She slammed her binder shut and rose with a sneer. "We're just dogs circling our tails. Meetings are rubbish. But you should read this—it has the history of our enrollments, curriculum changes, and marketing efforts over the past thirty years. A history of decline. At least you'll be fully informed." She dropped it onto my desk as if she were tossing love letters from an ex into a bonfire.

"I also have news about the Justice League," she said. That was a loosely organized group of white male students campaigning against white male privilege who had disrupted at least one class where Toni Morrison was being taught. Their complaint? A white professor shouldn't be assigning and discussing a book by a Black author. It was as ludicrous a charge as the name they'd chosen for themselves—they were anything but superheroes. "They've disbanded."

"That's a relief. Is there anything else?" I asked.

"Well, since we're meeting, I have an idea for a course called Reading in the Digital Age."

"Which would be—?"

She looked more animated suddenly. "Well, we want to make sure that students get their money's worth from their tuition but don't feel burdened by excessive textuality, right? The printed text is not always user-friendly, and so many of our students complain about their reading lists. Since they spend so much time online they'd be less resistant to digital texts."

"But can't they be more easily distracted that way?"

She ignored my question. "Digital reading puts readers in control and defies the patriarchy. And what's even better, students wouldn't have to be writing papers—they'd only do oral reports because writing is so hegemonistic."

"But what about the department mission statement? The one that says that English majors can get great jobs? Doesn't it say one reason is that they can write well?"

Ciska leaned forward. "Nick, the sky's the limit with a course like this," she gushed. "Think what we could do with analyzing narratives on Twitter!"

She seemed passionate about her idea, but it gave me the willies. I should have taken a wait-and-see attitude, but I was not feeling positive enough to hold back how I really felt. "Well, Ciska, from the studies I've seen, digital reading doesn't encourage critical thinking the way working with a printed text does. You can present a proposal to the curriculum committee, but I can't support something that undermines the mission of the department."

"Which means it won't fly if you block it."

"I guess not. What's an English department that de-emphasizes print books and writing?"

"You have no imagination!" Scowling, she marched into Celine's office and back out into the sterile hallway. Great. I had just pissed off my associate chair. That was not the swiftest move.

Celine appeared in my doorway, eyebrows raised.

I said, "I've never seen her this angry before. At the dean, and me."

Celine didn't seem surprised. "She's right, you know."

"Not about digital reading, I hope. About Professional Writing, or meetings?"

"Yes, the last two things. And right that trying to save the department with advertising or whatever else you come up with is like trying to stop climate change by buying an electric car. Too little, too late."

"So it's hopeless?"

"Most likely."

"And I'm the commander of a battleship that's just been torpedoed below the water line and won't get rescued?"

"Sounds about right."

Great. I had a year, maybe two, of gloom and doom to face as interim chair. Once again I found myself wishing that I had never said yes to the dean, and I wondered if he'd picked me because I had no feel for administration whatsoever and he wanted me to fail. He assumed I would make some terrible mistake that would disgrace me and get me axed—or force me to quit in humiliation. But then wouldn't *anyone* fail in this job?

Perhaps Bullerschmidt just needed a figurehead to preside over the department's demise and didn't really care who it was. There had been rumors for some time that we might be folded into Communications or merged with Journalism if we kept losing majors at this rate. But what was a university without an independent English department?

I spent the next hour on email and it left me dizzy. My meeting afterward with the department's financial officer promised to be more confusing still, partly because Aldo Kennedy didn't remotely look the part.

In his mid-twenties, Aldo was a walking hipster cliché: he had a dense auburn beard and mustache, wavy hair pulled into a man bun, and invariably wore beat-up Converse sneakers, super-skinny jeans or leggings, and flannel shirts. His neck was tattooed with a multi-colored garland of roses and I'd seen him in town at a coffee shop ostentatiously using a portable manual typewriter. He was barefoot then, with no shoes or sandals in sight. Sometimes he wore a black porkpie hat tipped back from his forehead. There were more and more guys around Michiganapolis who could have been his twin: the price of not conforming to the majority seemed to be nothing more than a different kind of conformity. On campus, Aldo's feet were covered, or at least he wasn't barefoot in our building, and at our meeting he was wearing checkerboard-patterned Vans. No socks, of course.

But truth be told, in middle age I envied his freedom and his youth.

He also had perfect teeth and I saw almost all of them in his wide grin when he shook my hand and sat down opposite me. I'd dealt with him briefly before when applying to be reimbursed for conference travel, but this felt very different.

"Where do we begin?" I asked.

He nodded as if he knew that was going to be my question. "What are your priorities?"

"My—?"

"Priorities. What's your vision for the department while you're interim chair and what do you want to accomplish?"

I felt my face turning red. "What am I *supposed* to do?"

He nodded again, but this time it was as if he was responding to an inner voice that likely said I was an idiot.

He launched into a fast-paced explanation, laying out all my responsibilities with as much care as a caterer insuring the buffet table was attractive and tempting. If there were going to be open positions, he explained, I'd have to decide exactly what the department needed and what I was looking for and write the job description to make sure it fit. A major task would be RPT at the end of fall semester. That stood for retention, promotion and tenure—and meant faculty evaluations at the end of the year and monitoring new hires to see how they were performing. I would be getting recommendations from the Salary Committee, with scores based on every faculty member's dossier. I'd review them for any inconsistencies, meet with the committee to establish a consensus, and then write letters that would go to the dean and then the provost.

"The process usually takes a few weeks," Aldo said. "You can't rush it."

I believed him.

"There should be a file of previous letters you can use as models." He pointed at some red-and-white Office Depot printer-paper boxes in a corner that Celine had brought in earlier in the day while I was on the phone. "You'll probably find them in there."

But there was more. Aldo said that I would need to meet with new faculty members, explain what the expectations would be for their three-year probationary period (basically publish a book). Then there was overseeing the budget, which was actually several budgets: grant accounts, general funds, and the travel budget. He went on for a good twenty minutes, adding more and more tasks and explaining the available resources. He clearly loved this.

But if my head had been spinning any faster it would have twisted right off my neck. I finally said, "Whoa! I can't absorb anything more."

Aldo leaned back sympathetically. "At the end of the day, a lot depends on your leadership style. How often do you want us to meet? How much responsibility do you want me to have?"

"What did the last chair say about that?"

Aldo shrugged. "He wasn't here long enough, but he was willing to give me a free hand. Ditto the previous chair."

"That sounds great to me." I realized then that I didn't know much about him beyond the surface, so I had to ask, "How'd you get into your career?"

"You mean because I don't look the part?" He smiled. "I was good at every kind of math from grade school on and by high school I was managing my mom's real estate business and handling the books for her. I loved the work. It's what I was born to do." He smiled again and it put me at ease. "Numbers turn me on."

"Wow."

"Can I call you Nick?" He fixed me with his luminous hipster eyes. "Nick, I'm here to help you any way I can, but whatever you let me take charge of, you're still going to have to make some decisions on your own that will piss people off. Being chair doesn't make you friends, it makes you enemies. And if unpopular directives come down from the dean or the provost, you have to implement them no matter what the collateral damage is."

Great. That was just what I needed: to be even more unpopular with my colleagues.

My face must have given me away, because he said sympathetically, "I know how sharp Celine is, and I can set up a meeting with her to start sorting things out for you, if you'd like."

"Please!"

"Then you and I can meet again afterward and really get started. You'll need some time to get used to how things work and what you need to do, but don't worry, you'll adjust, and Celine and I can keep things going until—" He shrugged, but I didn't need him to come up with a metaphor to describe my very steep learning curve.

"That would be great. Thanks."

As he left, I wondered if it was a mistake to admit my incompetence, but then would he have been fooled if I'd pretended to understand everything he threw at me? And why bother when he was so friendly? God, being chair was screwing with my head already.

Celine appeared in the doorway between our two offices, with the calm face of someone used to crisis intervention. "Aldo is terrific and one of the smartest guys at SUM. A good, sweet man to have on your side. But if being chair gets to be too much, or you hate it, you do know that you can always resign."

"I'd be ashamed to step down."

She nodded. "I get that. I think I would, too."

3.

OUR NEW MEDIEVALIST popped in and said, "Can I have a quick word?"

"Uh...sure." Roberto Robustelli was the last person I wanted to be talking to. He was on administrative leave while awaiting trial for murder, a situation that made everyone in the department nervous. We all wished he would stay off campus, but there was no way to bar him from the building or from his office. I think the university was afraid that he would sue if he felt mistreated in any way, which would generate even more bad publicity, so we all tried to pretend that nothing had happened and not make him feel stigmatized or demeaned. After all, he was out on bail because he wasn't considered a flight risk.

His arrest had ended a bizarre turn of events. The author of *Chaucer for Dummies*, Robustelli was a steal from Columbia University and SUM thought it was getting a rising star. Ebullient and in his mid-thirties, he dressed like a preppy and cursed like a rapper. He had a male model's cheekbones and jawline along with cinematically dark wavy hair and coal black eyebrows—but he didn't have the height. Today he wore less than usual of that spicy Lagerfeld cologne that was his signature.

"Nicky, I just wanted to tell you to ignore the motherfuckers who think you should never have been picked for chair. I mean what the fuck do they know about anything? I think you're going to do a great job. Your head isn't stuck up your ass like everyone else in this shithole department."

Nobody called me Nicky but I was not in the mood to correct him, because he scared me, so I just said, "Thanks." Why was he being nice?

He grinned, gave me two thumbs up, and left. Robustelli was the last person I would have expected to show up and cheer me on, but he was full of surprises. I guess everyone is. He had seemed too self-obsessed to be a murderer, but under the right circumstances, I guess anyone could be.

Celine leaned in, shook her head, and then went back to work.

After sorting through way more emails than I'd ever dealt with before, I arranged to meet Stefan in town for dinner at our favorite steakhouse, Chuck's, which was fairly new and had a Sixties Rat Pack vibe: red leather booths, dark paneling, and cool jazz playing seductively low on the sound system. There was seating for just about thirty people.

Stefan had been working at home all day on a new novel, so he was just as glad as I was to eat out somewhere familiar and reliable. We'd never had a bad steak there yet; he always ordered the ribeye and I ordered filet mignon. Both of us liked them prepared medium rare, both of us preferred potato croquettes to any kind of mashed or smashed potatoes, and we were happy with any seasonal vegetable. Reading the menu was just an idle exercise.

"Tough day?" he asked, as the shy server filled our water goblets and left us a basket of fresh-baked parmesan-cheese bread and a dish of olive oil. After telling us our waiter would be right out, he was gone.

Closing in on fifty, Stefan looked more and more like a Jewish version of Harrison Ford every year, though his new routine and trainer at our health club had helped him beef up considerably, so he carried himself like a wrestler now. I had bought a gun after last spring's assault; he had one, too, but had opted for making himself stronger and more imposing.

Stefan had warned me not to take the interim chairmanship, but promised that he would not say "I told you so" when I com-

plained about the workload or anything else. He listened sympathetically now as I took him through my meetings that morning.

"Celine is great," he said, "but will she be overworked
as department secretary on top of being your assistant for the
fellowship?"

"Well, she got a raise, and she thinks she can manage."

The old department secretary, who could have been Kathy
Bates's psycho sister in *Misery*, had taken a job elsewhere in the
university because she found ours "concerning." That seemed like
a gross understatement given that there had been two murders on
her watch, but it didn't matter. She was gone.

"Dr. Hoffman!" I looked up to see that our waiter was Peter
DeVries, an English major who was currently working with me on a
Henry James independent study. Before I could ask, he explained,
"I started here last week." From wealthy Bloomfield Hills near
Detroit, he was tall and as trim as a runner or cyclist, with vivid
blue eyes, a red-blond goatee, and masses of wavy blond hair. The
restaurant's uniform of black skinny jeans and black polo shirt
helped give him the air of an urban poet.

I was about to introduce him to Stefan when he said, "You're
Professor Borowski. I enjoyed your memoir. The prose was...
luscious." He laughed at his own word choice, but while Stefan
beamed I noticed a shadow flicker across Peter's face. He stood up
taller and said, "Can I tell you about the specials tonight?"

"That's okay," I said. "We know what we'd like."

He took our orders for the steaks and a bottle of Gigondas and
when he left Stefan said, "Nice kid."

"Very. And he's a good writer, thoughtful. He's exploring
James's stories about artists and writers. You remember I told you
about him." I was partial to all of James's short stories about writers because I lived with one.

"Those are good stories," Stefan said.

"That kid is a Henry James freak, a hard-core Jacobite. Didn't
you notice his tattoo?"

Stefan shook his head. "I missed it."

"On the inside of his right arm: 'Live all you can: it's a mistake not to.'"

"That's from *The Wings of the Dove*?" Stefan asked.

"No, *The Ambassadors*."

"The one set in France?"

I nodded. The line was part of famous advice from an aging man in *The Ambassadors* who had never done what he was recommending. I gave Stefan the whole quote: "Live all you can; it's a mistake not to. It doesn't matter what you do in particular, so long as you have had your life. If you haven't had that, what have you had?"

"Wow." Then he lowered his voice and asked, "Nobody's ever called my work luscious. Is he gay?"

"I don't know and it's none of my business if he is."

"Of course not."

"So tell me how the new book is going," I said. But before he could answer, someone headed for our table. He was a swarthy, dark-eyed thirty-ish man who looked like a black-suited bodyguard you'd see on TV following a politician, putting his index and middle fingers on his earpiece as he reported their movements. Tall, bald, muscular, he radiated quiet ferocity that his smile and jaunty "Hey!" to Stefan didn't soften.

Stefan introduced him to me as Boris Hernandez, and I recognized the name.

"You're in the dean's office," I said.

He nodded. "Guilty as charged." It was a joke, I guess.

Stefan and Boris exchanged some vague pleasantries and when he nodded at me and left, Stefan said, "I run into him a lot at the gym. He looks like a bruiser but he's pretty cool."

I had a brief flash of jealousy I suppressed because it was ridiculous, and asked Stefan about his book again.

Stefan filled me in on a subtle plot twist he was trying to work into his novel, and then Peter was back with our wine. He uncorked it expertly, let me sample the bottle even though it wasn't strictly necessary, and then deftly poured us each a glass.

We had ordered this Famille Perrin wine before because it was a classic Gigondas: powerful, elegant, and a little peppery.

Peter said, "I hope the meal will meet your expectations tonight," but now I sensed something darker in his mood. He'd been in my Edith Wharton seminar a year ago and also did an independent study on Sinclair Lewis, one of America's great neglected authors. I felt lucky Peter wanted to work with me since he was so much more dedicated than most students. Quiet, intense, he took feedback on his papers especially well, and used it.

Peter and I had already met once for his new independent study, and I continued to find him hardworking and perceptive. As we ate our terrific steaks that evening, I observed Peter serving other people and also when he returned to our table, trying to be discreet about it. He was clearly troubled by something, and trying his best to hide it behind his waiter's conviviality.

"I feel it, too," Stefan said quietly after we ordered dessert.

That startled me.

"I've been watching him just like you have," Stefan explained. "And I think your student is definitely in some kind of trouble."

Peter thanked us for the generous tip when we were leaving. But when I said, "See you tomorrow" because we were having a meeting to talk about a famous James story, he actually looked alarmed.

On the way out, we ran into the head of Film Studies, Carson Karageorgevich, heading in for dinner. He was a tall bearlike man who favored boxy suits and was supposedly in line to the Serbian throne if the monarchy was ever restored there, which seemed unlikely. But the connection—genuine or not—gave him a kind of crazy charm.

He stopped me and said, "I hope you remember what we talked about at the department retreat a few weeks ago?" He had urged me to invite the author of *The Danish Girl* to campus for my fellowship, hoping to teach the movie and improve his chances for promotion, but he needed a book for that, not a celebrity visit. And I didn't need to invite anyone, given that well-known authors were eager to apply. It paid well, $25,000 for a month of workshops and readings.

I nodded, wished him a good meal, and broke away. Now that I was chair, I was sure I'd be getting more requests of all kinds, and I was not looking forward to any of it. On the drive home, Stefan said, "He always reminds me of Lon Chaney, Jr. in *The Wolf Man*."

"I know, right? It's those big tragic eyes and that stare."

• • •

Peter was at my office Tuesday morning at 10:00 for his independent study, and the first thing he said to me was, "I need to close your door." Before I could ask why, he explained, "I don't want anyone else listening."

That was clearly not connected to the discussion we were supposed to be having on the elegiac story "The Middle Years." It was about a dying novelist who has felt unappreciated and longs to have a second chance to do more, to write as well as he believes he can.

"What I tell you has to stay confidential," Peter said.

I'm sure Stefan was used to moments like this because he taught creative writing which tended to be more personal and intense, and he got to know some of his students well. I'd had faculty members confide in me for various reasons—before I was the chairman, of course—but my students rarely shared anything heavy. That's what I assumed Peter wanted to do.

And I assumed that's why he was dressed as if he were applying for an internship. While Peter always looked neat, today he was much dressier in a white button-down shirt, steel gray cashmere cardigan, dark jeans, and dark gray Ferragamo loafers. I recognized them because Stefan had a similar pair, which he bought after his memoir became a best-seller, and I knew they cost close to six hundred dollars. Peter's parents were corporate lawyers, so that explained the expensive clothes.

"My administrative assistant is very discreet," I said. "She can keep a secret."

"This is something I don't want to tell anyone but you. I don't trust anyone else."

I hesitated, wondering if I deserved that kind of trust, then said, "Okay, go ahead."

Peter closed the door and then surveyed the two chairs I had for my students or anyone else who needed to speak to me. Low-backed and fairly comfortable, one was at the side of my desk, the other faced my desk. Peter usually sat in the one facing me, but today he studied it like it was new to him, then moved it a foot further away from my desk before sitting down. He had a spiral notebook with him which he placed in his lap, but he seemed intent on more than taking notes. Last night at the restaurant he had appeared unsettled or worse, but the expression on his square-jawed face this morning was hard, determined.

"I don't drink," he said flatly.

I don't know what I had expected him to say, but clearly that wasn't it. "Okay…"

"My parents do, all the time, to unwind from work." He shook his head. "They're always working, both of them. Email, phone calls, texts 24/7. Which means they drink a lot and it can get ugly." He paused and ran his hands nervously through his wavy hair.

I started to wonder if he was going to tell me about being the victim of abuse of some kind. Should I stop him right there and suggest he see a counselor? Or just listen? I sat there, nervously waiting for a terrible revelation of some kind.

When he hesitated, I bumbled a response: "That sounds rough." Even though I often felt like I was always on duty, I couldn't imagine the kind of life he was describing his parents lived, and the pressure that they took for granted. But then I suppose neither one of them had been involved in as many murders as I had.

It didn't matter what I said, though, because Peter seemed focused on whatever he was about to reveal, and me, I was already sorry I had agreed to him closing the door. I didn't like feeling cut off from Celine and even though I liked Peter and thought he had potential as a writer, I was uncomfortable with this kind of intimacy from a student. I know there were faculty members who went drinking with their students and liked to be "buddies," but that had never been my style.

Peter looked as blank then as someone in a hostage video ordered by his captors to be expressionless and give nothing away. "My mother can go through a whole pitcher of daiquiris and my dad loves crazy-expensive Japanese whiskey. Clients give it to him all the time since they know it's his thing."

I nodded and waited. His talk of drinking made me assume that violence—or worse—was somewhere in this story. And if Peter was being abused, I really would have to report it. That was university policy, even if it happened off campus.

"My dad is really strict. He's always bugged me about grades and wants to know how I do on every term paper, every exam." He blinked a few times. "I screwed up last week on an Econ test—it was his idea I should take crap courses like that—and he was furious. And seriously drunk. He said, 'We didn't pay all that money to get you into State for you to fuck up so bad.'"

What the hell was his father talking about?

In-state tuition kept going up every year, but it wasn't exorbitant, and it was definitely affordable for rich parents like Peter's.

As if he had followed my line of thinking, Peter said, "I reminded him that SUM wasn't as expensive as other schools in the state and that's when he lost it, called me a moron. Maybe I am...." Now Peter looked away and I thought there might be tears in his eyes. "I had lousy SAT scores even when I took the test a second time, which really pissed off my dad because the tutor he hired for me charged two hundred bucks an hour. I thought I might have to try a community college first." He shot me a quick, helpless glance. "I panic when I look at an exam. My mind goes blank. Sometimes I even feel like I'm going to puke."

"I was like that, too, back in high school." Well, all but the puking, but I was trying to be sympathetic. I felt like a fossil, though, because when I applied to colleges, I didn't have any help, paid or otherwise. I just took my SATs, wrote the essay for my applications, and hoped for the best.

Peter didn't seem to have heard me commiserating, or maybe

sympathy wasn't what he needed at the moment. Staring at the view from my window, he went on: "Then my dad asked me how I thought I got accepted at State with such bad test scores and mediocre grades in everything but English."

Where was this going?

"It was— It was a bribe," Peter said.

"What?"

Head down, he added very quietly, "My parents bribed some fucking greedy asshole at State to get me admitted." His face started to turn red, and now he looked me straight in the eye, defiantly, almost as if he were accusing me of something. "Some people donate to the university, you know, create a scholarship or whatever, donate to the Athletics Department, or contribute to a fund, to make sure their kids get in. But that's not the only way. I guess you can also just pay somebody. Secretly."

"Are you kidding me? Pay whom?" And why would he be so angry at whoever took the bribe?

He shook his head. "I don't know who. My dad wouldn't say. But it was two hundred and fifty thousand dollars. That's the going rate here."

I had read about wealthy parents bribing proctors to change test scores and bribing college officials to get their kids into Ivy League schools, but to pay $250,000 to get into SUM? What was the point? Despite some good programs, it wasn't a stellar university.

"They wanted me close to home," Peter said, once again seeming to know what I was thinking. "And they knew someone here at State who could make it happen even with my low scores and crappy grades."

How would a scheme like that work? Just thinking about it made me feel queasy. I knew some of the ways in which SUM was corrupt, but this scam was news to me, and deeply disturbing. I truly wished he wasn't telling me about it.

Peter sighed, set his notebook down by the side of his chair, stretched his legs out as if he had crossed some sort of boundary, and now felt relieved.

"They wanted me to stand out from the beginning, to look unique when I applied to college," he said. "It wasn't enough that I was on the debate team and joined the theater club, the school newspaper, and the model U.N. to demonstrate 'leadership.' "

"You didn't want those?"

"They made me join. They paid for bassoon lessons, which was a disaster, but they picked that because it was unusual and they thought it could get me into a college orchestra or at least stand out on my application. Because everybody plays the violin, right? They made me take immersion classes in Dutch because Russian and, Jesus, Mandarin, that's what everyone else is doing. They even had a friend of theirs tutor me in Dutch. And made me take a course in Amsterdam, but I was hopeless. I mean, what a fucking boring useless language." He rolled his eyes. "I like the beer, but Dutch is pointless and so what if that's my ancestry? It doesn't mean anything to me so why bother learning it?" He paused and looked away, crossed his arms. "My application essay was all about the river cruise I took from Basel to Amsterdam where I supposedly discovered my roots. I didn't even write that myself, I had a college consultant helping me because it was such bullshit. My parents paid him five grand."

I must have looked surprised about his needing writing help because he said, "Your papers, the ones I've done for you, everything I've written at State, that's all me, good or bad."

"You're a very good writer." I thought his work on Sinclair Lewis last semester was solid. I had assigned topics that were very idiosyncratic and not likely to show up on websites where students paid for essays, and I ran everyone's papers through a plagiarism app if anything made me suspicious.

"Yeah, I guess, when it interests me. I did go to Cranbrook." He added the last piece of information as if he'd done something shameful himself. "And I do like to read fiction."

Cranbrook, in his home town of Bloomfield Hills, was supposedly the best private high school in Michigan, and tuition set you back over $30,000 a year.

"So the cruise was a total waste of time?"

He glanced away. "I liked Amsterdam," he said haltingly. He didn't elaborate and I thought he probably went to the famed red light district there, not exactly what his mother and father had in mind.

"Do you know why your parents—"

"—cheated to get me into SUM?"

"Yes. Because if they had that kind of money to bribe someone, couldn't they have made a straight donation?" Not that *that* was much better, but it was legal at least.

Peter blushed. "They wanted to, but I guess they were told that nothing like that would get me accepted because of my record. Not money, stocks, art for the museum—nothing."

I hesitated. "Are you talking about a police record?"

He nodded, eyes down. "I got arrested for fighting in high school."

"What happened?"

He breathed in heavily. "It was stupid. I was hungover in class and somebody made fun of me and I hit him. Hard. Broke his jaw and knocked him out. His family sued. We settled out of court for half a million and I had to transfer to another high school. I got arrested for assault, but I didn't go to jail. My parents knew the right people, so all I had to do was community service and counseling. That's when I stopped drinking."

Was it true that SUM would have barred him for that arrest on top of bad grades? I had no idea what admissions decisions were like, who got screened out and why.

"I fucked up bad, that was real and out there in public, Dr. Hoffman, but parents spread shit about other people's kids, anonymously, and that's wrong."

"Parents do *what?*"

"If they know what schools someone is applying to, they send anonymous letters trash-talking those kids, dredging up stuff like pot-smoking and DUIs, or just making things up." He shrugged.

I had absolutely no idea what to say in response. He was describing a world that sounded frantic and insane. All that to get your kids into college?

I must have looked shocked, or worse. "I guess you don't have kids, do you?" he asked.

I shook my head.

"Dr. Hoffman, promise me you won't tell anyone what my parents did. Please. I need to keep this a secret while I figure out what to do."

"What do you mean?"

He frowned as if it was obvious. "I don't belong here. I got in unfairly. I took somebody else's place. What my parents did was dishonest. I feel better telling you what happened, but that doesn't make it okay. I think I should drop out."

"Wow."

"Isn't that the right thing to do?"

"How about some coffee?" I asked, playing for time. "I know I could use a cup." I rose from my desk to step over to the console table where I had a Bosch single-cup coffeemaker and a small revolving rack of Tassimo coffee discs. "Strong okay for you?"

"Yes. And black."

I made his Kona Blend in an SUM mug, aware of the irony, and handed it to him. He sipped expectantly, clearly waiting for me to get my own coffee and answer his question about dropping out. I was glad to have a little time to think while the second cup brewed, and remembered moments in movies where people facing a similar situation pause to get out a cigarette, light it, and take a long, slow drag.

When the coffee was ready and I'd cleaned up, I sat back at my desk, musing until it hit me what I needed to say to him, or at least what I *could* say to him. I remembered something I had recently said to myself. "In Judaism there's a concept taken from mysticism that's actually very practical—it's called *tikkun olam*. It means healing the world, repairing it because it's broken."

He frowned. "And that applies to me?"

"Yes. I mean, it can. You're not responsible for what your parents did, and you can't change it, but you can heal yourself and the world you're in."

"How?"

"That's for you to decide. You're here at State now, even if how you got accepted is—" I looked for the right word and only came up with "murky," which didn't seem adequate to the situation, so I left the sentence unfinished. "Ask yourself what you can do to repair what's been broken."

Peter drank down some more of his coffee. "This is good," he murmured, and I wasn't sure if he meant the coffee or our conversation. "What do you think Henry James would say?" he asked, and for a moment I thought he was joking, but then I realized he meant it.

I didn't hesitate: "'Try to be one of the people on whom nothing is lost.'" That was Henry James's advice to a young writer, but I had always thought it was more widely applicable than that.

Peter seemed to take that in, finished his coffee, rose and set the mug down at the edge of my desk. "Can we talk about the story next week?" He looked worn out from telling the truth.

"No problem." I didn't think I could shift focus to analyze anything at the moment anyway.

Peter retrieved his notebook from the floor, thanked me, and left. Celine was soon hovering in the doorway and she asked, "Is everything okay?"

"That's a good question. A very good question."

She nodded, and left me alone with my uncertainty.

Because I was department chair now, didn't that mean *I* was responsible? If I knew about something fraudulent affecting one of our English majors, wasn't I supposed to do something? But before I got very far with that, though, I heard raised voices in German from Celine's office.

4.

CELINE BUZZED my desk phone and told me what I already knew when I picked up: Heino and Jonas Bratfisch, the recent Digital Humanities hires, wanted to see me.

These twenty-something German wunderkinds were hard to tell apart because they were both slim, blond, blue-eyed, and almost always dressed identically. They were usually immersed in something online via their phones or else they were whispering to each other as if they were in their own world, their own universe even, and the rest of us didn't quite register.

Who knows, maybe it was all some kind of weird German performance art. But given their attitude to their colleagues, I sometimes wondered if they might be involved in that secret Committee of Public Safety and had really been hired to spy on the rest of us. I suppose everybody had something to hide, but our department didn't seem like a nest of anti-SUM renegades. And was that what the secret committee was actually up to? Nobody in the administration had said in public that it even existed, even when questioned directly by local reporters. And in pure doublespeak, our provost had said it was inappropriate to comment "due to privacy concerns."

"Wait a moment, Celine, and then send them in."

I made myself another cup of coffee, took a few sips, set the mug down and then moved the chair at my desk further out beside the other one, assuming they could sit together civilly without erupting into a brawl. I perched on the edge of my desk and crossed my arms. I had been expecting the twins, and now I was mentally prepared.

Today they wore black leggings, no socks, red sneakers, and matching red-and-black floral shirts that were so loud I suspected the fashion choice was ironic. But I did not let their attire distract me.

"We need to speak with you," they said almost in unison, then glared at each other.

"Please sit down."

They complied, but reluctantly. I knew exactly what was coming.

"Our office situation is quite intolerable," Heino complained. Yes, it had to be Heino because he was the one who had raised the same issue at a recent departmental retreat. Unless his brother was getting the jump on him?

"And it is unresolved," maybe-Heino continued. "You are the new leader of the department, and you must decide what is to be done."

I had a momentary flash of discomfort. One word for "leader" in German was, of course, Führer.

"I see no problem," his brother said airily. "The office is big enough for two people." That was Jonas for sure, since he'd been just as dismissive the first time I heard about their situation.

"Not when one intrudes upon the other's space. Jonas is still making a mess on my side of the office. I find food and coffee stains on my desk and sometimes crumbs as well. He sits in my chair, makes adjustment to the back and does not change it, he uses my trash bin as if it was his. As if it *were* his? No matter. It is quite disgusting, and—"

"—you've told everyone about the problem and I have the solution," I said, not waiting to hear Jonas's side of the story again or let the discussion escalate further.

Their enigmatic faces showed what might have been a smile (unless it was a flash of unease?) and for a moment, I wondered if this whole disputatious vibe of theirs wasn't some kind of put-on. I just could not read them at all. Was it a cultural thing?

"Here's my plan, guys. I've decided to move both of you out of that office and into separate offices elsewhere in the building."

They stared at me and one of them muttered, "Madness."

"It's the only fair solution. I did some investigating and there are available offices in the basement. There's no view, obviously, but each of you can have your own office and that should end the problem."

Heino, I think, sputtered something in German, then said, "I refuse to work in a crypt. The conditions in such a place would be insalubrious."

"Listen," I said, leaning forward. "I had a basement office back in Parker Hall one semester. That place was really run-down, you know that. These are much nicer. I checked downstairs myself. It's very clean down there, as clean as this whole building. The lighting is good, all the walls have been freshly painted, the furniture is on the newish side, and you'll even have nice carpeting." I assumed the basement offices were carpeted to cover up some defects in the flooring, but didn't bring that up. Most of the basement offices were actually used for storage of old furniture or occupied by graduate assistants and maintenance workers, so I was lucky there were some empty ones.

"It might be a better place to work on your book." I knew they had a contract with Oxford University Press for a study of the "*Bubikopf*," the hairdo in Weimar Germany's movies, magazines, and popular literature which Americans associated with Flappers. It seemed an unlikely topic for a book, but I guess the publisher thought anything connected to the 1920s had a potential audience. The contract meant that the twins would likely have it in press or at least finished by the time their three-year review came up, and then they would probably be here to stay. That was the kind of book that would get reviews in a wide range of publications even if it was scholarly, because the focus was fashion.

"It's the only fair solution," I said.

Silence from the twins.

"You'll be at opposite ends of the hallway down there and also have more privacy."

Still no response.

"Okay, then. It's settled. Please get it done by the end of this week," I said. "And if you need help with moving your books and files, talk to Aldo and he can make the arrangements."

The twins were both wide-eyed now and breathing heavily as if they were about to lunge at me, but I found myself unfazed. Their squabble over office space was ridiculous but disruptive, and the feuding had to end. It felt good to exercise my authority even over a matter as minor as this.

"Have a great day," I said as a gentle sign that the meeting was over, but as soon as I said it, I wondered if the twins might think I was being sarcastic.

They stood and marched out. One of them grumbled, *"Drecksau!"* I think it was Heino, but who could be sure when their backs were turned to me? I didn't know exactly what the German word meant, but it was clear they were unhappy because the other twin said, "He will be regretting this."

Well, it wasn't even noon and I had probably made two new enemies, as Aldo had predicted could happen. Still, I hoped the move would reduce tension in the department. And hell, if they managed to get into a tussle down there anyway, it would be out of sight from the rest of us.

My cell phone pinged. It was a text from Celine who had obviously heard the whole interaction: "Well played."

I texted back a happy face emoji. Then I sat back behind my desk and surveyed my domain, feeling proud of having resolved the problem of the twins, or at least moved it out of the spotlight, which might be just as good. If they couldn't behave like adults, at least it didn't have to be a spectacle for the whole department. Maybe the twins would even enjoy their isolation since they were so cut off from all of us anyway.

But then I wondered if I should have tried to arbitrate their dispute somehow rather than present a solution they might view as punishment. And was feeling good about my decision, feeling positive, actually the first little sign of creeping corruption? I wasn't powerful, not really, but I did have power over the faculty now and had just used it. Had I started out all wrong by making the twins move? Would the rest of the department see my choice as arbitrary? Our last chair had been despised for being capricious—would I already remind people of him?

And would moving them to the basement really help them write their book? What if the sparring and personal insults that seemed part of their relationship were integral to their creativity? I knew next to nothing about twins in general except that they supposedly had their own secret language and could simultaneously experience events when they were miles apart—unless that was just an urban legend.

I finished the now-lukewarm coffee left in my cup and it tasted strangely bitter. I was starting to feel mildly ashamed of myself. I usually discussed anything connected to campus with Stefan, but hadn't run this decision by him. Maybe I'd kept it to myself because I suspected he would disagree and point out the kind of regrets I was already having.

Being department chair was not remotely like being one of the faculty, and it was unsettling. I'd heard other people across the university talk about the transition to having their own secretary and how that broke their typical isolation, but thanks to the Nick Hoffman Fellowship for Visiting Writers, I'd already been working with Celine, so there was no change there. But being in charge was already starting to feel cumbersome and ill-fitting. I understood from Celine that I would have two roles as chair: a ceremonial one where I would have to show up at a wide range of events to represent the department without having to do or say anything, and a substantive one, making sure we conformed to college and university guidelines, served our students well, and somehow managed to stave off the academic equivalent of urban blight.

It was daunting, like going from being a private citizen to mayor of a small town.

I was trying to wrap my head around all this when Dean Bullerschmidt unexpectedly surged into my office.

"I was in the building and wanted to see how you were faring." His frigid grin didn't relax me at all because it was fake: there were never wrinkles around his eyes, which always stayed watchful, cold. Bullerschmidt was so imposing that I felt trapped, and somehow I had forgotten how tall he was, over six feet.

Nevertheless, seeing him take possession of my office just by standing there, I couldn't help but admire the beautiful cut of his dark gray suit with a super-subtle pin stripe, the spread-collar blue shirt, and purple tie in a full Windsor knot. He clearly received good advice about what to wear from somebody (wife? mistress? tailor?) because he didn't look like a fat man dressed well: he looked dapper, though he was larger than life, enormous and overbearing.

He surveyed my two chairs with a scornful glance and did not try either one. Picturing him sitting in one, I remembered a tremendously bad line from a David Baldacci thriller about a large man leaning back in a chair, "...his mass extrapolating outward until it fully engulfed the space." I tried not to smile.

The dean cocked an eyebrow at me, clearly inviting me to speak, and I said, "It's early days, I'm just settling in."

"But you're not moving."

"I've moved once already. And the chair's office isn't much bigger than this one."

"You'd only be going down the hall," he said, his eyes narrowing. It somehow sounded like a threat.

I nodded. "That's true. So why bother?"

And now he chortled like Sydney Greenstreet in *The Maltese Falcon*. His laugh was even more inauthentic than his smile. "Why bother, indeed?"

Celine appeared in the doorway. "Can I get you gentlemen anything?"

The dean frowned at what he must have felt was an intrusion, but didn't turn around.

"We're good," I said for the both of us. I did not want him lingering over coffee, tea, or even a glass of water.

Celine withdrew.

As if the question of my moving hadn't just come up, the dean said, "I understand you're getting a new desk for this office. I'll make sure your chairs are updated, too."

Why did he care about something as petty as my office furniture and how did he even know Celine had ordered a new desk for me? Was he tracking our emails? Was *he* on that secret committee?

"And your desk lamp could use replacing," he added, peering disdainfully at the green-shaded banker's lamp I'd picked up years ago and was very fond of for no special reason.

If Bullerschmidt wasn't there to try and bully me into moving, why *was* he there? What did he want? Had he somehow heard about how my student Peter got accepted into SUM? I wiped my sweaty palms on my pants and hoped I did so inconspicuously, but if he were a dog, his ears would have pricked up because he suddenly seemed to focus on me much more intently.

"Are you all right? Has something happened?"

To throw him off my trail, I said, "Heino and Jonas were here just now. And I told them I was moving them to separate offices in the basement."

Now his smile seemed more genuine and not quite so toothy. "That's an elegant solution. They can be a tad rambunctious, can't they? I would have done the same thing if I were in your shoes."

I should have felt relieved by his validation, but I wasn't.

"So...I understand that you refused to help the university by taking on the summer program in Sweden." He glowered at me.

"I wouldn't put it that way."

"That's the only way to put it. SUM needs you, and you say no."

"Other people passed, too."

"But you have expertise, you understand the culture and you study the language."

How many people in the administration were aware of that, and what else did they know about me? I could taste bile in my mouth and wondered if I might actually become sick.

"I'm very disappointed in you, Nick, after we give you this plum position."

It was beyond arrogant that Bullerschmidt was using the royal "we"—unless I'd been installed as department chair by more than one person in some kind of plot.

"And it's not just because of Sweden," the dean said. Then he drew closer and said almost menacingly, "You're very argumentative and uncooperative. Everybody says I'm the best dean Humanities has ever had and easy to work with—there's never been a better dean in the history of SUM. And I've never had trouble with any faculty member except you."

That self-assessment was unhinged. But the dean wasn't finished.

"Your refusal to move into the chairman's office is symbolic, isn't it? I'm sure you think that if you stay where you are, you're demonstrating some sort of spirit of egalitarianism. Trying to show that you don't think you're better than the other faculty."

After the detour to the summer program, I was surprised by his sudden return to the subject and couldn't think of what to say.

"If that's the case, Dr. Hoffman, then you're dead wrong."

With his use of "Dr. Hoffman" instead of "Nick," I felt like a teenager whose mother is calling him by his first, middle, and last name to demand his attention before launching into some sort of diatribe.

"You're the chairman. You're not anyone's *pal*," he said, his face twisting with disgust at the word. "Nobody liked you before and no matter what you do or say you're not going to endear yourself to anyone *now*. I can see right through your false humility. You're trying way too hard. You think that just because a student willed the university money for that fellowship and wanted it named after you, you think that makes you special. You're not special at all. You just got lucky. SUM is filled with jumped-up nobodies like you."

"Then why did you appoint me interim chair?"

He groaned as if I'd asked what two plus two equaled. "Are you an idiot? I picked you because you're *gay* and SUM needs some diversity out front, that's why. Nothing else."

I stood up, tired of being berated. Working hard not to raise my voice, I said, "I don't want to move, Dean Bullerschmidt. And I'm not going to move."

He squinted at me as if I had revealed something pitiable about myself. "I picked you for interim chair! I can remove you any time I want to!"

"Go ahead. Do it. *I don't give a fuck.* Get your fat ass out of my office!" I looked at my lamp and had to fight the urge to pick it up and bash him with it.

The dean's face turned dark red and his eyes were suddenly very small. Bizarrely, he produced that phony laugh of his again, but what he said wasn't at all amusing. "You will regret talking to me like that." And he turned and lumbered off.

I did regret it already. I should never have yelled at him that way. It was rude and it was wrong.

Celine hurried in. "Are you okay? What the hell was that about? People stopped out in the hallway when you were yelling."

"Great." Just what I needed: making a spectacle of myself fighting with the dean—and insulting him, too. My office was close to the elevators and who knew how many people heard the set-to. Even if nobody had tried to capture it for Twitter, it would be making the rounds of the department and campus within an hour and I'd be branded as a hothead—or worse. I sank back into my chair, exhausted, and Celine sat down in the chair Heino had recently vacated. Unless it was Jonas's chair.

"Was that gorilla testing you somehow?" she asked. "Was it some kind of game?"

I shook my head. "This place gets crazier every day."

"You've got *that* right."

"I mean, what the hell? First Lovelace pressures me to move out, then Bullerschmidt tries it. And he was so...vicious."

"I don't think sweet-talking is one of his talents," she said with a sour grin, and I could feel my heart beating faster. I wished that the day was already over so that I could relax with a glass of single malt while my West Highland White Terrier Marco snoozed in my lap.

"It won't make you feel better, but you have to know that people hate him in his office, across campus. I'm sorry he blew up at you, but that's how he is. I know Humanities' associate dean for undergraduate studies, Boris Hernandez, and if the dean screws up, he always blames his staff. Not that it seems to bother Boris at all. But Bullerschmidt never accepts responsibility when something goes wrong. That's why there's high turnover in that office."

"I just met him—how long has he been there? And is he part Russian? Boris is a Russian name."

"His heritage is actually half Dutch, despite that name. I think it's been five years or more for him working with the dean—he's been there longer than anyone else. The word is that he's bright and ambitious, though why he's an administrator here and not someplace more prestigious, I don't know."

"What do you mean?"

"I heard that he has degrees in Renaissance Studies from Harvard and Columbia."

"He probably couldn't find a teaching job—competition is fierce no matter what schools you went to."

"Well, I get the feeling that he's really the dean's right-hand man and the dean depends on him more than anyone else."

"But how does he stand it?" I asked. "Working with the dean?"

Celine had a ready answer: "I guess some people need to be followers, even if they're following someone like Bullerschmidt. He could be in thrall to the dean and might not be able to leave if he wanted to. There are lots of weird relationships on campus."

She wasn't exaggerating, since academics got very little supervision and administrators were virtually free of oversight.

"Boris is always around the dean, like a watchdog or something. It's a little bizarre. He's a nice guy but hard to read."

I heard what she said, but my thoughts had drifted in a different direction. "You know," I brought out, "the way Lovelace and Bullerschmidt acted about my staying here, you'd think there was some hidden treasure in this office and they needed me gone so they could start hacking at the floors and the walls."

"Anything's possible," Celine said.

We both surveyed the room as if we had X-ray eyes, then started to laugh. *Real* laughter, the kind that left us both with tears in our eyes. I needed to laugh badly because nobody in the administration had ever talked to me like the dean had, and I had never lost my temper with someone so much more powerful than me.

But things turned serious because Celine broke off to ask, "What's going on with the student who came to see you? Peter, right? It must have been serious if he wanted the door closed."

I stopped laughing. "He asked me to keep a secret."

"That does sound serious. Too serious. And it could be a problem if it's anything that might involve a crime." Her insight was painfully clear.

"I know. I have to think about it before I figure out what to do."

Was what his parents had done a felony? Was he implicated? If it came out would there be a trial?

• • •

On the way home, I stopped at our palatial health club to swim. Michigan Muscle was a chaotic agglomeration of brick, steel, glass, and concrete buildings and additions that had no real style and was not easy to navigate for newcomers. It was too big, too spread out, there were too many staircases and corridors and not enough signs. But all the equipment was top notch, the young trainers were as smooth and beautiful as androids, and everything down to the decorative tiles in the showers bespoke money lavishly spent.

The club was usually crowded in the late afternoon with

students who used their parents' memberships, retirees, and housewives in the weight rooms, racquetball courts, aerobic studios, and cardiovascular areas, but the pool was often empty for some reason. It was almost monastically quiet down there compared to the rest of the crowded club filled with chatter, shouting and whooping from spin class, the clang of dropped weights, Zumba class music, and even music leaking from people's headphones.

The empty pool and the time of day meant there was even less chance I'd run into another faculty member and have to make nice. I had discovered that SUM professors preferred either the morning shifts or else arriving near closing time. So swimming in the afternoon also meant avoiding the awkwardness of seeing a colleague in the nude in the locker room or showers, or else discovering that someone you knew had foul-smelling sweat.

I think Roberto Robustelli might have had the same idea, because as I headed to the pool, he was walking away from it, a fluffy white towel flung around his brawny shoulders. I'd never run into him before at Michigan Muscle and was surprised at how many tattoos he had scattered across his arms, legs, and torso. When he saw me, he slowed down to swagger past, grinning. He was built like a soccer player, and he knew it.

"Lookin' good," he said as he passed me, and he grinned as seductively as if he wanted to take me home, which was weird. I'd never picked up that kind of vibe from him before.

I now had even more reason to want to lose myself in the pool. I swam my best stroke, backstroke, for half an hour, mind blissfully blank as I went back and forth in my lane. I wasn't fast or especially graceful, but I'd been told by better swimmers that my form was clean. While I'd never been able to meditate, swimming came close and it usually worked so well that I would leave the pool feeling clearheaded and refreshed. That afternoon, though, I couldn't shake Peter's confession, and it was still on my mind even after I was showered, changed, and in my car driving home.

• • •

It was our second house in Michiganapolis, a two-story stucco Art Moderne house built in 1930 and set in a cul-de-sac filled with clusters of enormous, theatrical-looking weeping willow trees. The rounded walls and steel balcony rails echoed the curves of an ocean liner from that period, but I never felt a sense of movement there because it all felt so solid and peaceful.

The quiet was magnified by the protected wetlands beyond our back fence, which we had a view of from our dining room's window wall. We were only the third owners, and the house itself was like something from a Fred Astaire/Ginger Rogers movie, decorated boldly in orange and red, filled with glass brick, and black and white leather furniture original to the house and beautifully maintained.

The previous owners had updated the master bath with a soaking tub and rain forest shower and made the kitchen dramatic and bright with deep red Viking appliances, rose quartz countertops, and sleek white Italian cabinets.

Stefan liked to cook even more than usual when he was working on a book because it relaxed and refocused him, so dinner that night was stuffed cabbage and couscous with pimientos. Marco loitered hopefully by the kitchen table for a while, then trotted off to find a toy, and I could hear its squeak and his play-growling from the living room. He was good at entertaining himself.

We had opened a nice bottle of Beaujolais-Villages to go with the meal, and after my second glass of wine, I related my interaction with the twins.

Stefan didn't say anything for a moment, then came out with what was clearly a place holder: "Okay..."

"You think it was a mistake?"

"Well, it's risky. It could go either way."

"How?" I could feel my shoulders already hiking up in tension.

"Some people in the department will be thrilled, and some people will think you're a jerk for kicking Heino and Jonas out of their office."

"But the twins haven't even been around a full year."

Stefan sipped some wine, set his glass down. "Even if they didn't get along, that was still their office and they were attached to it, or why would they be arguing? You don't want to leave yours, do you?"

"It's not the same thing," I said.

Stefan shrugged. "You're being logical and logic is not a defining characteristic of our department." He snorted. "Probably not of any university department."

He was right about that. In our travels around the country, whenever we met other academics they would regale us with the foibles and bad behavior of their colleagues. And his dim assessment of how I would be perceived for moving the twins was probably right: I would look like a hypocrite given that I didn't want to leave my own office. And what the hell were we going to do with the chair's office? Why hadn't I even thought about that before?

"I'm sure as hell not taking it back," I said. "They're moving."

"Who gets their old office?" he asked.

That was something else I hadn't considered. I tried not to grind my teeth.

"I'll talk to Aldo and find out if there's anyone doubled up who might want to move in." Hopefully I could make somebody happy—unless there was more than one doubled office and I'd have to choose who got their own. Which would likely piss somebody else off.

And then there was the fact that both Dean Bullerschmidt and Dawn Lovelace were unhappy about my not moving to the office designated for department chair, though why Lovelace cared was beyond me. What sort of trouble could staying where I was make for me? I didn't know my position well at all, but I was sure that Bullerschmidt could make me suffer, administratively, if he wanted to.

Stefan poured me some more wine. "You look like you need it," he said. "And I know there's something you're not telling me."

5.

THAT'S THE PROBLEM with marriage—even if you're not an entirely open book, your spouse can still read between the lines.

Marco trotted in just at that awkward moment with a stuffed blue-and-white elephant in his mouth. It was almost as big as he was, and he shook it at me to entice me to play with him. The elephant was his favorite toy and I welcomed the change of focus, finished my wine, and leaned down to grab one end of the critter while Marco growled and tried to pull it out of my hands. I growled back at him while we did our tug-of-war.

I could feel Stefan's steady gaze and after a few carefree moments I let go of the toy, sat up straight, and without meeting his eyes said, "It was a terrible, horrible, no-good, very bad day. I kind of yelled at Bullerschmidt when he surprised me. I mean, he just showed up without warning. He's very intimidating. You know that."

Stefan waved the last part away. "Kind of yelled?"

I breathed in as if there was a way to delay the confession but even Marco seemed to be waiting. He was sitting there and staring up at me, the toy at his feet.

"I told him to fuck off. Basically."

"You told him to fuck off," Stefan repeated flatly. "Okay, now *I* need another glass of wine." The bottle was shot and he went to the wine fridge to get another. "Maybe two." When he had opened the second and poured himself a glass so full I thought it might spill over when he tried to drink it, he said, "What exactly happened?"

"He tried to bully me into leaving my office, you know, to move into the official department chair's office, and then he started mocking me. He said I thought I was better than everyone else because of the Nick Hoffman Fellowship. And he told me I was a dime a dozen at SUM. It was like some kind of kamikaze intervention. He was brutal." As I said it, I almost couldn't believe it, and I wondered if I was possibly in shock. Or maybe it was the wine that muffled what I was feeling.

"And he told me that I was just window dressing, I'm a token, because I'm gay."

Stefan muttered, "That fucker. You should report him."

"To whom? And for what?"

"Harassment?"

"That won't go anywhere. He can always say I misinterpreted what he meant. Even if it was sexual the university would bury my complaint. You know how things work at SUM. And anyway, I'm the one who was yelling."

We started clearing the table and stacking the dishwasher. It was calming to do something routine like taking care of the dinner dishes, but that didn't last long. "Why did he go off on me like that?" I wondered aloud. "It doesn't make sense. I mean, why appoint me interim chair and then abuse me?"

"He's a mean sonofabitch, that's why. He doesn't need any better reason than that. He treats everyone like shit. He loves power plays and humiliation."

We had silenced our phones during dinner, but as soon as we turned the volume back on, both of them were blowing up with texts about my encounter with the dean, and it was worse than what I had feared: I was actually trending on Twitter, being pilloried for losing my cool. It was an explosion without any context and ripe for parody. I already had my own Hashtag: #crazyprof. And even friends from other universities were texting me because they'd heard about the imbroglio.

I understood the dynamic: joining a Twitter mob to attack any-one was a quick high. It made you feel superior to judge someone else, it was cheap entertainment to wallow in contempt.

My phone had never seemed like something toxic before and I once again felt an urge to be violent. I wanted to hurl it across the room, but I knew it would likely break something, or just get broken, and it would alarm Stefan and Marco.

I didn't reply to anyone. I dreaded how Bullerschmidt would react to this shame fest.

We headed for the living room, sat on the couch and scrolled, and scrolled some more, and kept scrolling. I felt alternately hot and cold. The mockery was devastating.

"I should step down as chair," I said. "Before things get worse, before I'm on YouTube, before there's an anti–Nick Hoffman Face-book group, before Whoopi Goldberg is dissing me on *The View*."

Stefan took the phone from my hand, silenced it again and placed it on the couch face down, and then did the same with his. "If you resign, they'll call you a coward."

"That's not worse than 'idiot' and maybe this would burn itself out."

"It'll die down soon either way. You know what Twitter is like. Outrage doesn't last long."

"But it may be too late, and I don't want to be a meme!"

Some of the nastiest tweets had "Duh!" superimposed on my official SUM photo which people had grabbed from the depart-ment website, and that's all it took to make my smile look moronic. I know people had worse thrown at them every day on Twitter, but this was the first time for me and I wanted to lash out at some-one, anyone—or just hide. Other tweets had heads exploding or people going berserk and there were even some with my head photoshopped onto Rambo's body, which might have partly been a compliment, given the low general opinion of academics, but I wasn't sure, and they didn't remotely balance all the rest.

Stefan shrugged. "It's too late."

Marco had read my distress and jumped on the couch and

started licking my face. Lucky dog, even if someone made fun of him, he wouldn't care.

Stefan rubbed his eyes as if trying to wake up. "I'm sorry the dean pushed your buttons. But you know, Bullerschmidt has such a bad history at SUM, I'm surprised nobody's tried to off him by now."

"Don't say that!"

"Why not? I bet he infuriates lots of people on campus, maybe even *off* campus, too."

I toyed with telling Stefan that I had imagined bashing the dean's obnoxious face in with my desk lamp, but thought it might make me really sound crazy.

"I should kill him," Stefan said thoughtfully, "in my book."

"But you're not writing a mystery." Marco had settled down at my side, and I was lightly scratching the back of his neck.

Stefan shrugged. "No. But there's plenty of time until I have to turn it in. Even if it's not a crime novel somebody could get killed. Literary fiction is pretty violent at the moment. Starting with a corpse is a good way to get attention from reviewers and I bet my agent would be delighted."

Now that Stefan had produced a best-seller, I thought his agent and his editor would be thrilled with whatever he wrote—and hungry too. Because his career was so different from when he first started out: writing a book every year or two wasn't enough anymore. He had to produce "content" between the books: short stories, mini-memoirs, novellas, anything that could be launched on multiple platforms and keep his audience coming back for more. It was sometimes a grind, but this kind of acceptance and this level of sales was what he'd always wanted, so he was careful not to complain. Even when I could feel that the world of publishing was driving him a little crazy.

"Something weird happened with the dean, I mean, something I haven't mentioned yet. He knew that I ordered new furniture. How would he know that if he wasn't spying on me somehow?"

"Nick, I think you might be getting a little paranoid."

I shook my head. "Maybe it's true that there's a Committee of Public Safety and it's not just a rumor. Celine thinks so and she's really connected. Maybe all our offices are bugged. Maybe they're spying on our computers, too, logging every keystroke we make."

"Why would they bother? What would be the point?"

"Control. Intimidation. I mean, we don't really know if this is happening, but people are afraid it's true—well I am—and that could be enough. Create a climate of fear, anxiety, and you keep people in line."

"Well, it might have the opposite effect and make people angry." Stefan frowned. "If it's true that we're under surveillance, that violates everything a university is supposed to be."

"Since when did anyone at SUM care about that? And the world is slowly turning fascist—why should SUM be immune? Really, why should it be immune? Bullerschmidt's a tyrant. You listen to what the provost says and she sounds like it's just after 9/11. That's the new normal here."

"Well, we did have a mass shooting," Stefan said quietly.

"That's no excuse for turning the university into a police state. Which is where we're headed with all these rumors and threats."

Talking about spying and secrecy made me wish that I could tell Stefan about Peter's bizarre revelation, but the information was too new and too explosive to share with even him. But did keeping silent make me complicit somehow in what could actually be a widespread problem? Peter's parents couldn't be the only ones paying to get their kids admitted to SUM. I hadn't had any time to decide whether I should reveal what I knew to anyone in the administration, and I confess that was partly motivated by how I felt about the whole hierarchy including the president.

I wasn't alone in my low opinion of President Yubero, who was a dead ringer for our twenty-seventh president, William Howard Taft, right down to the mustache. Yubero was a multi-millionaire donor to the GOP and had been picked as SUM's president in a closed meeting of the Board of Trustees which violated precedent, but they didn't care. Rules were for minions, not them. Stefan called Yubero a "knucklehead" which was pretty accurate despite being a dated insult, since his public statements sounded either juvenile or overly scripted.

Yubero was a businessman with no background in education whatsoever, but being Hispanic was a huge plus at a university obsessed with *looking* diverse. More than that, the board loved his wealth, assuming he would be a good fund-raiser, and the trustees applauded the clichés he spouted about returning the university to "our core American values exemplified by the hearty and hard-working Pilgrims."

Yeah, I thought, that was just what we needed: an updated version of the Salem Witch Trials.

"Shit! I forgot to tell you about Sweden."

Stefan frowned. "What about Sweden?"

"Dawn Lovelace came to my office to ask me to take over Viktor's program next summer since he's retiring."

"That's great. No? It's not great?"

"No, it isn't. I can't take on a new summer program and be department chair at the same time."

"But you love Sweden. Well, the idea of it."

"Yes, but not now."

He nodded thoughtfully. "Point taken. My guess is she wasn't happy when you said no."

"She was not. Not at all. She wanted me to take one for the team, but the whole thing felt off somehow."

"Meaning?"

I shrugged and Stefan rose to pour us some spicy Bumbu rum. I dutifully sipped some when he handed me the glass. It distracted me, but it didn't ease my mind. "Okay, this may sound crazy, but I'm starting to wonder if they want me out of the country for some reason, and that's what pushing me to do the Sweden program is all about."

Stefan drank some rum, nodded, sipped some more, closed his eyes as if deep in contemplation, though he might have just been enjoying his drink. "Get you out of the country to do what?" he asked. "What's their plan?"

"I don't know. Obviously."

Stefan sighed. "Well, you're not going, at least not this coming summer, so it doesn't matter, does it?"

I almost snapped at him for seeming so calm about what they were trying to do to me, and then caught myself. *They?* Really? There was nothing special or nefarious about my being manipulated and treated badly, it was just Standard Operating Procedure at SUM, and I had to accept it or quit.

Stefan reached over, took my glass, set it on the coffee table and pulled me in for a hug. "I think we're both on edge, thanks to the shooting," he brought out. "You're worried about conspiracies, I'm thinking I won't be able to finish the new book, I'm not good enough."

I sat back up and cupped his chin with both hands so that our eyes were locked. "You always finish your books."

"But all of those were written and published before..."

I let go of his chin, took up my glass, and downed the rest of my rum. Then I reached over to the coffee table and poured myself an even bigger shot. I was not sipping tonight. "Maybe we should get trauma counseling." SUM had offered that to us after the shooting, but we hadn't been ready, and the university's counseling center did not have a great reputation anyway.

"Maybe," Stefan echoed.

After the shooting we had fled Michigan and the scene of horror to spend weeks in Italy, the south of France, and Belgium. The food, the museums and churches, the wine, and the immersion in cultures we knew but always loved re-entering went some way toward healing us. We slept extremely well there, almost as deeply as if we were drugged. We never discussed the shooting at all. When we returned, there was a new department chair and more chaos that absorbed any energy we had left over from teaching and just living our lives.

"Maybe not," I said, suddenly feeling myself as dizzy and

afraid as if I were trapped at the edge of a cliff and my only escape was to jump.

That's when my phone vibrated even though I thought Stefan had silenced it.

I hesitated, but Stefan handed the phone to me with a shrug. How bad could it be?

It was Peter DeVries.

"Professor Hoffman…" The words were slurred but I recognized Peter DeVries's voice. "I really fucked up," he said, and I thought he might be crying.

"Are you okay? What happened?" Images of a car crash or something like that filled my thoughts. I mouthed, "It's Peter" for Stefan.

"I got lit and I told my best friend here about the bribe. I've known him since middle school," he added as if that explained anything.

I didn't know if "lit" meant high or drunk in this case, but that didn't matter. I pictured Peter's revelation spreading across social media faster than the video of my outburst with the dean. This was a much juicier story and likely to spark cascades of fury when it went viral, which I was sure it would. The media had been chewing on stories of families using bribes to get their kids into college, but that had been for elite schools. Now there'd be a new, Midwestern angle.

"And it's really bad," Peter managed to say through what definitely sounded like tears now. "His father is a fucking newspaper reporter, for *Scoop*."

That was like a gut punch, because *Scoop* was a new, popular, irreverent weekly in town. It was stealing readership from the boring daily which was a bad clone of *USA Today*.

I didn't probe for more information, just asked Peter, "Are you okay?"

"I don't know. I guess. I just feel like a moron."

Consoling a student wasn't exactly in my repertoire, but I gave it a shot. "It's hard to keep secrets," I said. "Sometimes they hurt too much." I hoped I didn't sound like one of those fake quotes that always went viral on Facebook, something attributed to an unlikely source like Mark Twain.

"That's right," Peter replied, his voice steadier. "That's right."

I could almost see him nodding in agreement.

"And, you know," he went on, "I think I feel different now."

"Better?"

Stefan stage-whispered, "What's going on with Peter?"

I held up my free hand and mouthed, "Wait."

"I'm going to go see my girlfriend now," Peter said. "Thanks for listening."

"Sure." I let Peter end the call.

"Nick, what was that all about?"

I closed my eyes as if that could stave off what was coming, and said, "Trouble."

6.

"*HOW ABOUT* some coffee?" I headed for the kitchen.

Stefan followed, and his silence radiated disapproval in the classic way that introverts do. They manage to communicate a lot without saying anything and right now the messages were coming fast and furious, because he was likely imagining the worst.

I'm not sure he was wrong. I made myself an espresso, but Stefan passed on having coffee. We sat at the kitchen table and I told him everything that Peter had shared with me in confidence earlier today in my office about how his parents had bribed someone to get him admitted to SUM. It still sounded wildly improbable, even though stories like this about other universities had been in the media.

Stefan wasn't angry that I had kept it to myself. But the corners of his mouth were drawn down as if he'd just gotten bad news he'd been dreading to hear. What he said next was unexpected, but not surprising: "I'm glad we don't have kids. I couldn't deal with worrying about drugs, and school shootings, and this hysteria about getting them into the best college—or any college."

We had never really talked about the possibility of adopting because we traveled so much, and Stefan was always so absorbed in his career even when it hadn't been going well, but I understood how he felt. My favorite Joan Didion line was from her bleak novel *Play It as It Lays* and I was sure it applied even more nowadays when you had children: "In the whole world there was not as much sedation as there was instantaneous peril."

"Peter stole someone's place," Stefan said.

"No."

"Well, his parents did. When the story breaks, he might have to leave SUM."

"But he's a good student. He works hard, he writes well, he's focused, he's dedicated." I might have been over-zealous in my defense, but I was feeling sorry for Peter. He was the victim of his parents' misplaced ambition, wasn't he?

"And he broke the law. He assaulted somebody."

I couldn't argue with that.

Stefan crossed his arms. His eyes were narrowed, but he didn't seem to be looking at me. "He's a fraud, no matter what he's doing now. The real kid, the real Peter, wouldn't have been admitted to SUM, so his parents had to bribe his way in."

I wondered if this story was somehow triggering Stefan's adolescent discovery that his parents were Holocaust survivors. They had hidden their Jewish identity from him and pretended to be Polish Catholics, but of course the secret eventually came out. Rich material for him as an author, trauma for him as a person.

"Nick, you have to report him."

"*What?* Why?"

"You know why," he said, eyes locked on mine now. "You're the department chair, he's an English major who doesn't belong there and you know how it happened. If the story breaks—and it has to because he's told his friend—you'll be screwed if you haven't told anyone in the administration."

I glanced away and suddenly felt like I was in some kind of mob movie because I wanted to say "I'm not a snitch."

"As the chair, you have a duty to inform if a student's being sexually harassed or if a professor isn't meeting his classes, so this is the same kind of thing."

When I didn't respond, Stefan said softly, "I'm right. You know I'm right. You've gotten into enough trouble at SUM without adding this to your record. You have important information about something illegal that's taken place and you can't keep it to yourself."

"What if he's wrong and it didn't happen the way he told me?"

He sighed. "It has to be investigated just the same. You can't keep quiet."

"Shit." I knew Stefan was being sensible, but if I reported Peter, students would think I was just another tool of the administration, wouldn't they? I wanted to be liked, and the day's barrage of Twitter mockery was bad enough. I did not want to be despised. Maybe even worse: threatened, harassed. Anything was possible thanks to social media and people's untamed desire to pile on when someone was being trashed, whether they knew the truth of the story or not.

"And I don't know how these things play out, Nick, but you might be in legal jeopardy, too."

"That doesn't make sense. I'm innocent. I just listened."

"It doesn't have to make sense. You've read all those stories about parents being arrested for the same thing that Peter's mother and father did."

A line from a Hart Crane poem popped into my head: "I am not ready for repentance/Nor to match regrets." I had to do something right away. I picked up my phone and called Vanessa Liberati, one of the city's best defense attorneys, because she had helped us out before. I expected to leave a message but got her instead.

"Nick! It's been forever." With her strong Brooklyn accent, that sounded almost like "fuh-evuh." It had actually only been a week or so since we last talked (or "tawked"), but she was a very dramatic woman.

"I may be in trouble," I said.

"I assume you're not calling from a police station?"

"Not yet." My nerves made me laugh.

"You've got great timing. I just finished going over some transcripts and making notes. I could use a break, and if it's urgent, I could drop by now." Lucky for us, she lived just a few blocks away.

"Stefan thinks it is."

"That's good enough for me."

We cleared the table and brought the glasses and bottle into the kitchen, and Vanessa arrived in under fifteen minutes. I was surprised the doorbell didn't wake Marco up.

Tall and built like a model, Vanessa was green-eyed and freckled, with masses of pre-Raphaelite auburn hair, and was nothing less than glamorous in a town that tended to be on the subdued un-showy side. Tonight as usual she was dressed to kill, wearing a jaguar print silk pantsuit, high-heeled black sandals, and strands of honey-colored amber beads. Her Brooklyn accent delighted me because it reminded me of home, though I'm sure it bothered locals who mistakenly thought it indicated a less than agile mind.

As always, she appeared with a bottle. "This is a great Montepulciano rosé," she said, handing it to Stefan who went off for a corkscrew.

"In vino veritas?" he asked when he returned with the open bottle and three of our Orrefors glasses. He'd brought out our best crystal for her.

Vanessa grinned as she sat on the couch. "That's the plan." She crossed her legs and looked very regal. "So where's the little guy?" she asked.

"Snoozing," Stefan said as he poured. The rosé was delicious and surprisingly fruity, but I only took a few sips because I wanted to keep my head clear given what I'd already had to drink. I explained as carefully as I could to Vanessa everything that Peter had told me in my office and on the phone. She listened with complete stillness.

"What do you think?" Stefan asked as soon as I finished and before I could ask the same question myself.

Vanessa blinked a few times as if checking her memory for similar cases in her files. "It's a felony to bribe a public official in Michigan, with up to ten years in prison and five thousand dollars in fines. But I don't know for sure if that would include somebody at one of the state universities. I would have to look into that. I'm pretty sure, though, that the kid's parents could be charged with mail fraud at the very least. And then honest services fraud."

"I've never heard of that," I said.

She shrugged. "Who has? It means SUM was defrauded in offering its 'honest services' as a school reading admissions applications. The parents cheated the school, in other words. They committed fraud. And how much did you say they paid? A quarter million bucks?" She squeezed her eyes shut, then opened them. "Offhand that could be a sentence of at least two years in prison—but the judge has discretion in cases like this. And of course," she said, "there's the question of intent."

"What do you mean?"

She shrugged. "His parents could claim they thought they were making a legitimate contribution. Maybe they did think that. Maybe they thought nobody was getting hurt, but he took another student's place, someone who would have gotten in legitimately."

"That's what Stefan said."

"It seems like a victimless crime, but it's not. You know, a lot also depends on how the money was handled—there's always the possibility of a money laundering charge, too."

"Holy shit," Stefan muttered. "What a mess."

"And even if the parents accept responsibility, there's still a fine and probation. Fraud is serious. The federal government would be prosecuting even if local police were involved in the investigation. Did your student give you any more details?"

"Not really, just the amount," I said.

"Okay." Vanessa's eyelids fluttered briefly as if she had a mental checklist she was going through. "Well, I don't think this kid who confessed to you—"

"—Peter."

"I don't think that Peter will be charged with anything, unless it turns out that he lied to you and he actually knew what was going on. And obviously, whoever took the bribe at SUM could be charged with a felony, like I said, but none of this is on you."

"That's a relief."

"Not so fast, buster."

I grinned despite myself because my father used to say the same thing to me when I was a kid. It was a line he must have picked up from an old movie.

Vanessa didn't seem to notice because she was on a roll. "See, the longer you go before telling anyone at SUM, like I guess the dean of your college, the worse it could be for you. I'll have to check, but since you're in education, you may have some kind of mandatory duty to report a crime in the university community, or the suspicion of a crime. Failure to do so could mean you're charged with a misdemeanor, maybe even a felony. Again, I'd have to check what laws apply to your situation. This whole business with college bribery is pretty new, and I haven't dealt with it myself."

"The dean is my immediate superior and he hates me. We just had an argument. But if I go over his head and talk to someone else, that could piss him off even more." Now I held my glass out to Stefan for some more wine.

Vanessa did the same. "What did you argue about?"

"Moving from my office to the former chair's office. He wanted me to, and I refused. I like staying where I am, he thinks it's wrong for a bunch of reasons. It got kind of loud." I was too embarrassed to say there was footage of the incident on Twitter.

Her eyes went wide. "You squabbled over an office? Are you kidding me? Jesus, you academics are really something."

I nodded glumly. "We are, it's true."

Vanessa's advice to report what Peter had told me was solid, and the wine was even better, but none of that cut my unease at being enmeshed in a situation that could turn very ugly. I dreaded being caught up in another SUM scandal.

"What happens if somehow I get charged with a crime?"

"I don't see it happening, but we'll deal with that if it does. No worries, I've got your back."

Those weren't just words. Vanessa had won some pretty big cases and could defend me as well as anyone in Michiganapolis.

"But Nick, you need to take this situation up with somebody at SUM, pronto. Okay?"

I nodded, thinking of Odysseus trying to steer his ship between Scylla and Charybdis. There I was: Keeping silent about what Peter had told me wasn't remotely an option, but revealing it was going to be unpleasant, I was sure of that.

"Let's change the subject," Vanessa said, sounding like a party host announcing the arrival of a marvelous guest. "What are you guys binge-watching these days?"

• • •

Before Stefan and I went to bed, I texted Celine and asked her to get me a meeting with Bullerschmidt ASAP. I wanted her to have the request as soon as she checked her phone in the morning, and it was the right move because before I was even done with breakfast the next morning, she texted me that the dean would see me at 9:00.

Stefan tried cheering me up at breakfast, but it was pointless. He hugged me good-bye and advised, "Just keep cool no matter what he says."

I told him that I would try, but driving to campus, all I could think of was "The Charge of the Light Brigade." And just like the six hundred in Tennyson's famous poem, now I was heading into the Valley of Death.

Bullerschmidt's associate dean for undergraduate studies, Boris Hernandez, was loitering at the entrance to the dean's secretary's office at the end of a suite of offices. Even though I'd met him and Stefan seemed to like him, I found him very intimidating. There was something odd in his eyes when he said, "The dean is waiting for you." I couldn't make out the vibe at all and why did he need to even be there? As I passed, I noticed he wore a showy gold ring encrusted with diamonds, not the kind of thing you typically saw anyone on campus wearing. And some kind of large fancy watch.

The dean's mousy secretary waved me in as if she were afraid to look at me.

The dean was dressed all in black and he tore into me before I even sat down.

"Do you know who came to see me yesterday thanks to you? Those little Digital Humanities jerks from your department. Why the hell are you harassing them? Why do they have to move out of their office?"

This was surreal. Hadn't he been telling me that *I* had to move? And hadn't he thought it was funny that I'd decided to separate them? Was this early onset dementia? Or had I imagined his bemused approval?

"It's not harassment," I said firmly, sitting down. "They can't share an office, so I decided to separate them. They had a fist fight at our department retreat—they're incorrigible." I wanted to add that we had discussed this already, but worried it might enrage him.

"Do you know what they told me? They're going to complain to the German consulate in Chicago! They say you're prejudiced against them. They say you called them Nazis and said they should be buried in the basement."

"That's a lie!"

"Is it?" Sweat was beading across his forehead and he shook his huge head like a bear emerging from a pond. I was glad I wasn't sitting any closer or I might have been sprayed. "Why would they make up something so outrageous?"

"How am I supposed to know what goes on in their heads? Maybe it's because I'm Jewish."

"Oh, so now you're accusing them of being anti-Semitic. Terrific! What is wrong with you, man? Didn't I warn you to keep a low profile as chair?" he snapped. "How does creating an international incident do that?"

I should have walked out of his office right then and come back when he was calmer, or better still, not come back at all. But he was pushing my buttons and I was not going to be defamed for something I didn't do, so I decided I had to challenge his memory of our encounter.

"When I told you in my office what I decided about them, you said you would have done the same thing in my position, moved them to different offices."

The dean gave me a lizard-like glare. "You're wrong, I never said anything remotely like that. I don't get involved in trivial matters like office assignments."

If it was so trivial, why was he bringing it up now? And how was I supposed to reply? Call him a liar, too, even though it was true? I'd quickly get a reputation for being paranoid.

But maybe he wasn't lying. Maybe he had truly forgotten what he'd said to me yesterday. This was freaky. I had to unhook and move on.

"That's not why I asked to see you," I said as calmly as possible. "There's a situation in my department—"

"—and you're too incompetent to handle it yourself?" Now he was grinning. I suppose he thought his comment was witty.

I closed my eyes and pictured Stefan telling me to keep cool no matter what. I opened them and without raising my voice, said, "One of our majors has told me that he thinks his parents paid someone, bribed someone, to get him admitted to SUM."

The dean's mouth actually fell open. I could even see gold crowns at the back of his jaws. He was silent, then his mouth snapped shut.

Was this some kind of ploy? If so, I waited it out.

"How long have you known?" he asked.

"The student told me yesterday."

"What! Why did you wait so long?"

I was starting to feel as trapped as a perjury-prone witness facing an eagle-eyed prosecutor in court.

"Dean Bullerschmidt, I'm telling you now." Saying his name and using his title gave me a little breathing space, helped me focus on not losing my temper.

He squinted at me. "You should have told me *immediately*. Why did you wait? Did you need time to concoct a story? What exactly have you got to hide?"

His office door was open and I could sense an ominous quiet out among his various minions at their desks and laptops. Not a sound from anywhere.

"I don't know what you're talking about."

He shook his head as if pitying me. "You're not a very good liar."

Either he was being gratuitously insulting or the dean was misreading my unease about revealing Peter's story. I had needed time yesterday to mull over my next step, but I wasn't going to say that to a loathsome bully.

"Who's the student?" he asked.

I hesitated. "He spoke to me in confidence."

Bullerschmidt pounded a fist on his desk. "Where are your loyalties? Do you want to be known as an enemy of SUM? That's treason."

The charge was so deranged I didn't challenge it.

"Can't you investigate the admissions process without his name?" I asked.

"How do I know you're not fabricating this story? Are you ready for fire and fury? Because that's what this university will unleash on you if you don't cooperate."

His threat was crazy but it startled me so much that I blurted out what he wanted to hear: "Peter DeVries."

The dean's eyes widened like a cartoon character having an *Aha!* moment. "Your protégé. He's studying with you this semester. Again." His tone made it sound creepy, somehow.

I knew that the dean had been the last person to approve and sign Peter's independent study form, but he had to sign lots of those forms every semester—why would he remember Peter's name?

As if I'd actually asked him, the dean continued, "I know what *everybody* is up to in Humanities."

"I'm not 'up to' anything. Peter's doing an independent study—there's nothing suspicious about that."

"What's suspicious is your claim that you only found out yesterday about someone perverting the admissions process when he's been one of your students since last year."

My forehead felt hot and tight.

"I don't believe you," he said with a nasty grin, apparently delighted to think of me as dishonest. "I just don't believe you. Your veracity is hardly unimpeachable. You're lying to save your skin."

I breathed in deeply, exhaled, stood up, and said in a firm voice, "I'm done being insulted."

"But *I'm* not done. I'm over-ruling you. Heino and Jonas will not be moving. I told them to stay where they are. I've emailed your office manager, Aldo, and warned him not to touch anything of theirs no matter what you say."

It took a few seconds for that to sink in. Then I let him have it: "You'll be sorry you did this, I swear to God, you will be so fucking sorry!"

Now he was unnaturally calm, perhaps to goad me further. "You need to tell me more about this bribery story."

"Find out yourself, since you seem to be spying on everyone."

I stormed out of his office and the dean's suite, aware that people were staring at me from doorways and desks.

Boris Hernandez followed me out into the empty hallway calling, "Wait!" but I kept heading to the stairs. I was too angry to wait for an elevator. When he caught up with me and tried to grab my arm, I rounded on him and said, "Touch me and you're dead." He was younger and bigger than me, but right then I must have seemed way meaner. Looking shocked, he backed off, which was too bad, because if he had tried anything I would have done my best to knock the crap out of him. And enjoyed it.

Part
Two
. . .

7.

I WAS STILL FUMING when I got to my office, and I must have looked mildly deranged because Celine stepped behind her desk as soon as she saw me. Voice steady, she asked, "What happened?"

"Cancel all my meetings today."

Celine pulled out her cell phone and swiftly sent off a volley of texts. "All clear," she said after a minute or two, cocking her head at me in a silent "Why?"

"Because that bastard said I was a liar, and how could anyone even think I'd call a colleague a Nazi!? That's fucking insane."

"Nick, *who's* a Nazi? Slow down."

I stomped into my office and should have been pleased that the new furniture was already there: well-padded visitors' chairs, a gleaming new desk that might have been rosewood, and a desk lamp that was a good imitation of a classic Tiffany lamp with a fluted bronze-colored base and stem, and a bowl-shaped stained glass shade in orange, red, yellow, and green. It had two pull chains, was surprisingly beautiful, and as I looked closer, I saw that the colors formed a stylized dragonfly. Impressive and hateful. I hated all of it.

Celine followed me into my office and hovered anxiously near the door as if to make a quick getaway if I turned into the Incredible Hulk.

I fell into my office chair with a thunk and momentarily contemplated sweeping every damned thing off the desk, including the lovely new lamp. It would be satisfying to watch things fly and listen to them crash and shatter—until I had to clean it all up. And besides, Celine didn't need to be any more worried about me than she was already.

Sitting there, I noticed a wooden hourglass about a foot tall on the windowsill. "What the hell is that?"

"Jasmine brought it as a gift. I put it there because I wasn't sure where you'd want it."

"She *what*?"

Jasmine Aminejad was a frumpy, mean-spirited, half-Iranian professor of Shakespeare and creative nonfiction, one of the newer faculty, and she had never said a nice word to me or Stefan. He'd given her a copy of his memoir when she first arrived at SUM and she had never thanked him, just attacked it online in a blog review that was so vituperative it made Stefan laugh. She was a mediocre writer herself, so perhaps she felt threatened. I didn't know or care, but now that I was department chair, I'd have to deal with her more often and I dreaded it.

"That's what she said."

"Throw it out."

Celine cocked her head at me. "How about I put it in my office? And I can send her a thank-you note on your behalf."

"Whatever."

"Do you want to talk?" she asked softly. "Or should I leave you alone?"

"You can sit." She settled into the chair opposite me, still looking a bit wary. Or maybe it was concern. My vision felt blurry and my face was aflame.

If she had said anything clichéd right then like "Breathe" or "It'll be okay" I would have lost it, but she was wisely silent. She folded her hands in her lap and was nodding as if listening to music on wireless earbuds. There was something very comforting in her presence. She was the least malicious person I knew, as safe as a trusted therapist.

I plunged right in. "So yesterday when Peter DeVries was in here and asked to close the door, he told me that his parents bribed somebody at SUM to get him admitted."

She frowned. "Why would they have to do that? I thought he was a good student."

"He is. There were...reasons he might have been rejected. That's personal. It'll probably all come out if this situation blows up, but I don't feel comfortable talking about it right now."

"Is that why you wanted the meeting with Bullerschmidt?"

"Yup. If Peter got admitted to SUM thanks to bribery, he can't be the only one." I hadn't said it aloud yet, hadn't wanted to consider some widespread corruption of the admissions process, but when I did, it made me feel queasy. "The dean accused me of being involved somehow."

"Sweet Jesus," Celine muttered, "there is no end to that man's malice."

"That's not even what pushed me over the edge. He countermanded my decision to move Heino and Jonas to separate offices because they complained to him—they said I was a bigot. They said that I called them Nazis. I would never do that. Stefan's parents were Holocaust survivors. I don't throw around terms like that."

"I know."

"Bullerschmidt actually went behind my back and told the twins they're staying in their current office, and he also told Aldo not to move them."

"On what grounds? You did the right thing. If those two stay together long enough, one of them is going to end up dead."

Given the history of our department, that wasn't hyperbole.

"And why would the dean care about office assignments anyway?" Celine asked.

"He claims they told him they were going to complain to the German embassy or consulate or whatever in Chicago."

"Oh, right. Bad PR. I can see the headline: 'SUM is Hostile to Foreign Faculty' yadda, yadda, yadda.... With all the news about immigrants, it would make us look like thugs."

"Exactly."

There was a soft knock on the open door between my office and Celine's. It was Aldo. "Celine," he said, "we had a meeting, do you want to reschedule?"

"Come in," I said. "Please, you need to hear this, too."

He smiled a bit crookedly, looking perplexed, but he dragged the chair from the side of my desk to sit by Celine who patted his hand in warning as if to say, "Fasten your seat belt."

I wasn't entirely sure he *did* need to hear me, but Aldo felt so helpful and simpatico I wanted him fully informed. And frankly, I was starting to enjoy his sense of style: he had purple leggings on today and a matching knit cap, a vintage Madonna T-shirt, a black cardigan, and black-and-white Converse sneakers. He was quietly giving the old farts on campus the finger and that made me smile.

But it was fleeting because I launched into the short version of my interactions with the twins, the dean, and Peter DeVries. Repeating the whole mess didn't lighten the load, it only made me feel more trapped.

"The dean's complaints are totally bogus. You didn't do anything wrong," Aldo said. "It's not even like you went more than a day before you told him."

Celine jumped in: "Nick texted me the evening he found out so that I could set up a meeting with Bullerschmidt ASAP."

"Even better, then—you have nothing to worry about." He looked as happy as a lottery winner, and though his reaction was a bit too cheerful, I appreciated his optimism.

"But all the same, the dean despises me," I had to point out.

Aldo shrugged. "He despises everyone. He's a hateful man and a stone-cold creep. Every time he sees me he asks why I don't dress like an adult—or something insulting like that."

Celine said, "You should tell him to stop."

"Right, and get fired for some trumped-up reason. And you know how conservative this administration is anyway. I bet plenty of people would be glad to see me gone. It's not like I have a strong union at SUM to defend me, and at the end of the day, it would be my word against his. That man is crazy, vindictive, and never lets go of a slight. He's an ogre and he's cruel to his staff."

Celine nodded. "That's what everybody says."

Aldo was as animated now as I'd ever seen him. Eyes blazing, he said, "Bullerschmidt is a monster, but they're insanely loyal to him in his office no matter what he does."

"How is that possible and how is he still around?" I asked. "He must have made dozens of enemies across the university over the years."

Celine looked disgusted. "Some people like to grovel. They need a big bad daddy to tell them what to do and what to think, to make them feel like they're important, to feel special because they believe in him."

SUM's own Mussolini.

"Well, shit," I said. "I don't see how I can stay here as chair with someone like that breathing down my neck."

Aldo urged me not to step down from the chairmanship. "SUM needs decent administrators." He hesitated, then went on. "I'm sorry about the mess with Heino and Jonas. When Buller-schmidt emailed me and said to forget about their move to the basement, I didn't know what the hell was going on. He even told me not to bother double checking with you, that his word was final, and warned me not to say anything to you until he shared the news. I'm really sorry, man."

"There's nothing to apologize for," I told Aldo. "You can't go against him."

"I'd like to," he added with unusual steel in his voice and Celine studied him, looking as surprised as I was. "I'd like to bring him down. Remember what Arnold Schwarzenegger says in that first Conan movie when they ask him what is best in life?"

Despite everything, I was amused because I'd seen the movie many times and loved to quote the line he was referring to: "'To crush your enemies, see them driven before you, and to hear the lamentation of their women!'"

Celine grinned. "That movie rocks!"

In that moment I felt like the three of us might be forming a kind of pact.

"There's something else," I said, because they had to know it all.

Celine and Aldo studied me, looking extra attentive.

"Peter called me last night at home and told me he blabbed to his best friend about the bribe, and that guy's father writes for *Scoop.*"

They both looked deflated by that news.

"Damn," Aldo said. "It would all come out sooner or later, but this could happen really fast now." He seemed to be weighing possibilities and said, "Peter's a student of yours and you might get called by that reporter if anyone thinks it's a big story and they take the time to track down all his professors."

"What do I say if I get a call?"

"No comment," Celine suggested. "And hang the hell up."

"Won't that make me sound guilty?" I asked, feeling like a candidate running for office who was hashing over strategy with his consultants on the verge of a scandal going viral.

"Just pretend it's a robo-call," she said flatly.

Aldo grinned at her even though she was serious, and the gleam in his eyes made me wonder if he had a kind of crush on Celine, though he knew she was married. I could see why: she wasn't just handsome and magnetic, she radiated competence where the opposite so often reigned supreme at SUM despite efforts to mask incompetence as creativity, innovation, dynamism.

What Celine said next surprised me. She asked Aldo, "Is there anything else? Anything else about the dean?"

Aldo coughed, fell silent, and nervously scratched the back of his neck.

"There is, isn't there?" she said. I had no idea what she had guessed at, but I trusted her intuition.

Aldo brought his hands together and up to his mouth as if he was about to pray. For guidance? Courage? He dropped them and crossed his arms as if he might be cold.

"Okay, yeah. I haven't told anyone this because it's— It's embarrassing." Without looking at either one of us, he went on, "At those receptions for visiting lecturers which the College of Humanities holds to broadcast collegiality and show what a great community of inquiry and learning we are, all of it bullshit of course, Bullerschmidt would say some really inappropriate things to me when nobody was close enough to overhear."

"More than slamming your clothes?" I asked.

"Yeah. On more than one occasion, he'd tell me I should be a model or an actor. And that I have great bone structure, and beautiful eyes. He'd even talk about my beard, that it looked really soft." Aldo started to blush, but he kept his head up.

I don't think I had paid much attention to Aldo's eyes before because his wardrobe was always so attention-getting. But I had to admit they were luminous and very blue, the blue of a clear spring sky.

"I'd just kind of laugh it off or eat another crummy canapé or claim I needed to talk to someone across the room."

Celine had a face like thunder, as a romance novelist might put it. "Has he ever *touched* you or tried to get you alone?" Her nose twitched in disgust.

"No. Never."

"It's still wrong," I said. "Totally out of line."

Celine said, "Amen. He's a pig. SUM is lousy with them."

I said to Aldo, "I know he's married, but do you think he's a closet case?"

Aldo perked up as if he'd been asked to explain some arcane accounting procedure. "Here's the thing. I don't know how he sees himself or what he really is, but that's not the point. When he makes comments about how I look, it doesn't really feel sexual at all, which in a weird way is even creepier. It feels like he's just asserting his power, putting me in my place, telling me that I'm an object, something he can assess and comment on, like I'm on display in a museum. It's dominance. It's dehumanizing."

"If you went public," Celine said, "There would probably be other people saying the same thing has happened to them."

Aldo rubbed his beard with one hand. "If I went public," he said after a few moments, "he would crush me. It doesn't matter that I'm straight, he would say I was gay or bi and making it all up for whatever sick reason. He'd find someone to dig up any kind of dirt he could, and SUM would back him."

"You think so?" I asked. "Wouldn't they want to oust him as soon as possible? Look at all the universities with sexual abuse scandals across the country."

"I'm sure he would sue me, or SUM would. It would be a juggernaut and I'd get annihilated. I'm not going that route, no way. And besides, what happened to me isn't like rape or sexual abuse."

"No, but it's *wrong*," Celine countered. "I didn't mean to pressure you, though. Everybody has to make the choices they can live with."

I knew her well enough to know that wasn't a passive-aggressive attempt to get Aldo to change his mind. Celine was a straight shooter who did not play games.

My office phone buzzed just then and we all stared at it as if it were the timer for a bomb. I picked up the handset gingerly.

"Is this Professor Nick Hoffman? I'm calling from *Scoop* and I'm doing a story about SUM."

The voice was as smooth and mellow as a radio announcer's and I thought it could be a very disarming tool, but luckily I was on guard. I mouthed "reporter" to Celine and Aldo and switched to speakerphone, set the handset down gently. He'd hear the difference, but he wouldn't know there was anyone in my office.

"Yes, I'm Nick Hoffman. Who are you and what do you want?"

"My name is Fabian Flick and I cover local news for *Scoop*."

Flick? That ridiculous name must have been hell for him as a boy, and even worse for his kids.

Celine was saying softly, "Hang up, hang up." Aldo held up a hand to indicate "Wait."

"And why are you calling me, Mr. Flick?"

"Sources tell me that there may be something going on with SUM's admissions process, and I wondered what you could tell me."

Boy, he was parsing his words very carefully, I thought, and trying hard to draw me out. Did he really have more than one source, or was he just blowing smoke to make me think he knew more than he did?

"I have nothing to do with admissions," I said, determined not to engage with this man on anything more than a superficial level. "You should call that office and speak to someone there." Of course he'd be stonewalled, but that wasn't my problem.

"Professor, how would you feel if you knew that students were being admitted to SUM who didn't exactly go through the normal admissions process?"

I was silent.

He persisted: "As chairman of the English Department, how would you feel if you discovered that someone majoring in English had bribed his way into SUM and into your department? Someone who really didn't belong there? Someone who had, in effect, stolen the place of another student?"

He was clever not to mention a name, but I'd dealt with reporters before.

"Well, Mr. Flick, that's really a hypothetical and it's not my field. Try the Philosophy Department." I hung up.

Celine quietly applauded me, but I knew this was just the beginning of something truly horrible. I felt like a D.C. politico brushing off an insistent reporter who was digging for the truth— or at least a good quote. Hanging up just delayed whatever was coming, whatever mess I'd already been dragged into. First by Peter's confession, then by the dean's wild accusations, and now by the reporter's phone call.

Mr. Flick would be calling back, because there was a juicy story just waiting to be devoured by a public that was always thrilled to see someone torn apart for any reason whatsoever. Twitter was the new Roman Coliseum.

8.

"THE REPORTER'S NAME IS FLICK?" Aldo asked, frowning.

"Yes, why?"

He sighed. "There was a story about him online somewhere when he started writing for *Scoop*. That guy used to write for some paper in Boston and he's won a Pulitzer, or almost did, something like that. Maybe it was just a nomination…"

Aldo was clearly more plugged-in to local events than I was.

"Why is he working at a newspaper in Michiganapolis?" I asked. "Was he fired or forced to leave?"

"That would be really good," Celine brought out. "I mean for us, you." She looked a bit sheepish, but I nodded. She was right. One defense against anything hostile Flick might write about me would be to question his ethics—if we could—or bring up something iffy from his past.

I brushed aside what that said about how corrupt my thinking had become, and how quickly. We were only a short way into my tenure as department chair and I already felt embattled and defensive—that was not a good omen. What was next, "oppo research"?

Aldo shook his head. "Flick is originally from Grand Rapids, moved to the East Coast when he and his wife divorced, but he quit his reporting job back East to be near his son because of a drinking problem that he doesn't think his ex-wife takes seriously enough."

It sounded like something from a soap opera.

"You read all that online?" I asked. It amazed me how confessional people were now, baring their souls on YouTube and everywhere else.

"No. This is a big campus but it's a small town—I overheard people talking about Flick and his son in a Starbucks. But I did want to read more about him, and from what I learned I think we're in trouble. He's got a reputation for being worse than a pit bull when he's on a story."

The three of us were silent, and I assumed we were imagining the violence those dogs had a reputation for doing.

But it wasn't a beast who called out, "Hello?" from Celine's office at that moment, it was Peter DeVries. Celine went out to talk to him, but he pushed past her and entered my office, weaving a little, looking disheveled in the same clothes he'd worn yesterday, and smelling of sweat and alcohol. He was either hungover or still drunk.

Aldo rose and moved to the deep windowsill to the right of my desk and sat there after moving the hourglass to the floor, while Celine asked Peter softly, "Do you need some water?" I guess if we were English we'd have been offering him a nice cup of hot sweet tea. Maybe that would be Celine's next choice.

Peter nodded dismally and sank into the chair she had vacated, but hardly seemed to be aware of her or Aldo. Celine nabbed the hourglass and went off to the water cooler in her office and returned with a full glass of water which Peter downed greedily. She set the empty glass on my desk and lifted the other chair over to set it by Aldo.

Sitting there, the two of them were trying to be quiet and inconspicuous, but I don't think Peter cared. Studying his ravaged face I thought of lines from a poem by my favorite poet, Lord Byron: "in my heart/There is a vigil, and these eyes but close/To look within." This was clearly a tormented young man.

"What's going on?" I asked.

"I lied to you," Peter said brokenly, eyes cast down. "Yesterday. I'm so sorry."

"On the phone or in my office?"

"Both, I guess. I didn't tell you everything."

"You *knew* about the bribe?"

He sighed, eyes down. "I knew my parents were desperate to get me into SUM because they thought it would keep me from drinking again." He sneered. "Like that was ever going to work..."

"And?" I hoped that prompting him didn't sound cold, but I needed him to tell me everything.

"You know, you hear things in high school," he said. "You hear about ways to get admitted to universities that wouldn't accept you otherwise. Sketchy ways." Now he met my glance and his eyes looked haunted. "I figured my mom and dad had plenty of money to throw around and they were going to use it. They know all kinds of people at SUM, they went here as undergrads and they're members of the alumni association, go on trips together with other rich alums. When I got admitted, I was sure their money made it happen, but I didn't want to know the facts. And now it's all going to come out—because of me."

I glanced over at Celine and Aldo, both of whom seemed as struck by his condition as by his story. I wasn't sure what to say next, but Peter had more to share.

"I guess it doesn't really matter," he said. "We're all going to die anyway. The water, the air, everything's fucked. Alaska's melting, Australia's on fire, the whole planet is fucked and there's nothing anyone can do—it's too late to save it."

I confess I had started to tune out news about climate disruption because it was too disturbing. Wildfires, superstorms, droughts, floods, and heat waves were accelerating across the country, across the globe, and Michigan was already experiencing changes in its climate, just like the other Great Lakes states. Our average temperatures were going to keep climbing in the next few decades, according to climatologists, and our rain and snow storms would become more intense. They already were. Waves on Lake Michigan were higher than ever before and the resulting erosion was changing Michigan's western coastline. Many houses had already been severely damaged by the rising levels of Lake

Michigan or had even been swept away. Luckily for me and Stefan, our condo in the lakeside town of Ludington was far enough from the shore to still be safe. And the state wasn't facing anything as dire as the hurricanes hitting Puerto Rico or those raging fires in California.

Contacting Congress or state legislators, signing petitions, coming out for Earth Day demonstrations, any and all of that seemed pointless when there wasn't enough political will nation-wide to try to stop our race to destruction.

But despite all that, I somehow hadn't lost hope, and maybe that was just denial. I probably would have felt different if I were Peter's age and bombarded by bad news from every media source, news that sounded like the latest disaster movie, news that paint-ed my future as impossibly bleak.

"Is that why you're drinking again?" I asked. "Despair about the future?"

He nodded. "One reason, anyway. That. And the bribery. And my parents driving me crazy." He almost smiled at that.

"Have you tried seeing a therapist?"

"Yeah. It doesn't really make a difference. I'm so tired of talk."

"Maybe you need a break from school," Celine suggested gen-tly. "A vacation."

"Go someplace you can chill out," Aldo said. "That's what I would do."

It didn't sound like a bad idea. I asked, "Is there someplace you really love? Where you feel at peace?"

"I don't know...I kind of like Santa Fe."

I was about to suggest that he go for it and take a leave of absence, but then it hit me. Encouraging Peter to get away could be seen as abetting a criminal if he was more involved in his parents' plan to get him admitted to SUM than he had already revealed. And that was very possible, given that he'd lied to me once already. I disliked being suspicious and even fearful, but wasn't that the national mood right now for a large part of the population?

"Did you tell anyone else?" I asked. "Besides your friend?"

"I don't think so. But he's got fifty thousand Instagram followers."

"Wonderful," Celine muttered.

I felt the same way and didn't ask for details of Peter's friend's Internet celebrity. It could be something utterly trivial or something important, the reason didn't matter. What counted was his friend having an audience, and what was the point of having one if you didn't play for it? Once you got on that particular path you had to keep feeding the beast. Stefan's agent and publisher were constantly pushing him to boost his presence on the Internet, and he wisely resisted: "I'm a writer, not a clown."

"You probably need a lawyer," Aldo said to Peter from the windowsill. "Separate from your parents, just in case."

"No worries there." Peter smiled crookedly. "We have plenty of lawyer friends. If I don't leave."

I found myself thinking about a break myself. I closed my eyes and for a moment let the sounds of the university wash over me: bikes whizzing by outside the building, the nearby elevators dinging insistently as doors thumped open and closed, footsteps in the hallway, some determined, some hesitant—those were probably students searching for a professor's office. Phones were ringing, too, and somewhere there was the faint, sweet arpeggio of a wind chime in someone's office window.

I wondered then if my hope that I could make a difference at SUM as a department chair was all just a fantasy, maybe even narcissism. I was a teacher and an Edith Wharton scholar, but none of that had prepared me for this voyage into lies, treachery, and rage that I seemed to be on. Honestly, sitting there with Peter I felt helpless and clueless myself. Suggesting a time out for him wasn't even a Band-Aid, it was simply the equivalent of sending someone "thoughts and prayers" after they'd lost everything in a disaster.

"I'm going back to my dorm now," Peter said. "Thanks for listening." He turned to Aldo and Celine. "Thanks for the advice."

He seemed to mean it, but there was something furtive in his eyes.

"What's your dorm?" I asked as casually as I could.

Peter's head jerked back in surprise. It was an odd question, I guess, but he said, "Clinton."

"Just curious," I brought out, and he left, much steadier on his feet than when he had arrived, and with a determined set to his shoulders. He didn't seem distressed or conflicted at the moment, which surprised me because I couldn't imagine what had changed for him in our conversation. Was it simply the relief of unburdening himself?

Celine and Aldo gathered around my desk and the air was still heavy with Peter's distress.

"I'm glad my daughter got into Georgetown the old-fashioned way," Celine observed. "Great test scores, straight A's, and her father went there." She smiled disarmingly.

Aldo said, "My girlfriend doesn't want kids at all, and I'm fine with that." And then he added, "I'm not big on day drinking, but I wouldn't mind a few shots of Wild Turkey right now, and a couple of episodes of *Portlandia* so I can detox."

I knew the satirical show about life among Portland, Oregon's hipsters only by reputation, but I nodded. I think we all needed some kind of restoration and relief.

I asked Celine, "Can we find out who the resident assistants are at Peter's dorm? Or just one?"

RAs were upper-class students who supervised dorm life. They arranged social events, advised students in their care on everything big and small connected to life on campus, dealt with things like study problems and feelings of isolation, mediated roommate disputes, gave informal seminars on crucial topics like diversity, and made sure that all rules were followed so that dorm life was peaceful and fun. They were crucial, under-appreciated members of the university community. RAs really strived to *create* community—unlike the administrators who just put out press releases and left it at that.

"I'm on it," Celine said, pulling out her phone and heading to her office.

Aldo looked at me curiously, and I held up a hand and said, "Wait."

Celine was back with a phone number and I called it, got a Jeremy Lewis who sounded absurdly chipper, which was a good sign, I thought.

"This is Nick Hoffman, chair of English, and I just wanted to ask you to keep an eye on Peter DeVries. He's on your floor? Terrific!"

Lewis's bass voice practically vibrated my phone: "Is he in trouble? Is he a danger to himself?"

"Not that I'm aware of. He's an English major taking an independent study with me, and he's been a student of mine before. He's dealing with some heavy issues right now." I thought that was enough of a warning without betraying Peter's confidence.

"Have you recommended the counseling center?"

"I did suggest therapy, yes."

"Okay, cool. Thank you for calling." He ended the call and I hoped he took my concern seriously. No, he had to, that was his job.

"Was calling the RA a mistake?" I asked Celine and Aldo, suddenly realizing how worn out I was after the imbroglio with Dean Bullerschmidt, the call from *Scoop*, and now Peter's revelations. What a day, and it wasn't even lunch time. God, I needed a nap.

Celine and Aldo both gave me a firm "No."

"You're the chair," Aldo said. "You need to look out for the majors, or any students who have problems. You can't ignore them, it's part of your job, whether it's in writing or not. Most chairs on campus really couldn't give a shit. They want power, they want more majors, they want some kind of larger role on campus. Students are an afterthought."

"You did great, Nick," Celine said with feeling. "Now we have to hope Peter gets the help he needs, whatever that turns out to be."

"Listen," I said, "if you guys want to take the rest of the day off, feel free. I'm going home. I feel dizzy and I don't think I could do any real work today."

Celine nodded sympathetically. "I'll stay and man the barricades and call you if there's something you need to know—or would you prefer a text?"

"Either is fine, Celine. You decide."

I hadn't even had a chance to unpack my made-in-Detroit Shinola messenger bag, so I was good to go.

"Celine and I can have a lunch meeting," Aldo said. "We'll order Chinese, and if I can't hang on after that, I'll head home. Thanks, Nick." He shook my hand and Celine looked like she might want to give me a hug, but then she backed away and just patted my back as I left, feeling like a passenger deplaning from a really bad flight.

Marco whined with excitement to find me coming home early. I fed him lunch, took him for a walk, and lost myself in watching him encounter the world through his nose. This wasn't a brisk walk, it was a meander as he snuffled one mailbox or shrub after another like a doggy detective. And that gave me time to bask once again in how calm, quiet, and lovely our subdivision was. Laid out first in the mid-1920s, its variety of homes built at different periods was eye-catching and soothing: Cape Cods, split-levels, Tudors, ranches, brick Colonials, our own Moderne, and several Prairie-style houses by students of Frank Lloyd Wright. There were no sidewalks, which gave it a bucolic feel, as did the mammoth blue spruce trees that bound together the disparate plots which were almost all beautifully landscaped. Magnolias, variegated spirea, and hydrangeas were particular favorites.

It wasn't a wealthy neighborhood but a popular one for its color and the quality of the homes. People might take jobs elsewhere but when they returned to Michiganapolis they would buy houses in this same neighborhood, and there were families whose kids had only moved a street or two away. Even in a bad real estate market, houses here sold quickly because of the quiet, the lovely homes, and the old trees. The songs of chickadees, robins, cardinals, and mourning doves filled the streets, counterpointed by the squawking of crows.

Though we didn't have close friends here, we knew at least a dozen dog owners and their dogs, and Marco loved to socialize. I preferred chatting with the owners to spending time with my ostensible colleagues because I'd been considered suspect when I started teaching in the department for too many reasons. Stefan, even as writer-in-residence, had also felt quietly sneered at by faculty members who prized theories about fiction over actual fiction. At one faculty party someone now dead and gone had said, "Your career isn't especially distinguished, is it?"

Of course our neighborhood wasn't idyllic: there were careless neighbors who couldn't control their dogs and berated you if you expressed concern. One of them, a chunky, nasal woman with badly dyed blond hair, had a few years ago yelled at me to get control of myself when her unleashed Black Labrador lunged at me and Marco and I whipped out pepper spray to defend myself. I didn't need to use it, luckily, because she finally got her own dog under control, but I would have if he'd attacked us or come any closer. She had the nerve to tell me to "Take a chill pill" when I told her she needed to watch her dog more closely.

Stefan was at the gym and when I got back, I welcomed the quiet as I sprawled on the couch, with Marco joining me for another snooze. He crawled up onto my chest, rolled onto his side and was soon gently snoring. As I wondered so often, why couldn't my life be that simple?

I thought I might be able to nap, but my head was filled with scenes: the dean's contempt for me, Peter's multiple confessions, and shadowy images of the coming juggernaut of bad publicity that might flatten me. I had no doubt I was in trouble, even though I was only peripherally involved in the scandal of Peter's admission to SUM. The university leadership were all hypocrites. Threatened by bad publicity, they would shoot up phony, distracting flares to demonstrate how responsive they were to the crisis of the day, how sensitive and caring. And that meant somebody would have to be the fall guy. How could I prevent that from happening?

I was warming up some lasagna for lunch when Stefan came home and gave me a big hug. "You look like you've been through hell," he said, setting his gym bag down in the kitchen. Laundry could wait, but I could tell he was ravenous for something to eat.

"I'm *in* hell." As the Anglo-Saxon poets put it, I unlocked my word hoard and updated him on the day's turmoil.

"Walk away, Nick. Just quit. Today. Right now. You don't need the aggravation of being chair."

I wanted to. I really wanted to. But I imagined the mockery that could erupt on Twitter. It would look like I'd been bullied out of my position, and this perception could easily launch savage, demeaning take-downs on a range of sites from *BuzzFeed* to Fox—and who knew where else.

Some U.S. senator had once said, "Each one of us can make a difference, together we make change."

If I didn't try to make a difference, how would the university ever change?

"If I step down, the next chair might be happy to throw Peter under the bus. I know his situation is very murky, but maybe there's something I can do as department chair to help him—more than if I'm just another professor."

"Nick, you are *asking* for trouble."

I tried to make a joke. "I don't have to ask. Trouble always knows just where to find me."

Stefan didn't seem to think that was funny. Marco started to howl.

9.

AND THEN, as if we were in a horror movie, the doorbell rang and Marco's howling intensified. He raced to the front door and went wild, barking and scrabbling as if a monster were outside. Stefan hurried after him, picked him up, brought him to the kitchen and sent him out into the backyard through the dog door where he would quickly be distracted by chasing squirrels and chipmunks.

We crossed paths as I answered the door.

"I'm Fabian Flick."

He wasn't at all the grubby man I imagined. He was younger than I, over six feet tall, lean, rosy-cheeked and blue-eyed with copper-red hair slicked straight back, and his dove-gray suit was immaculate. That and the lavender open-necked shirt and blue paisley pocket square made him look like a high-powered consultant of some kind.

Or a very smooth criminal.

I recognized his cologne: Davidoff Cool Water.

I was about to close the door but he said, "There are serious allegations being made about you and I think you might want to get your story out there." His voice was so toneless it was almost robotic.

I stepped back. "What allegations?"

Stefan came in from the kitchen and echoed my question, then asked, "Who's this?"

"Fabian Flick." He held out a hand and Stefan just stared at him till Flick dropped his hand and shrugged. This was clearly not the first time he'd been treated with disdain by a member of the public and he seemed not just used to it, but impervious. As if it gave him more power.

"Can I come in?"

My curiosity outweighed my suspicion and I ushered him into the living room and pointed to the least comfortable chair.

He sat without commenting about the room or even seeming to see it. He took out his phone and asked, "Can I record our conversation?"

Both of us said a firm "No."

He put it away.

I sat on the arm of the couch opposite him and Stefan stood in the doorway, looking as threatening now as a bouncer eyeing a customer one drink away from being thrown out of the club.

"Why are you here?" I asked. "I'll talk to you only if it's off the record."

A flicker of annoyance ruffled his façade just a little, but he suppressed it. "There are rumors you're involved in a bribery scandal at SUM."

"What the fuck?" Stefan growled.

"I have sources telling me that."

"Your son?" I asked.

He didn't flinch or even blink. "I don't reveal my sources."

"Well, I know that a student of mine told your son about what he thinks happened."

"So you're saying it's not true?" he asked flatly.

"I don't know. How can I be sure? I just know what he told me." But had Peter told me everything?

"Are you saying your student might be lying?" His eyes narrowed.

I could feel my cheeks flaming hot. "Do not put words in my mouth."

"Fair enough," he said, cool and imperturbable. I thought he could make a wonderful torturer, and pictured him never breaking stride even with his victim's blood splattered across that lovely suit and rosy complexion. "But whatever your role in what happened, there is a strong possibility of administrative malfeasance at the university. Students who shouldn't have been admitted to the university had influential officials helping them unfairly." He smiled. "That's a euphemism, of course."

Flick wasn't saying anything that hadn't occurred to me already, but I sure wasn't going to tell him that. "Who else have you talked to?"

"Your dean, for one." And now he almost smiled.

"He doesn't like me."

"I'd call that an understatement."

"I don't like him either," I said, realizing it sounded childish. Stefan said, "Easy, Nick."

Disregarding caution and sense, I said, "If he's been trashing me, I'm happy to return the favor. He's a little fascist. He's despised across campus, and you might want to check into how he interacts with staff." Maybe Aldo wasn't the only guy he'd been creepy with—or woman for that matter. He could be an equal-opportunity harasser.

Flick nodded as if he'd expected me to take that tack. "Well, his staff actually said that you threatened him."

"Bullshit."

"Really? This is a quote: 'You'll be sorry you did this, I swear to God, you will be so fucking sorry!' Did you say that to the dean or not?"

"I was angry. He was accusing me of all kinds of shit and insulting me. *He's* the one you should be investigating."

"I'm not a cop, Professor, I'm just a reporter putting a story together. And witnesses said you looked out of control."

I took a deep breath. "Since when is speaking truth to power being out of control?"

He grinned. "Good answer."

"Feel free to quote me on *that*," I snapped. "And now you should leave. If you want anything else, contact my attorney."

"And that would be—?"

"You're a reporter, figure it out."

He didn't wait to be led to the door, but rose and left without looking back. Stefan slammed the door after him.

"Shit, Nick, what was that all about?"

I sunk my head in my hands. "I know, it was stupid to say anything to him, and insult and accuse the dean on top of it. I'm beyond stressed—I'm overwhelmed."

The doorbell rang again a few moments later and I thought of Dorothy Parker's famous quip, "What fresh hell is this?"

"You get the door," I said. It was unlikely to be Mormons or people with a petition to sign this early in the day.

"We could ignore it," Stefan said.

"Whoever's there probably just saw Flick leave the house, so I think that's not going to work."

Stefan acquiesced. The next voice I heard at the door chilled me. It was my true nemesis on campus, Detective Valley, and that meant the bribery scandal was already on his radar.

Wonderful.

We'd had way too many run-ins over the years. Valley thought that SUM professors were thugs, wastrels, and fools. That was on a good day. He'd made it very clear that if the university was shut down and the faculty exiled *en masse*, he would be very happy. And if he had a shit list, I was surely at the top for having been involved, one way or another, in so much campus crime. Maybe he thought I caused it?

"Professor," he said coldly.

"Detective."

Cops had scared me as a kid the way some people get freaked out by clowns, though I had no explanation why. Was it the uniforms? More recently, the run-ins Stefan and I had with campus and local police had deepened my distrust. Likewise learning about all the different ways police across the country were abusing people's rights. And even though my rank at the university had changed in the last few years, Valley still sometimes could make me squirm.

Weirdly, he was dressed all in brown from head to toe and looked like some sort of UPS functionary.

Valley waited for me or Stefan to invite him to sit down, but we let him stand. He was lanky, going gray, and showing crow's feet and deep frown lines. Though he was physically fit, he seemed wearier now than ever before and I was glad to see that he was tired.

But then I relented and waved him to a chair and asked if he wanted some coffee, because it hit me that I had to clear myself of any involvement with the bribery ASAP, and this was the place to start.

"Coffee?" he asked, as if I were offering him something outlandish. Well, I was: my hospitality. I represented everything he despised about SUM, whether that was a fair assessment or not.

"Yes," I said. "We have Swedish, German, Turkish, whatever you like." I might have been imagining the last one.

He studied me, perhaps to see if I was mocking him. I smiled as warmly as I could manage, and Stefan caught on, saying, "I'll put up a pot, it takes just ten minutes. Or I could make you some tea…?"

Valley shook his head and squeezed out, "Thanks, I'm good."

I sat opposite and said, "I want to make it completely clear that I had nothing to do with what's going on."

He glared at me. "Of course you're involved. There have been credible accusations against you for making threatening statements."

"Wait. *What?*"

Stefan waved a hand at me to stop. Valley was clearly not there to ask questions about how Peter DeVries got admitted to SUM. This was about my morning's high-volume meeting with the dean.

Shifting mental gears, I tried to sound as innocent as possible when I asked, "Threatening whom?"

He grimaced as if even the sound of my voice was working his last nerve. "The Dean of Humanities for one, and an associate dean, Boris Hernandez."

I was stumped trying to think of how to handle this situation. Stefan sat down next to me and filled my awkward silence: "The dean has a pattern of abusive behavior and Nick was on the receiving end today."

"Why haven't you lodged an official complaint?" Valley shot.

I almost said, "Why do you think?" but modulated my annoyance down to saying "Because he's a powerful person and I'm not, that's why. The dean's been insulting me ever since he appointed me to the position of department chair."

Valley looked scornful, as if it were my fault the dean behaved the way he did. I was getting a tiny taste of what women experienced when they didn't report sexual harassment or worse—and it was making me very uneasy.

"If it's that bad," Valley said, "you have a responsibility to speak out. SUM's Code of Safety applies to faculty as well as staff and students." He paused as if he was about to quote from the Constitution: "'No one on campus shall verbally harass, intimidate, cause or threaten physical harm to another, or endanger the physical safety of another campus citizen in person, via mail, electronic media or any other form of communication.'"

"I take it that's a direct quote?" Stefan asked.

Valley nodded.

When I didn't say anything, Valley continued: "Professor Hoffman, the dean also says you threatened his associate dean."

"And what did he say? Boris?"

Valley cleared his throat. "Boris Hernandez denied it, but other witnesses confirmed the story."

Something was off here but I couldn't guess what, exactly. I did threaten Boris, so why was he telling Valley something else?

"Well, he tried to grab me," I said, confused by Boris's silence. "Who? How?"

"Boris did, when I was leaving."

He nodded. "Did he actually make contact with you? Did he hurt you?"

"He was going to! You saw what he looks like." I sounded ridiculous to my own ears, but the moment had been real. I did feel he was going to attack me. Or something. Unless I had totally misread the situation. It wouldn't be the first time.

"And that's why you threatened to kill this man?" Valley's expression was a blend of contempt and boredom, which made me wonder if he'd had conversations like this with other SUM faculty before.

"It was a figure of speech. I was warning him not to touch me."

"And did the dean try to touch you, too?"

"Well, no, but he—"

"—he what?"

Stefan coughed, warning me not to say anything about the bribery issue and I knew he was right. It was actually smarter to wait till Valley brought it up, whenever that might be, so I tried to steer the conversation back to what I felt I could discuss.

"Are you investigating me? Is this official?"

"It's preliminary. SUM takes the safety of everyone in the community very seriously."

"Investigating on whose behalf? Campus police?"

He looked incredulous, which should have surprised me, but then I realized a possibility. This was my chance, so I asked, "Is there really a Committee of Public Safety? Is everybody on campus under surveillance? Is our email being monitored? Are there cameras besides the ones we can see outside buildings? Hidden inside offices? Can the Committee have people arrested if they're considered dangerous? Who gets to make that decision?"

When he didn't reply, I asked, "Are you on it?"

He repeated what he'd said before about SUM taking people's safety seriously.

"That sounds like a yes to everything," I said.

Valley scowled. "I'm not confirming or denying what you said."

"Why not?"

It was good to have him on the defensive again, and I was damned tired of feeling scrutinized, blamed, and attacked. Then I thought, "Watch yourself," and could feel Stefan radiating the same message. The last thing I needed now was to blow up at

Valley and prove I was some kind of risk to anyone, on campus or off.

"What are you planning on doing?" Valley asked me.

"I don't understand."

"You've acted in an unprofessional and alarming manner to your superior and a member of his staff."

"I wouldn't put it that way." And neither would Vanessa if this turned into a court case or I was brought up before some panel at SUM.

"Again. I'm asking you: What are you planning on doing?"

I looked at Stefan who seemed as baffled as I was.

"You need to show contrition."

I heard Stefan quietly gasp but I was afraid to look at him because I thought I might laugh at the bizarre turn the conversation had taken.

I suddenly pictured someone who couldn't be any less like me, King Henry II of England as played by Peter O'Toole in the movie *Becket*, walking barefoot and shirtless into Canterbury Cathedral to be whipped by monks for having incited the death of his beloved and hated counselor, Thomas à Becket.

Valley was mumbling something impatiently under his breath and the only word I thought I could make out was "idiot."

"I've been instructed," he said aloud, "instructed to make you an offer. The dean is prepared to forget the incident involving him and the associate dean, if you apologize. Not by email or a phone call. In person."

I understood it in a flash: Bullerschmidt didn't just want to humiliate me, he wanted to bury what had happened because there was always a chance it could make *him* look bad, not me.

"And you're the dean's messenger?" I asked, not trying to keep the scorn from my voice.

He shrugged. "More like an ambassador. Think about his offer. But don't take too long. I'll show myself out." As Valley left, we heard Marco burst into the kitchen through the dog door. He raced towards the closed front door to pour scorn on the departed detective. We didn't try to quiet him down.

Did people really say "I'll show myself out" anywhere but in movies and TV shows? I guess Valley did.

After two barbed encounters in under a few hours here at home, I felt deflated. Was the dean serious? Could he be trusted? I could see him secretly recording my apology and turning it against me somehow. The whole thing was deeply suspicious.

Stefan fell back heavily against the couch. Flinging his arms wide across the cushions as if settling in to binge-watch a favorite show, he said, "Oh my God, we have truly gone down the rabbit hole." He seemed to be perversely enjoying the crazy spectacle of the last hour or so.

10.

"SO WHAT DO YOU THINK?" I asked Stefan. "Should I do it?" I honestly felt at sea and wasn't sure what made sense anymore—the day had left me exhausted and dizzy. The idea of an apology to the dean was outrageous, but maybe it would be a way to move past the current craziness with a clean slate.

His eyes went wide. "Apologize to that maniac? Are you kidding? He'll make sure everyone on campus sees it."

"I can stipulate that he can't record my apology in any way. I can pick a neutral spot, it wouldn't have to be at his office."

"Nick, Nick, Nick. Listen to yourself. The dean doesn't negotiate, he demands. He won't accept your terms."

"How do we know that?"

Stefan leaned forward as if to hypnotize me. "*Listen.* Just raising the question of where the meeting takes place is giving in to him. Once you do that, you'll be a kind of slave even if he doesn't record it—which he could do surreptitiously."

"Slave? Isn't that hyperbole?"

He shook his head vigorously. "A man like that will eat people's souls if they stay in his orbit long enough, if they succumb to his will. Is that how you see yourself? A minion?"

The word "minion" made me think of Dracula and how he turned Renfield into his shivering creature.

I understood Stefan's objections, but having lost my temper was making me think that I *should* apologize. I felt ashamed of how I'd behaved in the dean's office. That was not the way I wanted to act or be perceived on campus—or anywhere else for that matter.

Stefan took my hand and clearly was reading my mind again. "I know you're embarrassed about blowing up at Bullerschmidt and Boris, but that doesn't mean you have to debase yourself. See a shrink if it's really troubling you, but don't get caught up in the dean's mind games. Don't try to negotiate with someone who can't be trusted. Look how he's been treating you—do you really think an apology is going to change anything?"

We discussed my dilemma all the way until dinner, with an intermission to walk Marco and further breaks to check Twitter, Facebook, and Instagram. Well, *I* checked them and Stefan didn't try to stop me. I guess he hoped the obsession would burn itself out. And it did, sort of. The results were actually a relief because the uproar over my yelling at Dean Bullerschmidt in my office was already dying down—just as Stefan had predicted. Social media had more important stories to capture people's attention and turn them away from my little scene: pop star rivalries, white supremacists going nuts in Walmart and Mexican restaurants, people almost coming to blows over flag burning, white homeowners threatening Black kids seeking donations for their high school sports teams.

There was thankfully no hint whatsoever of my latest shouting match going public.

But I still knew that even if that incident never became widely known, there was still always the chance that I'd take my place on the Internet as another example of "everything that's wrong with academia" based on that one clip someone in Shattenkirk had posted. If I were paranoid, I'd be launching a quiet investigation, because the originating account didn't have a name or information that revealed the poster's identity. I knew that there were ways to unmask a person trying to stay anonymous on Twitter, but even if I could find someone to help me do that, wouldn't it be Nixonian, and what would I do with the information anyway?

"I hope people don't think of me as a crank," I brought out.

"There are worse ways to be remembered," Stefan said.

"Sure, I could be a war criminal."

We defrosted some veal stew for dinner and Stefan picked a bottle of Stone Hill Winery's Norton, a big full-bodied red that tasted like something from the south of France. The winery in Missouri was over a hundred and fifty years old and we'd often talked about driving out there to sample the wines and enjoy the German restaurant onsite, but never seemed to get going. I wouldn't have minded being on the road right then. I was feeling like the title of that Mona Simpson novel: *Anywhere but Here.*

I suggested going out to see a movie that evening but everything we checked at our closest theater seemed to be a remake or a superhero flick, so we turned our phones off for the night, took the remaining half bottle of wine to the living room, and settled down to watch a DVD of *Midnight*, a classic screwball comedy with Don Ameche and Claudette Colbert. We had barely gotten into the opening scene when the doorbell rang. This time *I* was the one who suggested not answering, but our evening caller was very insistent and I remembered the Oscar Wilde line about someone ringing in a "Wagnerian manner."

Marco barked, though not very heartily, and Stefan carried him to the door, opened it, and I heard his surprised question: "Ciska?"

What the hell was she doing there?

"I hope I'm not interrupting anything," she replied in her silky voice. "But this is important departmental business and it can't wait until tomorrow."

I turned off the TV and wondered if she had tried texting me, but I didn't have time to check before she, Stefan, and Marco entered the living room. She was looking regal but businesslike in a purple coat dress and square-toed pumps, a string of black pearls, and her hair drawn back into a loose ponytail. She was wearing a very floral perfume that was so strong it made my eyes water a little and I wondered if I was going to sneeze.

Stefan and Marco settled beside me on the couch. Ciska sat

opposite us, folded her hands, and didn't wait for a question from me or Stefan. "I have to tell you that what I've heard about today's events is deeply concerning."

"You mean the drop in the Dow Jones because of our trade war with China?" In the middle of the day's chaos I hadn't forgotten to check how our investments were faring. Not the wisest remark, but then strategy wasn't the keynote of my day.

She frowned. "This isn't a time for jesting."

Her presence struck me as ominous and her observation annoyed me. "Of *course* it is, Ciska. This is the *best* time. Who needs humor when life is going smoothly?" I wondered if she was still steaming about my response to her digital reading course idea.

"It's not good for the image of the department—or our morale—when the new chair gets into a shouting match with the dean. Your encounter today casts doubt on the seriousness of our mission as educators."

I think she really meant my own seriousness was in question, but was perhaps trying to sugarcoat the poison a little. Ciska seemed as aloof as usual, but I could sense a hamster wheel spinning frantically behind the calm façade.

"And you know about my 'encounter' how, exactly?" I asked.

"The dean called me and explained everything."

Bullerschmidt had called her? Why? I could feel Stefan bristling at this new information. If I were Marco, I would have been growling at this point. He, of course, had jumped off the couch and was already asleep by the fireplace.

"The dean called you," I said flatly.

"Yes. And he suggested that as associate chair, I intervene."

"Intervene? To do what exactly?"

She gave me a smile so sincere-looking it had to have been practiced in a mirror more than once. "To recommend that you step down as chair if you're not willing to apologize to him."

I exchanged a glance with Stefan, who was generally good at keeping his cool, but right now his face was turning red and he looked daggers at Ciska. If she and Detective Valley both knew about the dean insisting on an apology from me, was there anyone on campus who wouldn't know by tomorrow or the day after at the latest? Even without the help of social media, our campus was what Aldo had called it: a gossipy small town.

"I can understand your reluctance, Nick. You've embarrassed yourself enough already by the way you've behaved in a position you're clearly not suited for. I'm happy to fill the gap," she said blithely, as if we were talking about something anodyne and lovely like origami, not a coup. "You'd probably be happier back in the classroom full-time and vetting authors for your fellowship anyway." She flashed that smile again and I marveled at her movie star teeth—so big, so white, so shiny.

A line from *Evita* came to me: "Dice are rolling, the knives are out." Any doubts I had about being department chair were squashed at the moment by Ciska's apparent lust for power, which was really pathetic because being chair of our English department wasn't any great prize—even with the extra income and reduced teaching load. But then academia was filled with bald men arguing over a comb, and maybe launching the new digital learning course really meant that much to her.

"If you're so eager to help," I said, matching her cheerful tone, "why don't *you* apologize to the dean?"

Now it was her turn to flush. "That is insulting and sexist."

"Really? How so?"

"The fact that you don't understand how you're abusing your power as an agent of the patriarchy right now, well, that doubles the offense. Can't you see how oppressive your rhetoric is? And honestly, how could you have spoken to the associate dean the way you did? It's disgraceful. Boris works harder than anyone in the college and he's a wonderful human being. People absolutely adore him."

That was the first time I'd heard that Boris had a fan club and I found her assessment hard to believe, given that Boris seemed so imposing and fierce. But maybe that was just me. And Celine *had* reported he was well thought of at SUM, despite apparently being under Bullerschmidt's thumb.

"Boris didn't deserve to be treated so badly, *nobody* deserves that." Her intensity made me wonder if she and Boris were lovers or at least dating—or had some kind of past together. But before I could respond, she forged ahead. "Nick, you're behaving reckless-ly. You really can't afford to make new enemies."

I assumed that Ciska meant herself.

"Are you threatening me?" I asked, which I realized was way too ironic given that I'd warned Boris in violent language not to touch me.

"Not at all. I'm being honest and objective."

I wanted to tell Ciska that she was being a bitch, but that would be grossly impolite and impolitic and would get me into even more trouble than I was in already. So I settled for sarcasm: "Thank you for your honesty. I'm sure the dean keeps you very busy and you must have other calls like this one to make. He's so lucky to have you on his team."

That's when a thought crossed my mind that gave me chills: What if my accusing her of working for Bullerschmidt wasn't just a figure of speech, what if she really was in cahoots with the dean? It could be even worse than that. What if both of them were on the Committee of Public Safety—and I had become their latest target?

"It's been a long day," I said pointedly.

But even though I was clearly asking her to leave, Ciska didn't move, she just sighed. "You know, Nick, I would have come to talk to you even if Bullerschmidt hadn't reached out to me. I find your behavior as chair very troubling and self-centered. We all have to do whatever we can to preserve the great name of this university. It's our foremost responsibility."

With that stirring and bizarre call to arms, Ciska rose and paraded to the front door. She left without quite slamming it, but she closed it behind her more firmly than was necessary, which woke Marco up. He barked once, a little halfheartedly, and Stefan shushed him.

At that moment I couldn't imagine anything better than a cruise around the world where nobody would mention SUM or anything even remotely connected to it. Or lying on a quiet beach, dazed by the sun with a totally blank mind. Martin Cruz Smith had a line in one of his thrillers: "What a relief to think of nothing, to be a rock in a field and never move again."

"Oh my God," I blurted out. "Oh. My. God."

Stefan started laughing helplessly. "Ciska," he said, trying to stop. He managed to finish his sentence without choking: "Ciska is delusional." Getting that last word out seemed to sober him a little.

"Does she really believe that crap about protecting SUM? If she does, she's gone over to the Dark Side."

"And if she doesn't believe it?" he asked.

I shrugged. "Then she's playing a long game and wants more than being department chair. I bet she'll say and do anything that clears a path. The university is full of people like that, on the make."

"What's she shooting for? Dean? Provost? President?"

I nodded. "My guess is that she wants to go all the way. She's got the look, the lean and hungry look, that's for sure."

"Then you need to watch your back."

"Nothing new there," I said, briefly wishing I'd chosen a different career and stayed on the East Coast to follow it. After all, I'd had no experience with crime before moving to this bucolic Midwestern college town that was really a nest of criminality.

"Let's watch the movie."

We did, and laughed at *Midnight's* hilarious situation, the glamour, and the glittering Billy Wilder dialogue, both of us expressing a wish to have been there when it was being filmed. It changed the whole tone of the evening. But soon after we finished, took Marco out to potty one last time, and thought about getting ready for bed, I got a call on my cell phone, which I'd turned on just in case after the movie, despite Stefan's frown.

It was Boris Hernandez.

"I need to speak to you," he said.

I had no idea why he was calling me, but with my newfound, intermittent paranoia and the dean sending people to coerce me into apologizing, my first thought was that Boris was recording the call and wanted to catch me saying something incriminating.

This had to be some kind of trap, likewise his not telling Valley what the detective wanted to hear about our interaction. I put the call on speaker phone so Stefan could hear both sides of the conversation which was already as weird as anything else that had happened so far that day.

"It's late, Boris." It was almost 10:30.

"I know, but this can't wait. It's urgent. I was trying to talk to you this morning when you left. Can you meet me at my office in Humanities as soon as possible?"

"Now? What about one of the Starbucks?" I asked. There were two near campus and I knew both stayed open till midnight to cater to students doing all-nighters.

"Too public. I don't want to be seen with you."

Well, that was charming.

"I know what's going on with admissions," he said. Then he added, "But don't ask me to come to your house. Someone will see me."

His voice was steady but he sounded more paranoid than I was.

"Boris, do you think someone is following you?"

"I'm sure of it. It's those German twins in your department. I think they're spying on people for the dean."

Given how bizarre the duo's behavior was, I had wondered before if it was a cover for something else, so I couldn't dismiss the possibility. Their behavior was so outrageous, who would take them seriously as agents for the administration? Many of us worried about electronic surveillance, but in a closed community like SUM, old-fashioned spying by actual spies made just as much sense.

"Please," he said. "I'll be waiting for you at my office."

Stefan was waving his hands at me and mouthing "No!"

"The building's locked at night," I said. "They all are." Well, except for the library, and that would be closing at midnight.

"I have a key and I'll leave the main door open. Really, you have to meet me there."

Boris sounded desperate and I agreed. And before Stefan could remonstrate with me, I said, "I'm not going alone. You come, too. That'll be two against one."

"Okay, but I don't think I'm bringing my gun." Stefan still had the Walther PPK .380 a friend had given him, and he was a good shot. I'd seen it.

"We're not in danger," I said. "I think this is a Deep Throat kind of situation."

"And the dean is Nixon?"

I shook my head. "Beats me, but if Boris has something to tell me about the bribery business, I want to hear it."

"This morning you thought he was trying to hurt you."

"I could be wrong." I closed my eyes to picture those brief moments in the hallway of the Humanities building. "Maybe he really wanted to stop me to tell me something, not threaten me."

• • •

SUM's campus at night was ghostly and beautiful. Every path was irradiated with soothing, yellow light from gorgeous, Victorian-style lampposts with peaked, copper-edged globes. Their light seemed to pool at the feet of a vast multitude of trees like a mythic horde of gold coins. The trees themselves were even more beautiful at night because they seemed more mysterious, less revealed in the colors of the trunks, branches, and leaves, while their shapes shifted depending on your line of sight. They seemed to take command of the hundreds of buildings they sheltered, and the sound of their leaves in the slightest breeze and the fragrance they exuded was intoxicating.

Every now and then you'd find a raccoon scurrying away from you up to safety in a tree where it would hiss if you got too close.

It was being on campus at night that often made me wish I'd had the talent to be a painter. I would have loved to capture the play of light and dark that turned trees into sculptures and took them out of their quotidian life. The vast array included willows, red and sugar maples, black cherrys, aspens, red oaks, white pines, birches and more exotic varieties—all of them labeled for horticulture students and maybe former big-city dwellers like me who needed to be educated on their strolls across campus because we weren't always sure which was which, or were simply dazzled by the splendor and forgot. The students and bikers who moved among them at night to and from the library or on a date felt tiny and insubstantial by comparison.

One of the older buildings on campus, the sandstone nineteenth-century home for Humanities looked like a fairytale castle in this light with its pointed turrets and rusticated stone walls. We parked in the empty lot and headed to the front of the building. The main doors were under a low, wide recessed arch where someone could have been lurking, but I forged ahead regardless and Stefan followed.

As promised, the door was open, and we headed to the elevator across the small, dimly lit lobby. With its thick walls and small windows, the building never seemed noisy, but late at night it was eerily quiet.

When we got to the dean's suite of offices, light spilled from just one of them and we followed the glare to the doorway of what I assumed was Boris's office. Stefan was right behind me when I stopped in the doorway.

Boris was slumped over his disordered, gleaming desk.

"We have to call 911," Stefan said, his voice tight. "Sweet Jesus…"

I could feel my pulse pounding in my ears. My eyesight was suddenly as blurry as if I'd been on the road too long and just driven into a misty rain that grayed everything around me. I was afraid to even blink in case I lost my balance, but I must have started to sway because I momentarily felt Stefan's palms at the center of my back steadying me.

I pulled out my phone, but my hands were shaking so much that I dropped it, transfixed by the bloody wound on the side of Boris's head.

Part
Three

. . .

11.

THERE WAS BLOOD pooling on the desk and I thought I saw spatters on the bookcase behind him. I looked quickly away as if I could delete the sight from my mind like a bad sentence from a draft of an essay, but I knew that was hopeless.

Stefan picked my phone up, murmured, "The screen's okay" in a voice stripped of emotion, and made the call, which I knew would be routed to SUM's own police station like all emergency calls on campus. The GPS in our phones kept track of wherever we were, which meant we had no real privacy—but what was the alternative, going off the grid?

He got right through and said, "I'm in the Humanities Building and I think there's a dead body in a third floor office. I'm pretty sure it's Boris Hernandez. He's an associate dean." There was a pause, then he said, "My name is Stefan Borowski. No, I'm not injured and I'm not alone, I'm here with my spouse, Nick Hoffman. We're both professors in the English Department. What? Yes, we'll wait for the police, of course." Another pause. "How did I find him? We were supposed to have a meeting. Yes, I know it's late."

To me he said, "Her name is Melanie and she says the campus cops are on their way and to stay right here." Expressionless, he led me to a battered wooden bench in the hallway which got just enough light from Boris's office and sat me down. I knew where I was and yet I felt totally disoriented, as if I'd somehow been dumped into an ocean liner's life raft and set adrift with no hope of rescue. Safety was back on that vanishing ship and I was slipping further and further away from it.

How could this be happening to me—*again*? And so soon?

People would say I was cursed, and maybe they'd be right. After a night like this, how could I not end up on the cover of the *National Enquirer*?

Stefan set down my phone, took out his own phone, shot off a text and got a reply in under a minute: "Vanessa's preparing for a trial tomorrow," he reported, "so she's sending over an associate from her firm who lives right near campus."

"Okay. I mean, good." I wasn't exactly sure what he was talking about because the word "associate" took a while to penetrate my fog. When I grasped what was happening, I realized that we had never met any of the associates at her firm, so I asked who it was.

"Gideon Rosen," he said, handing me back my phone. I ended the call and he didn't seem to notice.

Gideon Rosen. Jewish, I thought, and that was oddly comforting. But anyone would have been fine. Like me, I was sure Stefan didn't want to be alone with cops—we'd had more than enough of them for several lifetimes.

Stefan was shaking his head. "We just fucking saw him the other night. He's always at the gym. How is it possible?" He looked very pale and I didn't know what to say.

Even though we were alone just then, the silence around us wasn't total. I could hear faint creaking and popping from the floors and pipes that sounded like an old man's low-level grumbling. And I'd never noticed before that the Humanities Building smelled moldy and stale, which was a sad commentary on the state of those disciplines at SUM. Most other colleges like Business, Engineering, and Law were housed in newer buildings where the walls had no cracks and the air smelled only of money. Lots of money.

Stefan just sat beside me and wisely said nothing more.

Remembering instructions from an old yoga class, I tried

breathing in and out very slowly, counting to four each time I inhaled, holding it for four, then breathing out for another four, hoping to relax and keep my mind still. But it felt like a kaleido-scope in there: wildly shifting, jagged images of Boris, Lovelace, Ciska, Bullerschmidt, and Peter DeVries cut into and overlapped each other with dizzying rapidity.

I know that in movies and TV shows, people in a situation like mine almost always puked their guts out, but my body felt locked up tight. I wasn't experiencing nausea or chills or anything visceral like that. I was flattened, stunned. I kept circling back to the bizarre reality that this was the second time in weeks that I had found someone dead—at least I assumed Boris was dead.

As if he knew what I was thinking, Stefan said with all the assurance of someone who'd been on a battlefield, "He's dead, all right."

And I thought, yes, blunt force trauma most likely. But should we have tried to search for a pulse? Or would that have contam-inated the crime scene? I sure wouldn't have been able to touch Boris's body.

It didn't take long before we heard sirens tearing the night apart.

Then the stairwell echoed with the thunder of boots and the hallway was suddenly swarming with campus cops in their new, intimidating black uniforms, black boots and caps. Their duty belts were loaded with handcuffs, radios, batons, Tasers, flashlights and other equipment I couldn't identify. And guns, of course. Glock 22's. That's what the campus newspaper had reported they now carried in an article about heightened security at SUM. It had pro-filed the Glocks as rugged, dependable, safe, and affordable, with a fifteen-round capacity. These facts unreeled in my mind like a magician's multicolored scarf being pulled from his fist.

The article had appeared after the last murder I'd been con-nected to and felt like a puff piece because it praised campus police for "keeping us safe." I guess that didn't include Boris.

"I'm Sergeant Taylor. Who placed the 911 call?" one of the

cops asked us. He was beefy, bearded, with a spray of acne across his broad forehead, and he looked as young as my students.

Stefan tapped his chest and mumbled, "Me."

"Okay, stay right where you are, both of you." His eyes turned cold as he walked off. And soon we heard him on his radio or phone calling for a command officer and asking for CSI to be notified.

Two cops took up positions in the hallway, one near the elevator and the other by the open stairwell as if there was a chance we might try to flee. They were as big and broad as NFL offensive tackles. Neither of them looked directly at me or Stefan, but I felt that the slightest twitch would make them pounce on us and hurl us to the floor. *You haven't done anything,* I thought, and yet with a corpse nearby, a history connecting me to murder on campus, and surrounded by so many police officers I felt guilty, guilty, guilty.

"We shouldn't have agreed to meet Boris," I whispered to Stefan. "Here. At night."

Stefan did not point out that I was the one who wanted to come, and I was grateful for that. But he did say, "It's not our fault that Boris is dead. It can't be."

"Why does this keep happening to me?" I asked.

He sighed. "Wrong place, wrong time."

That was an understatement, but as good an explanation as any other. With all the police activity around us, I was amazed by his composure, given that last spring he'd been insulted, humiliated, and abused by a Michiganapolis SWAT team that a stalker had sent to our home to torment us. The stalker was eventually killed, but even though we'd moved to help banish the memories of having our house invaded, you don't recover from an experience like that quickly—if ever. Yet Stefan didn't seem devastated the way I was now, but calm. Maybe when the worst thing you can imagine actually happens to you, nothing that follows can shake you in quite the same way.

Stefan was studying his phone, reading a text, and then he

whispered into my ear, "Gideon's almost here. He says don't talk to anyone and absolutely do not go off with the police unless they arrest us. And even if they do, we don't have to answer any questions. That's our right."

"Why would they arrest *us*?" I asked too loudly and the cops monitoring us jerked their heads in our direction.

"I would love to arrest you," Detective Valley said, striding briskly up the stairs and over to us. "Just for screwing up my evening."

I supposed that was some kind of grim joke, but I just felt myself being sucked into another whirlpool. I was a professor, an Edith Wharton scholar, a nice Jewish boy from New York, what the hell was I doing being involved with the police and death—yet again? This was not the life I had dreamed of in graduate school, nor the one my parents envisioned for me either.

Despite his griping, there was a jauntiness in Valley's attitude. He seemed almost triumphant, as if he had been tracking me for years and finally caught me.

I'd also never seen him dressed so informally: faded jeans, a dark turtleneck sweater, and Reeboks. He was followed by a young detective in an ill-fitting olive green suit and horn-rimmed glasses who looked more like an overwhelmed expectant father in a maternity ward than an investigator. His face was awash with fear, which made me wonder if Valley had chewed him out for some reason on the way over here, or if he was just bullying him out of perverse enjoyment. Unless the younger man had never encountered an actual murder before and Valley didn't know how he would respond. Perhaps *he'd* be puking his guts out.

"Trouble just follows you around, doesn't it?" Valley said, and I couldn't disagree or try to defend myself.

Valley ordered his junior to make sure that the crime scene was secure, then turned back to us with a basilisk glare. "Stay here, and do not post photos on Twitter or Instagram or Snapchat."

"Wait a minute," Stefan snapped. "We're not idiots. We'd never go online about this."

Valley snorted derisively, sounding like a mustache-twirling villain in a Victorian melodrama. "Nothing you professors do would surprise me. I've seen it all."

As he turned from us and headed to Boris's office, a paramedic bounded up the stairs. He was so short and thin, his enormous red shoulder bag emblazoned with a white star looked like it could pull him over if he took a turn too quickly.

He was followed by a man I guessed was Vanessa's associate, who told the police guarding us, "I'm their lawyer." They let him pass.

"Nick? Stefan? Hi. I'm Gideon Rosen." His smile was brisk and no-nonsense. He shook our hands and managed to give us each a business card without seeming awkward. He was lean, round-faced, thirty-something, with an untamed mass of dense black curls that reminded me of Ellis Island immigrant photos from the early 1900s. In his blue blazer, loafers, and chinos, Rosen looked dapper and confident. The ribbed aluminum briefcase he set down near us was like a marker. He was claiming the territory, staking it out for the three of us.

I felt a bit safer with him there.

"Who's in charge?" he asked. I pointed to the hallway.

From where I sat, I could see the flash of phone cameras as Valley and his junior recorded what they were seeing. Someone was probably filming the scene, too. This was just the beginning, and I knew the local drill all too well. Boris's office door would be crisscrossed with crime scene tape, a rookie cop would be posted to guard the scene, and someone would interview us—or try to. Then the on-duty Crime Scene Investigator would arrive from the state police to take more photographs, examine the scene in minute detail, and process all the evidence. Lastly, a prosecutor would appear to guide a search of Boris's office. I saw the various stages unreeling like a sort of film, but that didn't give me enough distance, since I was still trapped in the middle of it. And so was Stefan.

The paramedic was soon leaving, head down. I couldn't

imagine what it was like to deal with death as a natural part of your job.

Gideon set his briefcase down next to me on the bench, opened it, pulled out a tablet, sat on the wide arm of our bench and started typing furiously while checking his watch. He was studying us, the hallway, everyone and everything with fierce intensity. "I have to keep a record," he explained.

He didn't add "for later" but I knew that's what he meant and it gave me chills.

The voices of close to a dozen men now eddied around us, though our two guards remained silent. I understood Valley's scornful remarks about not posting to social media, but if he was worried about the press getting ahold of the story or it appearing on clickbait websites like *BuzzFeed* and *The Daily Beast*, nothing could prevent that from happening.

It was just too explosive a story: ANOTHER DEATH AT THE STATE UNIVERSITY OF MURDER.

And I was at the scene—once more.

"Let me handle everything," Gideon said without glancing up while he typed. "There's no need for you to say a word."

A born introvert, Stefan had already withdrawn into his own world, his inner reveries, and barely seemed to acknowledge Vanessa's associate's presence. Me, I found myself wondering who would want to kill Boris. I didn't know him, but the obvious motives for murder crossed my mind: revenge, money, sex, secrets. There was plenty of all of that at SUM, but who knew what kind of personal life Boris had, or what was buried in his past. Lines from a terrific mystery by Joseph Kanon came to mind: "It's the ultimate mystery, isn't it? People. Not who done it. Who they are."

Celine had called Boris bright, ambitious, and well-liked. But she'd also said he was the dean's watchdog in a peculiar sort of way. It was easy to picture Bullerschmidt as an academic version of a Mafia don and Boris as his consigliere. What if this murder was a message to the dean? Or he'd been killed because he knew something he shouldn't, something dangerous?

In our many years together, Stefan and I had found that our thoughts often ran on parallel tracks, and that night was no exception. He suddenly leaned over and said as quietly as he could, "I bet somebody killed him to shut him up. A man in his position would know where the bodies are buried." He stopped. "God, I can't believe I said that, but you know what I mean."

Gideon shushed us. I heard Valley talking to someone about search warrants and then he was back before Stefan and I could trade notes. He looked anything but casual now after having seen the body.

Gideon rose and introduced himself. Valley said coldly, "I know who you are." He did not take Gideon's card and added a curt, "No photos here. None." Then he spoke directly to us: "I need statements from the two of you, separately, so I'd like you to come over to the station."

"My clients have no wish to answer questions," Gideon interjected.

Ignoring the lawyer, Valley kept talking to us, his tone softer, almost wheedling. "Hey, I'm just a civil servant doing my job to protect the public. Every second counts in a case like this. The sooner you tell me what you know, the better. Come on, don't you want to be good citizens, don't you want to do your civic duty?"

Nice try, I thought. Next he'd be singing the football team's fight song. Or "America the Beautiful."

"They don't have to speak to you," Gideon repeated more firmly this time, his tenor voice mellow and soothing. For me, anyway. I knew what he said was true. I had read it enough times in articles about people's rights when dealing with the police, but hearing it made it seem more than just real. Spoken by a lawyer, the words had the power of something carved into the base of a noble statue or over the entrance of a columned public building.

Valley leaned forward to us as solicitously as a mother comforting her children who were afraid of the dark. "Listen, guys, this really isn't all that complicated. You'll just tell us when you got here, what you saw, why you're here so late at night, and then you can go."

That was utter bullshit because who would believe anyone would meet on campus after hours when so many of us couldn't wait to get away from SUM? Our being there in the Humanities building was grossly suspicious. And then there was my morning run-in with the dean and Boris....

I could see that Valley wanting us at the campus police station was an obvious attempt at intimidation, and failing that, he wanted to squeeze us for information on the spot. In that same unctuous tone, he asked, "Unless you have something to hide? Because not answering simple questions makes you look like suspects. Why else would you call a lawyer?"

I said, "There's nothing to hide. And we'd like to go home now. You can speak to Mr. Rosen if you have any questions."

"Him?" He put as much contempt as possible into that word.

Now the two cops who'd been left in the hallway were glaring at the three of us as if we were suspected terrorists who'd just blown up a building. They radiated hostility.

Valley said a little less genially, "Professor Hoffman, you're known to have threatened Boris Hernandez and now he's dead. I would think you'd want to talk to me and explain what you're doing here."

Gideon worked to control his surprise.

Stefan rose, and I followed, grabbing my phone. Gideon nodded his okay at us, though he looked troubled, and said to Valley, "My clients are going home right now. Otherwise, you and your department will be on the receiving end of a lawsuit. And by the way, our firm has never lost when we sued the police."

Valley's face flushed and his eyes went as wide as if he'd been slapped.

Gideon said to us, "I'm staying here to keep an eye on things. We can talk in the morning. Vanessa's going to be in court all day tomorrow."

We thanked him and walked around Valley. When the cop at the stairs, who looked even bigger close up, wouldn't move out of the way, I said, "Really?" He smelled of sweat and Old Spice aftershave and ignored me.

But Valley must have signaled the goon, because he grudgingly let us pass. We headed down the stairs and out to our car just as a white SUV with black-lettered CRIME SCENE UNIT on its side pulled up in front of the building to join the cruisers whose roof lights were flashing blue.

"Shit" was all I managed to say on the ride home. Stefan said nothing, and I didn't try to prompt him out of his silence. He was breathing heavily, like someone just back from a hard run, and I could tell he wasn't only upset about Boris's death—it was Valley and his small army back there. Stefan now had to be reliving how we'd been treated by cops before.

Both of us really should have started therapy after what happened to us last spring, and though I'd emailed a psychologist in town about a possible consultation because I'd heard he was good with trauma, he didn't respond, so I took that as a sign to move on as best I could without professional help. I was relieved, too. I wasn't ready to go down that rabbit hole right then, and neither was Stefan. Despite being born and raised in New York, where therapy is like a religion, I think that in our decades of living in Michigan, we had absorbed some of the Midwestern wariness of talking too much about yourself, and especially to a "stranger." It was as unseemly there as raising your voice in public—except at sports events—or honking your car horn at any time other than an emergency.

Home, we were both exhausted and after giving Marco time in the yard we headed up to bed. Stefan was out right away before I even turned off the lights. He could do that, he could *will* himself to fall asleep in a crisis. I joked sometimes that he was just like Marco, who was snoring lightly in his dog bed near the bathroom door.

Me, I didn't want to close my eyes to begin with, fearful of picturing Boris at his desk. To dim that apprehension, I took some melatonin, put in earbuds and listened to sea waves till I eventually zonked out, but I didn't feel at all rested when I woke the next morning.

• • •

Even before going to the john Thursday morning, I unplugged my phone from the charger. At the top of my Inbox was something Ciska Balanchine had sent to the whole department:

> Please join me at 4:00 this afternoon in the conference room for an informal gathering where we can share our feelings about the untimely passing of Boris Hernandez, a sterling representative of everything that's best about SUM.

How the hell did she know that Boris was dead? Who had told her? Valley? One of the cops? I woke Stefan.

Stefan didn't curse much, but he kept shouting, "What the fuck!" when I showed him my phone. I asked him to stop because he was disturbing Marco, who was inching away from our bed, his ears pulled back and eyes narrowed in what I read as fear.

"It's a power play," I said, feeling surprisingly calm. "She's building a base."

"She really and truly does want your job," Stefan said downstairs as we prepared breakfast. He was toasting rye bread and cooking bacon, while I was scrambling eggs with cream, chives, sugar, lemon juice, and Parmesan. I didn't know if I could eat anything, but working at the stove eased my mind a little, and when the bacon was ready, I found I was ravenous.

Eating something delicious made me feel alive. And while I savored my food I felt absurdly free, not like I was trapped in a car that had fallen into a gigantic Florida sinkhole with no hope of being saved.

Stefan ate his meal hunched over, like someone in a homeless shelter trying to stay inconspicuous and guard his food at the same time. We talked about the day ahead of us in fits and starts, but avoided any foray into the previous evening's nightmare.

After we finished and put breakfast dishes in the dishwasher, I sat down at the kitchen table with my laptop to email the department. I had to do an end run around Ciska without making it look like I was angry or petty. After a second cup of Dallmayr coffee, I came up with what I thought was an elegant solution:

> We're all shocked by the death of a mainstay in Humanities who was so well loved. To guide us in our shared grief work, a team of counselors will be available at this afternoon's session.

Stefan read it over my shoulder and said, "What are you doing?"

"It's a gamble. Let's see if it pays off."

It did. Within half an hour everyone in the department was hitting Reply All to say they were too busy or couldn't cancel class or had a doctor's appointment or family issues that couldn't wait or meetings that couldn't be canceled. Two claimed they had migraines (and honestly, who wouldn't have a migraine in that department?). Pretty soon everyone had bowed out, except Ciska of course. And I got a text from Roberto Robustelli saying "Bro, you're a fucking genius." I could almost smell his cologne when I read those words, and I wished he would just disappear.

Stefan still looked puzzled. "I don't get it."

"The last thing these people want," I said, "is to have intimacy forced on them by professionals. They keep their soul searching to themselves—if they even do any."

"You made up the part about counselors, didn't you? The grief work? To scare faculty off?"

I nodded.

Stefan grinned. "That was brilliant."

But he looked grim again when my phone rang and the ID read Fabian Flick. I let the reporter leave a message, which I played back right away.

"Good morning, Professor, this is Fabian Flick again from *Scoop*. I'd like to talk to you about the memorial service in your department for Dean Hernandez. I'm wondering if you can clarify your role and explain why the head of the Counseling Center doesn't seem to know anyone on her staff is participating. The planning for this event seems somewhat haphazard, wouldn't you agree?"

Ciska, I thought. Ciska wanted to supplant me since I wasn't giving up the chair and wouldn't support her new course, so her plan was obviously to undermine me and make me look bad. First she called a meeting as if she were already the head of the department, challenging my authority while raising doubts as to why I hadn't done it myself. And then she contacted Flick and forwarded my email, whose facts he started checking for himself, as any good reporter would.

Who else could it have been if not Ciska? Stefan had warned me about her, telling me to watch my back.

But it was too late. She was clearly out to get me, and I didn't see anything I could do to stop her. I was sorry now that I'd had anything more than a cup of coffee for breakfast because I felt queasy. If Ciska knew that Boris was dead before the story had broken, then she probably knew that Stefan and I had discovered his body.

That was powerful ammunition for a smear campaign—if she chose to use it.

"Did you smell anything?" I asked.

Stefan squinted at me. "What? When?"

"In Boris's office."

Stefan shook his head, clearly not following.

"I just remembered that there was something weird and sweet in the air. Sweet, but also like one of those copper saucepans we don't use much. Metallic."

"And?"

"I think it was the blood."

A lean, stoop-shouldered, gray-eyed veteran of World War II

who was at one of my parents' cocktail parties years ago had said out of the blue, "You don't ever forget what it's like to have to be surrounded by corpses in battle. You don't ever forget what it's like to feel that the smell of death is like a scarf that's choking you." It stopped conversation. For a while, anyway.

My evening wasn't remotely like anything he'd experienced, but I didn't think that the bloody vision of Boris at his desk and the scent of his blood would ever fade from my memory.

12.

CELINE CALLED me while I was wandering around the house in a daze, feeling as if the image of Boris at his desk had become as enormous as one of those ravenous wide tornados that devours the sky. Marco followed after me, tentatively wagging his tail as if this was some new game. He stopped a few feet off while I spoke to Celine, standing in the middle of the living room. Phone calls always seemed to fascinate him.

"The police were here," she said. "That nasty detective, and some bruiser in a uniform. I wouldn't let them go into your office or touch anything without a search warrant, but he asked a lot of questions."

"What did he want?" I could feel my shoulders and neck tightening as if I were sitting in a tiny commuter plane, crushed against the window by someone twice my size.

"It was mostly about you and Boris. What's going on?"

I told her about Boris's phone call and how Stefan and I had found him dead.

"Wow." There was a moment of silence and I figured she was shocked, but she sounded as unflappable as ever when she asked, "Should I let Aldo know?"

"Please. So what did you tell Valley?"

"I said you and Boris barely knew each other, which was true. And that you were both highly professional and well respected across campus. Also true."

Well, that last point about me was a stretch, since I probably had more detractors than fans on campus (except for my students), but I was grateful for her vote of confidence.

"He tried to get me to talk about what happened at the dean's office yesterday and I just said that SUM was a place where rumors spread as fast as head lice in a kindergarten."

"I'm really sorry he was hassling you."

"Shit, police don't scare me." Celine almost never cursed and it was a sign that she was furious at Valley. "I hope you have a lawyer, Nick, because he's out to get you, I'm sure of it. He is a menace."

"I do have a lawyer. You've met her before, Vanessa Liberati." I didn't add that it was after the shootings in our old building. Celine and I never mentioned surviving that attack.

"Oh yes, of course. She's terrific. Now, you take the day off," she said. "You hear me? You need rest. I can handle anything that comes up."

I thanked her yet again, realizing that I risked being called an absentee chair the way I was going.

And as soon as I ended that call I took one from Aldo who said without any preamble, "Don't worry, Nick, I've got your back. I didn't tell the police anything." Then he laughed. "Well, I don't know anything, really, so it was easy."

"What did Valley want to know? It *was* Valley?"

"Yes. It was Detective Valley in the flesh."

This was harassment, plain and simple. Valley was trying to get at me through Celine and Aldo because I wouldn't answer his questions last night. But Valley's behavior was not entirely new. He'd disliked me from the first day we met, when I was a relatively new hire in the department, and everything that had happened at SUM in the years since had only confirmed his worst opinion of me.

"He is one cold dude, Nick. He studied me like I was a circus freak."

"That's his shtick. He gives everybody the stink eye. I don't know why he stays here if he's so miserable."

"Haters gotta hate. But Nick, he's got some idea that you had a vendetta against Boris. You know, like maybe you made a pass at Boris and he rejected you."

"That's insane." I could suddenly feel sweat at the base of my spine.

"Tell me about it. Straight guys like Valley have no imagination, no nuance. To them, if you're gay, then the only thing you care about is sex. It's kind of pitiful."

It could partly explain Valley persecuting me or anyone I knew or worked with. "So I killed Boris because he turned me down?"

"Like you said, insane. But I do think Valley is serious." He paused. "He was asking me outrageous personal questions like are you promiscuous, do you and Stefan have an open relationship, do you take drugs, are you and Stefan thrill seekers? God, what a cheap mind he has. I didn't say a word because I figured whatever I said he'd use against you somehow."

Valley had wondered about my sex life before in a previous investigation, even though it had nothing to do with the case. And thrill seekers? Did he think we were psychos like Leopold and Loeb?

"He's like Javert from *Les Misérables*," Aldo said. "He's out to take you down."

It was an apt comparison. Too bad there wasn't a nearby river deep enough for Valley to drown himself in, the way Javert jumped into the Seine.

"You know, Nick, I have to tell you that I'm surprised Boris is dead, because everybody likes him. Liked him. I would've thought if anyone in Humanities ever got whacked it would be the dean."

"Whacked?"

Now Aldo chuckled. "*Mi scusi*, sorry, I've been watching too many mob movies."

I wanted to smile, but couldn't. I felt horrible about Celine and Aldo being pounced on by Valley, dragged into his interrogation, and wondered what the hell Valley was planning to do next to get under my skin.

"I know Celine was going to tell you that you should take the day off. I agree. We've got everything under control here. Try to chill out. If you can."

His kindness, following Celine's, moved me to tears and I ended the call before I lost it completely.

There was no time for me to recover or fill Stefan in, because the doorbell rang and I felt certain it was Valley. As Marco started barking, the medieval "Dies Irae" theme ran through my head. I knew it from music of Rachmaninov, who was obsessed with it. Day of Wrath.

Stefan hurried out of the kitchen to put a leash on Marco and pull him back. I stomped over to the front door and yanked it open.

Valley stood there with one of the uniformed cops who had guarded me at the Humanities building, who now seemed even surlier and more imposing in daylight. His gleaming gold badge looked ominous this morning and today I could read the nameplate over his right pocket: Grimm. It was too fitting and momentarily distracted me from the police cruiser at the base of our driveway. The red, white, and blue lights in the light bar on the roof were spinning and pulsing as if our house was a crime scene and our driveway had to be blocked because we might attempt to escape. A hulking black Chevy Tahoe was behind it. Valley's, no doubt. God knows what any neighbors who were home were thinking.

I fully expected Valley to handcuff me and recite my Miranda rights while he led me down to the cruiser, but he said almost amicably, "Professor Hoffman, you need to understand something. The longer you refuse to answer questions, the more people will think you're guilty. I know your lawyer wants you not to cooperate, but your lawyer is giving you very bad advice. That's what they do. That's what they *all* do at times like this because they want to earn more money." He held out his arms as if we were long-lost relatives meeting for the first time at an airport. "Why not come in and clear your name? You can even take a polygraph test and we can end the suspense."

Marco snarled somewhere back behind me and Stefan shushed him.

"Your assistant and the office manager have been very helpful in my inquiry. Do you want to make them look bad?"

It was a bluff, and not a very good one, either, since I'd just spoken to Aldo and Celine. But I didn't tell Valley that. I didn't say anything, and he shook his head in disgust.

"You'll regret this," he said.

"Is that a threat?"

Valley grimaced and looked like he would have happily knocked me out for daring to challenge him. I shut the door, enjoying myself immensely.

From the living room window, Stefan and I watched them drive off. Then we sat and I shared what Celine and Aldo had told me about Valley's interrogation.

Stefan's broad shoulders drooped and he seemed too weary to be angry. "I'd complain to his superiors if it would do any good."

"The hell with that," I said, "let's go to the condo." I had a sudden, deep longing to see Lake Michigan. "I want to get away from that asshole."

On sabbatical, Stefan's schedule was wide open, but he didn't jump at my suggestion, and I understood his reluctance.

"I know you like writing at home better than anywhere else, but you could take a break just for a day or two, couldn't you? It's not like you're behind schedule anyway, right, so let's just pack up and go."

And so we did.

. . .

Ludington was a small, scenic former lumber town on Lake Michigan, only two and a half hours away, and we'd owned a small condo there since before the Crash of 2008. It was a perfect getaway: there were pretty beaches, a lovely harbor, and Michigan's most beautiful lighthouse at the end of a half-mile concrete and boulder breakwater. Automated, four-sided to deflect Lake Michigan's waves, and shaped like a skinny pyramid, it wasn't officially considered a lighthouse since no one had ever lived there, but the difference didn't matter to me because it was so picturesque.

Being at the lake reminded me of growing up in New York and summer vacations nearby. It was fresh water but I often imagined the wind coming off the lake had a tang of salt even though that wasn't possible. The sight of that deep blue water apparently triggered those sense memories of beaches on Long Island as a child, and I treasured that trace of my past.

Best of all in Ludington were the gorgeous sunsets and the sand dunes which were part of the world's largest freshwater dune system. Standing there you felt part of something wondrous, especially at sunset, which we also enjoyed watching from our tower bedroom.

There were eastern hemlocks in the dunes along this shoreline whose thick canopy sheltered deer and many smaller critters, a reminder of the town's past when hemlock trees were harvested for a multitude of uses from roofing to boxes. Now, they made you want to touch their thick, ridged, orange-brown bark and feel connected to an industry that had flourished for so long but then faded. That was ironically Ludington's good fortune and why so many older picturesque buildings and homes were still standing.

Stefan said Ludington put him in the mindset of aristocratic refugees from the Russian Revolution living in reduced circumstances in Paris, say, after 1917, making life as beautiful as they could while they longed for return. He found it mildly melancholy in a soul-stirring way.

What moved me was what Michiganders called The Big Lake itself, as vast as an ocean in my eyes since you couldn't see the other side, though not as wild. It evoked tranquility, openness, escape from the quotidian—though neither of us had sailed on it or had even taken the ferry across to Wisconsin. The possibility was what charmed Stefan and me.

Our condo's building was a former brewery, red brick with a square tower at each corner. The condo had one large room

downstairs with a sleek open kitchen, and it wasn't really made
for entertaining, which was fine by us. We treasured the privacy. The condo had thick walls, high ceilings, enormous rounded
windows, red oak floors, and no knickknacks, wall hangings, or
shelves to dust. The décor was very spare and contemporary—
nothing like our home in Michiganapolis, which made it extra
special.

In Ludington we tended to sleep late, bike, walk the beaches,
and feel as far away from Michiganapolis and SUM as if we'd left
the country.

It usually wasn't until we were actually on Route 10 heading west to Lake Michigan that I began to unwind. In the car on
that trip we listened to Gary Numan's eerie and hypnotic *Dance*,
then Madonna's greatest hits, and rode into Ludington on jaunty
Baroque waves of Telemann.

Ludington was less than a tenth the size of Michiganapolis,
and without the ego, a town devoted to tourism, boating, fishing.
Yes, like almost everywhere else in the country it had its outlying
stretch of mini-malls, motels, and fast food outposts, but driving
past them into town was always a treat as we passed guest houses
that had once been Robber Baron mansions. All that colorfully
painted gingerbread was such a sharp contrast to Michiganapolis,
as were the commercial buildings with ornate decorative Victorian
stonework around the windows and the rooflines. And we always
slowed down as we passed the big square sandstone courthouse
built in 1893, which was dramatic and romantic, especially at
night with the huge white clockface up in the tower looming like
a second moon.

I tensed up, though, when a police cruiser raced past us to
catch a speeder, but we were soon settling in, with Marco happily
sniffing his favorite corners and racing up and down the stairs to
the bedroom until he wore himself out. The condo's pets policy
had thankfully changed recently and he seemed to love the change
of scene as much as we did.

The whole condo was infused with lavender and rosemary

potpourri my cousin Sharon sent us on a regular basis. She liked sending me expensive gifts. Breathing in the sweetness and piney tang together was like the feel of warm hands massaging the base of your neck, and it matched the Gregorian chant CD we set on repeat as soon as we got unpacked.

Stefan defrosted a flank steak which we broiled medium rare and ate with baked potatoes smothered in sour cream and snipped chives. Nothing fancy, but solid food served with a hearty Australian Shiraz. We weren't even halfway through dinner and I was already floating on a magic carpet of relief. The murder, the chaos at SUM, the harassment I'd received from Bullerschmidt and then Valley was feeling as inconsequential as the pale square left behind on wallpaper when a picture is moved and nothing replaces it. I could feel myself becoming calmer, as smooth inside as the gray bark of the American beech trees that also grew near the shore here.

As I often did at the condo, I imagined what it would be like to retire early and spend more time in Ludington. We could afford to now that Stefan was so successful. He would have more than just the long summer breaks to write, but would I get bored without the stimulation of teaching, of creating a community in the classroom, of sharing knowledge with young minds? The flip side of leaving SUM was that we might get to know more locals than the waiters and bartenders at various restaurants. We might feel more rooted in Ludington, maybe even part of the community at some point, turn it into a true second home.

After cleaning up, we took Marco for a short walk which thrilled him thanks to all the new and unfamiliar scents. When we returned, he settled onto his favorite Eames chair, and we decided to head out for some kind of nightcap. We took a leisurely fifteen-minute walk over to the Jamesport Brewing Company, a big, relaxed, high-ceilinged bistro-ish restaurant off the main drag that was always crowded and always friendly. The door was enormously heavy and shrieked when you opened it, but the food inside was great.

They gave us our favorite booth where we had privacy, something I needed badly after the last few turbulent days. Hopefully nobody here knew about our latest misadventures, hopefully we were in no danger of being photographed. We each ordered a pint of their Altbier, a traditional German-style ale. Sitting there, I breathed in the familiar aromas of the restaurant—sirloin in cherry bourbon sauce, fried perch, roasted chicken—and felt so relieved we had left Michiganapolis behind us.

I wanted my life to be like this always: warm, relaxed, convivial—and yes, even aromatic, redolent of good food, good friends, good times. I wanted my life *back*.

We talked about Stefan's current novel-in-progress, thrashing out some plot points between sips of beer. It was sometimes easier to work out kinks in his books either chatting in the car or here in Ludington. The key thing was being away from his desk and his PC because doubts about whether he could keep the story moving always hovered around him but were much worse at home, like a swarm of mid-morning gnats on an early summer day.

Having finally achieved financial and critical success hadn't made him remotely cocky or overconfident. If anything, he worried now about matching what he'd already accomplished, which we both knew was always iffy. I liked quoting Henry James, whose dying author in "The Middle Years" sums up his creed: "We work in the dark—we do what we can—we give what we have. Our doubt is our passion, and our passion is our task. The rest is the madness of art."

In today's climate, I thought the "rest" was the madness of publishing. People were more likely to land big contracts now because they were young, attractive, or goofy, and had massive followings on Instagram as "Influencers" than by writing a great book. I felt sorry for his creative writing students who hoped to become successful authors.

Stefan would have hated to start out in the current state of publishing. He chafed against his agent's insistent pleas to build more of an online presence, to capitalize on the thousands of reviews he now had on Goodreads. Stefan was fine with getting his website updated but he had no interest in being visible on any platform, and refused the idea of hiring someone to run a Twitter feed for him. These were not my problems, of course, since my expertise was Edith Wharton and nobody expected me to turn myself into a carnival.

Halfway through his beer, Stefan interrupted my talk about James and Wharton, subjects that I easily fell into after years of reading and teaching both authors.

"Don't turn around," he said. "I think we're being followed."

At first I thought he was joking and pretending that we were in a movie as a way of amusing himself, but his face was so set and his eyes so fierce I knew it was for real.

"Where? Who?"

"At the bar. I'm sure it's that cop who was with Valley today at our house. Grimm?"

I nodded.

"He's wearing jeans and cowboy boots, and a flannel shirt, but I'm sure that's him. I'd recognize that bullet head anywhere. He looks like a Nazi."

I had to see for myself and I leaned out of the booth to check.

As if he could hear us over the contented buzz of the restaurant, Grimm turned towards us and made no effort to look away. He just stared, as expressionless as a sniper in a war movie. It was chilling. He either hated us or was doing a very good imitation.

Then he left some money on the bar and sauntered out. Stefan rose and went after him, weaving through the clusters of tables, and I heard the door shriek twice more, but he returned from the street disconsolately and trailed back to the booth, sitting down again heavily.

"That arrogant strut of his was just for show," he said. "Grimm was parked outside and he jumped in and drove right off before—" He shrugged. "I don't know what I thought I could do. Tell him to leave us alone?"

I would have said "Fuck off!" but maybe that was just a fantasy.

"I'm sure he was driving Valley's Tahoe," Stefan said. "It was black wasn't it? In front of our house today?"

"Maybe that's standard issue for their unmarked cars. But can he do that? Can *they* do that? Can they follow us all the way out here? I thought only the state police could do that."

Stefan shrugged. "I guess he thinks he can." Stefan brought out his phone. "I'm texting Vanessa and Gideon to tell them where we are and what just happened."

"You put Gideon's number in your phone?"

He looked startled. "You didn't? You should."

I slipped Gideon's card from my wallet and entered his info on my phone.

Gideon replied first before Stefan had finished his beer, and he handed me the phone so that I could read the long text for myself:

"Cops have no jurisdiction beyond a mile outside the county line. On their own time they can follow anyone. They can lie about where they've been. It happens. You're lucky he didn't stop you for some bogus reason. He could've planted drugs in your car and arrested you."

What fucking country were we living in?

Vanessa's reply to Stefan's text was short: "Be careful." There was a second text: "TTYL." Talk to you later.

Before we called for our check, Stefan asked, "How did they know we'd be here?"

"Drinking or in Ludington?"

"Both."

It was a good question. Had the campus police or the Committee of Public Safety bugged our house and overheard our conversation about leaving town? Or was it just an educated guess based on trolling through my social media where I'd posted photos of the Brewery and our condo? Unlike Stefan, I didn't mind having an online presence, but right then I was considering backing off, maybe even eliminating it altogether.

Then simultaneously, we looked down at our phones and at each other. This was the moment in a movie where people on the

run threw their phones out the car windows so they'd be crushed
in traffic.

"You read that *Washington Post* article about colleges tracking
students 24/7 to make sure they're attending classes and not hol-
ing up in their dorms and missing meals and whatever?"

"But that's students, and we're not on campus."

"You don't know what kind of tech SUM has access to."

Well, however they'd tracked us, I wanted to get back to the
condo as soon as we could and lock the door. Once we were in
our home-away-from-home, with Marco sleepily wagging his tail, I
felt safe again. Maybe it was the castle-like feel of the building we
were in, those super-thick walls, but I was also glad we had good
light-blocking window blinds because we closed them all. Street
lamps, sunlight, none of it could get through.

"It's a pressure tactic," Stefan said as we washed up and got
ready for bed. "They want us, they want *you* to feel intimidated."

I sighed. "Remember that Jack Nicholson line from *As Good
as It Gets*? 'Sell crazy someplace else. We're all stocked up here.'
That's how I feel tonight."

It was a fine quote, but very premature.

• • •

I was in one of those moods where I didn't want to try anything
new so I was re-reading Graham Greene novels and that night in
bed I was just partway into *The End of the Affair*, a book that Stefan sneered at. He wasn't a jealous person and didn't like reading
about adultery and other romantic entanglements. He wouldn't
even watch the more recent adaptation with Ralph Fiennes
and Julianne Moore even though they were two of his favorite
actors.

"But that's what most of life is about," I said. "Clashing
dreams, broken hearts, poison in the blood."

"Jesus, you should write a romance novel and get that out of
your system."

We slept as well as we always did at the condo, lulled by the
lake air and the luxury of not feeling scheduled. It helped having

kept our phones off and not checking email—both of which felt as impossible at home as not scratching a mosquito bite.

After feeding and walking Marco that Friday morning, we went out to breakfast at our usual diner, Sophie's Lakeside Café, where I ordered more food than normal: a western omelet *and* corned beef hash *and* a homemade double baked biscuit—plus a side of bacon. Stefan raised his eyebrows when I was done ordering and the waitress moved off.

"I'll swim extra at the club," I said.

"You might need to swim the English Channel to work off that much food."

"What can I say? I'm eating my feelings. It's cheaper than a shrink—and more satisfying."

He smiled faintly. He had ordered coffee, French toast and orange juice, nothing more.

This casual spot was quirky and fun. Hung with lighthouse prints and artwork, the wallpaper had a nautical border that was matched by nets, wheels, and wooden anchors hanging on the walls. The waitresses knew our names and always greeted us cheerfully, commenting on whether we were there late or early, and the locals typically nodded hello. As usual, we could hear people at other tables chatting jovially about boats, barns, the weather, arthritis, grandkids, and their cottages.

Halfway through our meal, Grimm showed up, dressed the way he was at the bar the night before. He walked over to our table and said, "You boys enjoy your breakfast," gave us a carnivorous grin, and left. The dissonance between his words and his attitude left a kind of stink in the air, like the memory of some foul deed.

Attention had turned to us from other tables when he appeared but left us when he was gone. I doubt anyone was speculating what it was all about since the incident was so brief.

Stefan shook his head. "I don't think he gets it. Shadowing us disturbed me yesterday, now it just seems almost childish. He's just a bully."

"Yeah, a bully who has a gun, and a bully who can arrest us."

Stefan nodded dolefully at the truth of that.

But despite Grimm's intrusion, I hadn't lost my appetite. If anything, I wondered if I had ordered *enough* food. I wolfed down some more of the savory, salty corned beef hash, wishing I were the fiction writer in the family. Because I would have loved to put both Grimm and Valley in a book—appropriately disguised—and inflict a gruesome demise on each one. Perhaps death by Zombie Apocalypse…

13.

DRIVING BACK from Ludington was always a mixed experience. I felt as sated as if I'd had a five-hour tasting menu somewhere in Europe with wonderful wines in a convivial atmosphere. And I was glad to be home, but even those few short days spent at the lake reminded me of time passing and made me wonder how much of it we had left. And if I was spending it the right way. Was there something else I should be doing with my life?

Teaching had been my passion for years. I'd had great mentors in college and in graduate school, professors who modeled how to teach. They understood that one of the most important things in the classroom was sharing your excitement about the material at hand and about learning itself. I often felt as if they were sitting there in the front row of a classroom, nodding as I made good points, but more importantly, smiling when I helped students make progress in their understanding of the topic at hand. It was the life I had dreamed of (well, without the crime, of course).

On the drive home that Sunday morning Stefan wanted to listen to some Steve Reich trance music so we played *Six Marimbas* and *Drumming.* Then I chose classic David Bowie and Lou Reed, which reminded me of being a kid, knowing that I was different somehow, and feeling like those glittering rock stars pointed the way to a life of quixotic achievement.

Traffic was light when we hit Michiganapolis, though our usually quiet street was unrecognizable. When we turned onto it, we saw a strange car and three news-station vans with call letters and logos parked at the curb near our house and across the street. As soon as Stefan hit the button on the rearview mirror for the garage door to go up and we pulled into the garage, three women reporters with microphones rushed up the driveway and three men with shoulder-cams scurried along after them. The reporters were all young, blond and blandly pretty, the cameramen chunky and wearing plaid shirts. They were so similar that they looked like actors answering a casting call for a TV show. Or maybe a comedy troupe.

I didn't know what they were after but I hurried to unpack the car and get Marco out into the backyard. I wasn't fast enough, though, and neither was Stefan.

The sextet swarmed to the top of the driveway with the reporters shouting overlapping questions and shoving each other to get closer. I was too frazzled to understand what they were saying. Marco went nuts in his car seat, snarling and scrabbling, obviously feeling under attack. And of course we were. I realized then that it had been a mistake to cut ourselves off from the Internet for as long as we had, because we were clearly at the center of a storm. But I had no idea where it had come from and what it meant beyond the obvious: trouble.

"What do you want?" Stefan snarled, when he should have never turned to face them. That moment was going to end up on the news and framed as something ominous and incriminating.

Before they could start up again, Fabian Flick appeared, pushing through their scrum. Dressed as elegantly as the last time I saw him, he asked with a face radiating concern, "How does it feel to have SUM police ask the public for help in finding you?"

Stefan and I both stepped forward as if he was a confounding mirage and I blurted out, "What?" Something about Flick had stilled the other reporters, and then I wondered if this moment had been staged.

He nodded. "Yes, they said you were being sought for questioning about the murder of Boris Hernandez."

Stefan and I backed away from him as if he had a bomb vest

strapped around him and Stefan slammed his open hand on the wall-mounted garage door opener. The door folded down with Marco still barking his head off. We could soon hear knocking at the front door as we brought our bags into the house and finally let Marco out into the yard to pee. Then the doorbell started up. We ignored it even though the doorbell sounded demanding and invasive. Eventually it ceased but I could feel a ringing in my ears between its echo and Marco's fury.

Stefan headed straight to the kitchen, past the landline in the hallway, its message light blinking furiously. He dropped his bag by the kitchen table, opened the freezer, and took out the bottle of Icelandic Reyka vodka which he only poured from under extreme stress. He got out a shot glass, slammed it down on the nearest counter, filled it sloppily and drank. And then again.

Reyka had a zero-emission geothermal distillery, but Stefan cared more about the taste than its carbon footprint. And right then I think any vodka would have been fine for him.

Stefan drank some more and paced while I turned on my phone to find dozens of texts and emails from Aldo, Celine, local TV and radio stations, Flick, Vanessa and Gideon, Dean Buller-schmidt, various members of my department, Detective Valley, and on and on. This was the immediate aftermath of the news about Boris Hernandez's death, followed by SUM's press release which mentioned, of all things, that I was being "sought for questioning."

Utter bullshit. I had simply refused to talk to Valley, which was my legal right, but the public didn't know any of that. Instead, I was being branded as some kind of suspect. It was beyond infuriating. But Vanessa had told us more than once that the police lied with impunity.

As I sampled the torrent of texts, messages, and emails, I quickly felt my chest pounding from the barrage. I felt under siege. But it was Ciska Balanchine's terse email that made me really furious: "Don't you think you should step down before you disgrace the department any further?" She was relentless and had cc'd it to the entire department. Weirdly, it provoked an email to me and the department from the German twins: "We do not believe in the interference in duly appointed officials."

Was that support for me? Criticism of Ciska? Or were Heino and Jonas pursuing some other agenda? Whatever they were after, it didn't cancel my outrage thinking about Ciska's challenge. I had a fierce desire to drop the phone and stomp on it, but that wouldn't change anything in the department or anywhere else.

The police were screwing with our heads. They hadn't needed any help finding us. They knew exactly where we were—and worse, had tailed us there. They obviously wanted to make us, make *me*, look bad and look guilty. And Ciska was piling on.

I contacted Vanessa first and she said with quiet steel in her voice, "It's not a good idea to leave town at a time like this."

"We didn't leave the country, we just went to Ludington."

"You need to be here right now and keep your phone on even overnight. I don't like clients being out of touch." That was the closest she had ever come to reprimanding either one of us. She added, "And I say it from a place of respect."

I didn't hear any irony in her tone.

There were no new developments in the case, she reported, warning me not to speak to journalists likely to ambush me, even if I felt uncomfortable saying "No comment." She went on: "And they *will* ambush you. You're a hot story."

"I haven't *done* anything." But I knew that didn't matter. I'd been involved in more than one murder at SUM over the years, had survived a mass shooting, and that was enough drama to make me newsworthy for all time. Those events would swamp my work on Edith Wharton in any obituary Michigan newspapers might publish when I died. And truth be told, many students signed up for my courses, which were always full, precisely because of my colorful past at SUM, not because I had good teaching reviews online. I apparently offered students a taste of danger and excitement—in complete safety.

"Stay put," Vanessa said, "and we'll be in touch."

Then a call came through from Fabian Flick, and I took it so that I could berate him, but before I could launch into a tirade he said, "I know the cops are out to get you. It's obvious. Talk to me, Professor. Let me help you get your story out there. The news is like politics and everything else now, man. The best narrative wins. Don't you want to be a winner?"

"I'll get back to you," I said, surprisingly tempted by his appeal. Isn't that what lawyers said, that you won in court if your side told a better story, no matter what the evidence was? And TV talking heads were always going on about "narratives" when they covered political campaigns or the shambolic White House. It was the new buzz word.

Stefan put away the vodka and said, "I know what we need to do. I don't trust the SUM police to handle this case right. They could even plant evidence or frame you some other way. We need to call Aldo and Celine and sit down to figure out who would want to kill Boris and then find the fucker ourselves. We need their input, they're smart and they know SUM in different ways than we do, maybe even better."

"Won't investigating that be risky?"

Stefan shook his head. "I have a gun. So do you."

We both had carry permits, given the mass shooting we'd survived, but I couldn't see myself using the gun for anything other than self-defense.

"It's Sunday," I had to point out.

He smiled. "I think Celine and Aldo both like you enough to want to help—even on the weekend."

A murder investigation was way outside their job descriptions, but it was worth trying. I made the calls and they both said yes to coming over for an early dinner of pizza. Celine had been to our old house for a party but hadn't seen the new one yet, and we had only seen Aldo at department parties, so I was actually glad he could know me a little better, though I wasn't thrilled by the catalyst.

By the time we had unpacked, fed Marco, and reheated some turkey chili for our late lunch, I was starting to unwind, and the vans and car had disappeared. Of course they could always be lying in wait for us to emerge. But the commotion had not gone over well with our neighbors—well, at least one: Sophia Lebedev, our neighbor across the street who lived in a pretty 1940s white Cape Cod cottage with sky blue shutters. Checking to see if there might be a police cruiser or that black Tahoe parked in front to hassle us, I saw her come charging across the street and marching up to the front door, wearing a pink track suit and a red-and-pink crocheted shawl. Marco was in the yard and I opened the front door before she could ring or knock.

That seemed to startle her. Small, stocky, with purplish-red hair, she glared at me. "I am…poet," she said haltingly.

I wasn't sure how to reply to her announcement. I knew her name from the neighborhood association address book, and we nodded at each other now and then, but that was all.

"I need quiet for writing. Is too much noise today with trucks and with crowds." I guess when you wanted to concentrate on *le mot juste*, half a dozen people could constitute a crowd.

Her thin lips trembled. What was a Russian poet doing in Michiganapolis of all places? I was tempted to ask, but she seemed too annoyed. I tried not to stare at her colorful hair.

"I'm sorry, Mrs. Lebedev, but it wasn't my fault."

"Okay, yes. This I know." She stepped closer as if to impart a secret: "Police they come yesterday and ask me about you."

"What?"

"Yes! They say I should watch to see what happens here. I say nothing. I am Russian. I spit on police." I must have grimaced because she assured me, "Not for real. Is figure of speech."

I wondered if I should invite her in for tea or coffee to find out more, but she nodded as if to say Mission Accomplished, and bustled back to her house. I called after her, "I like Joseph Brodsky!" He was the only Russian poet I'd read.

She turned and shook her head regretfully. "*Nyet.* Pushkin is best."

"What was that all about?" Stefan asked when I closed the

door. I filled him in, thinking he might head back to the vodka, but he seemed utterly calm now.

"They're riling up the neighbors," he brought out. "It's more harassment. We just have to ignore it."

"Her first name is Sophia," I noted.

Stefan smiled. "That's Wisdom in Greek. And she came to warn us. I'd never put that in a novel—too symbolic. That's what's so great about life. It's believable even when it isn't."

"I hear the vodka talking," I said. "Do you want some coffee? And what do you think about my doing an interview with Flick about all this? I know Vanessa said not to talk to journalists, but the longer I'm silent, the more the cops can turn me into a fall guy."

Stefan sighed. "Flick could do a hatchet job on you, or he could treat you fairly. It's a gamble. But it sounds like you trust him?"

"I don't know. Maybe 'I need him' is a better way to think about it. Maybe I can get him on my side."

"Then go ahead. We're so screwed right now anyway, can it get worse? Wait—ask Vanessa what she thinks."

Well, in a quick text exchange, Vanessa said she knew Flick a little and thought he was fair. I should go ahead, be as straight-forward as possible and not complain about the police because it would make me seem unsympathetic and whiny. She signed off with more advice and a warning: "Don't give long answers, keep it simple, and don't say anything that can be misconstrued."

That last bit of advice seemed impossible—couldn't anything be taken the wrong way?

I found Flick's number and texted him that we could do the interview right now if he was free, and I put up a pot of Sumatra-blend coffee. Stefan and I each had a big mug's worth without cream and it seemed to work pretty fast. I felt clearheaded and determined.

Thanks to Michiganapolis being relatively small as cities went, Flick arrived half an hour later, and we met in the living room. He asked if he could record the interview and when I agreed, he set his phone down on the table between us, after passing on coffee or anything else to drink. I marveled at how unruffled he seemed in his midnight blue suit, pale blue shirt, and brown oxfords. Marco surveyed him without interest, then wandered off to stare out a window from the comfort of a cushioned window seat.

"Professor Hoffman, do you feel that you're in control of your department at the university?"

I hadn't expected him to start there, but I didn't flinch. "No, I'm not in control and that's never been my goal. I'm not a lion tamer in a circus." I realized that was a bad image because circuses conjured up clowns, but I didn't try to salvage the remark.

He smiled. "But there has to be leadership, no? There's talk that you're not up to the job of being chair."

I shrugged. What was the point of responding to "talk"?

"No comment?" he asked.

"Everyone needs time to learn the ins and outs of a new position. There's nothing unusual about that."

Flick crossed his legs, looking at that moment a bit like a Bond villain, elegant and knowing. I told myself to ignore his attitude and stay focused on telling my story accurately.

"How well did you know Boris Hernandez?" he asked.

"Not at all."

"Then why did you threaten him?"

"I don't know what you've heard, but it wasn't actually a threat. I was leaving the dean's office and I thought he was trying to prevent me. SUM is not a police state, people should be allowed freedom of movement." I hunted for a way to put the incident at the dean's office in the most favorable light. "I misspoke. It happens."

He nodded genially. "So saying that you were going to kill him if he didn't get out of your way wasn't what you would call a real threat?"

Stefan brought me a cup of coffee and with his back to Flick said very softly, "Quit before it gets worse." But I plowed on. If

Valley was trying to put pressure on me, maybe I could return the favor with Flick's help. Stefan shrugged and left the room, but I was sure he was listening.

"Can you think of any reason why someone would want to kill Boris Hernandez?"

I shook my head. That was the question I intended to ask Celine and Aldo when they came over. Surely with their network of friends and colleagues across campus they would have some ideas.

Flick cocked his head at me as if prompting me to say something, anything, and I said, "SUM is a complicated community."

"And you've seen more than your fair share of controversy there, wouldn't you say?"

"I can't judge that." But he was right. I was great tabloid fodder.

"How do you think that's changed you?" he asked.

"I guess you'll have to wait to read my memoir to find out."

He laughed. "Good one." Then he became serious again. "SUM police asked the public for help finding you," Flick said. "Why was that?"

"You'll have to ask them. Especially because an SUM police officer followed me and my spouse to Ludington. We have a condo there."

Flick's eyes went wide and he uncrossed his legs. "Are you sure you were followed?"

"No doubt about it. I recognized the cop and he even spoke to us. His name is Grimm, if you want to check his whereabouts for the last few days. I'm sure campus police keep track of where their officers are." And if they didn't, that would be both sloppy and even more newsworthy.

"Did anyone else see him?"

"Yes. He was at the bar at the Jamesport Brewing Company and the next day walked in when we were having breakfast at the Lakeside diner. Tall, burly, cowboy boots, flannel shirt. Hard to miss." I felt momentarily chilled talking about Grimm, but suppressed that.

Flick grinned and I wasn't sure why.

"I'm not making this up," I said. "It really happened. He was driving a black Tahoe."

"I believe you. Okay, so this cop followed you to Ludington, while back here we were all being told SUM's police didn't know where you were?"

"Bingo."

Leaning forward like Oprah probing a guest for a confession, he asked, "What did he say to you? Did he, uh, threaten you?"

"He barely said anything, but he let us know he was there." I reminded myself that Vanessa had urged me not to complain, so I sidestepped the question. "Don't you think it was weird that he showed up out of uniform at our favorite restaurants in Ludington? Was he following orders or is he some kind of loose cannon? Seriously, what's going on with SUM's police? Some people might call this harassment. I can't be the only person at SUM who's been treated this way. Are they hiding something?"

"What do you mean?"

Trying not to sound like a conspiracy nut, I went on, "Maybe there's some problem they're trying to cover up and they need to get people looking in the wrong direction. Politicians do that all the time."

SUM had a history of embezzlement and sexual harassment scandals, so it really was possible something was about to break. And maybe orders had come down from the top to create a diversion even bigger than Boris's murder to hide what might be about to explode regarding the bribery Peter told me about.

I didn't want to suggest homophobia as a possible reason for what was happening to me because that was exactly the kind of statement that would rile conservatives on campus and across Michigan. I would end up being charged with bigotry and prejudice myself. That was a common tactic now across the country, like telling the target of racism that she's racist herself.

"You think pointing the finger at you is a smokescreen, a deflection?'

"It could be."

Flick's eyes glowed and his hands twitched as if he were dying to start typing. He stood up, grabbed his phone, and clicked off the recording app. "So you were followed to Ludington, which is way outside the jurisdiction of SUM's police. That is one hell of a story. Can I get back to you if I have more questions?"

"Absolutely."

I walked with him to the door and let him out, hoping that I had thrown a grenade into Valley's camp. Stefan had heard most of the interview and he said he wasn't convinced that I had, but maybe he was wrong, and anyway it was time to get ready for Aldo and Celine. I set the kitchen table, and brought out an aromatic, fruity Sauvignon Blanc from New Zealand while Stefan ordered a Detroit-style pizza because he liked the extra-crisp thick crust. I confess I liked it because it was baked in a rectangular pan—so different from the pizza I'd known in New York.

"With mushrooms instead of pepperoni," he said to me, "in case either Aldo or Celine's a vegetarian."

They arrived just a few minutes apart, Celine in jeans, flats and a man's purple dress shirt with rolled-up sleeves, Aldo in a long-sleeved gray T-shirt that stretched almost to his knees, super-skinny jeans and a broad-brimmed black hat. They both fussed over Marco before settling down to eat, drink, and strategize. I felt heartened that they'd come, and much less alone. The aromas of cheese and tomato had Marco licking his lips and even though we had just fed him his own dinner, he planted himself under the kitchen table in anticipation of crumbs falling his way.

"You saw the news?" Aldo began after we'd sat down and Stefan had served everyone pizza and I'd poured wine for us all. "No?"

My mouth dried up faster than I would have imagined possible. I was afraid to ask, assuming the news would be about me. Aldo handed me his phone where the *Michigan Now* website had a big fat headline: ADMISSIONS SCANDAL BREAKS AT SUM.

14.

"HERE WE GO," Aldo murmured, cutting into a square slice of pizza while I scrolled through a short article that didn't have much content. What it did say, though, was explosive. It quoted anonymous sources who "claimed" that some students had been admitted to SUM because of bribes paid to university officials. SUM police were investigating and the FBI might become involved as well. Questions from *Michigan Now* had been referred to the university's legal office which had no comment. The article ended with links to similar admissions scandals at other universities around the country.

The photo of an especially bucolic part of campus that accompanied the article made the headline seem even more disturbing. There was no way a story like this wouldn't eventually go national and morph as the media also covered the response to it on Twitter. Another black eye for SUM.

I handed back Aldo's phone and poured myself more wine even though my glass was half-full already. I downed most of it, glad I wasn't going anywhere that night and equally glad I was at home with people I trusted.

Now that the story was "official," I felt tainted just by having been confided in by Peter, but also free to openly discuss everything I knew with Aldo and Celline, so I did.

"I don't know how common it is," I added. "Parents are nuts."

Celine frowned. "I would never do that. Never. No matter how desperate I was. The law is the law."

Aldo said, "Admissions bribery is happening at other universities, so why not here? How much did they pay?" he asked.

"Two hundred and fifty thousand dollars."

"Okay, that's insane."

"I know, but it happened." I wondered if Peter had told anyone else beside his friend when he was drunk. "How long do you think it'll take before Peter's name comes out," I asked, "and what's going to happen to him?"

Everybody shrugged.

Even though Peter had known he was benefitting from a bribe, I still felt sorry for him, and for everyone else like him for whom college was a giant hurdle to jump. "When I was his age, tuition was so much less expensive, and there was never this kind of hysteria about getting admitted into a school you just had to go to—or that your parents insisted on. It just blows my mind."

"Who received the money?" Aldo asked.

I told him I didn't know, Peter hadn't shared that.

Aldo chewed thoughtfully, then he said, "You said Peter told Flick's son, right? He must feel really guilty. So maybe leaking what happened is part of atoning for what his parents did."

Stefan had a different idea. "What if Peter's being used to get at somebody? Maybe the whole thing was a set-up from the beginning? Like a kind of sting operation."

Anything was possible at SUM, I thought, but that would mean I'd been unwittingly roped into the sting with Peter "confessing" to me. If that was true, then he was a terrific actor—and I was a chump to fall for it. That would make continuing to work together on his Henry James independent study difficult. "I can see the possibility, but it seems kind of convoluted. What if Peter's been advised by a lawyer to lay the groundwork for his defense by helping get the truth out?"

Celine was on a different track altogether. Setting down her knife and fork, she asked, "Do you think Boris's murder has anything to do with this admissions mess?"

We all turned to her and it was as if the lights in the kitchen had been dimmed until that moment.

"Good question," Stefan said. "Maybe Boris was going to expose the scandal and he got killed before he could talk." Then he said almost to himself, "Though I can't see how he would have been involved in the dean's office. Admissions has to be where the problem is."

That's when I realized I had no clear idea what Boris—or anyone—actually did in his position of Associate Dean for Undergraduate Education. So I asked.

"Okay." Celine took a deep breath. "There's a lot. First of all, that person provides leadership in the College of Humanities for undergraduate education, like the title says."

"What kind of leadership?" Stefan asked.

She started ticking things off, one finger at a time. "Program delivery. Program evaluation. Curriculum development. Faculty development. Institutional assessment and improvement. Facilities planning. Facilities management." She took a breath and went on. "Then they chair a committee for undergraduate affairs that oversees adding or dropping courses, course descriptions, degree requirements, and so on, et cetera."

When she paused, Aldo jumped in. "Whoever's associate dean is also the chair of task forces, and the leader for strategic planning, boosting academic innovation, ensuring academic accessibility for all students, fund-raising for the college, which sometimes means handling crabby donors, and—"

I waved at him and Celine to stop. "So given all that, who did he have regular contact with? Department chairs and other administrators in the college—including Bullerschmidt?"

Celine said, "There's also a Deans' Council for the whole university and the associate dean sometimes attends that in place of Bullerschmidt. The provost and associate provost are also there."

I could just imagine the pomposity level at a meeting of so many SUM bigwigs.

"Well, where would he have been clashing with anyone?" I

asked. "Who would be pissed off enough at him to kill him or at least attack him without having planned to kill him?"

"I don't know about clashes," Aldo said, "but it's a fairly big circle. He would have been in contact with all those people we mentioned, along with the Associate Dean for Graduate Education in Humanities—"

"—Wait," Stefan said, "isn't that somebody new?"

"That's right," Celine said. "The previous associate dean died in a car accident and this guy is just getting settled in, so I don't think he had much interaction with Boris."

"Does that mean we cross him off the list?" Stefan asked the three of us. "Being new doesn't mean being above suspicion, does it?"

None of us had an answer to that one. I thought of Peter Sellers as Inspector Clouseau saying, "I believe everything and I believe nothing. I suspect everyone, and I suspect no one," but I kept that to myself.

Celine said she agreed with Stefan. "His first name is Dean, if you can believe it, and all I've heard about him is that he's overwhelmed, given how the graduate programs are hemorrhaging students. Boris would also have had contact with the Admissions Office, too, and possibly the Registrar's Office as well. But Bullerschmidt most of all," Celine opined. "Even though he was popular, some people said he was Bullerschmidt's lapdog. Maybe the dean decided to put him down." Then she shook her head. "Sorry, that was ugly. I didn't mean anything against Boris. I liked him." She closed her eyes for a moment as if saying a brief prayer or remonstrating with herself. Then she returned, cut herself another bit of pizza. "This is really good, thanks."

"So what could Bullerschmidt or anyone else in that crew have against Boris?" I asked.

Aldo's eyes were narrowed as if he was making out a sign in the distance. Then he turned to Celine. "The lapdog thing is news to me, and I don't know that I've ever heard complaints about him, either."

"That seems unusual," Stefan said, reaching down to scratch the back of Marco's neck.

Celine smiled. "There *are* good people at SUM—they just don't make waves, so people don't talk trash about them."

"Well," I said, "Somebody killed Boris, right? The police haven't released details, but there's no way it could have been suicide. Somebody wanted him dead for a reason—unless it happened during an argument." For a moment my vision blurred and my chest tightened remembering the sight of Boris at his desk, seeing the spray of blood behind him and blood pooled on his desk, and that cloying scent in the air.

"My money's on Bullerschmidt," Stefan said. "He's obnoxious, he's cruel, and he has a terrible temper." Then he added, "I can see him exploding—but I can't imagine what it would be about. Maybe Boris was after his job the way Ciska wants yours. Boris could have been scheming to damage him somehow. Just because he seemed nice doesn't mean he really was."

"When somebody's murdered, isn't the most likely suspect their spouse or partner? Was Boris married? Living with someone? Straight? Gay?" I asked, picturing his ostentatious diamond ring but unable to remember which finger it had been on.

Nobody had the answer. Aldo pulled up Facebook to see if Boris had posted personal photos, but he didn't have a page there and he wasn't on any other social media platform either.

"Isn't that weird?" Celine asked.

Aldo shook his head. "Privacy is the new black." Then he flushed, and started to apologize for using the word "black."

Celine waved it off. "Honey, please. Just enjoy your pizza and your wine and let's help Nick stay out of jail."

"Thanks," I said. "Was he dating anyone on campus?"

Aldo nodded. "You know, I think I might have heard a rumor that he was screwing Dawn Lovelace—someone in Study Abroad told me that was the buzz there. But stories like that circulate on campus about lots of people and most of them are bullshit."

"Lovelace is married to that guy in fund-raising," I said. "So maybe she and Boris were having an affair and her husband killed Boris out of jealousy."

Stefan looked intrigued. "Very possible. Or Dawn could have killed Boris because he wanted her to leave her husband, or maybe she broke it off and Boris was stalking her. Everyone keeps saying how nice Boris was, but maybe there was another side to him?"

I nodded. "So that's two possible suspects. Well, three if you include Bullerschmidt, but don't bullies enjoy tormenting people? Wouldn't the dean have wanted to keep Boris around? Killing him would end the fun."

Again, nobody had a response.

"What task force was Boris leading?" I asked.

Aldo knew. "Digital Humanities. He went to the DH conference in Utrecht this past summer. I heard him talking about it somewhere on campus, and he was disillusioned but I couldn't make out why."

Stefan and I exchanged a look. "Heino and Jonas," Stefan blurted out. "I don't know what beef they could have had with him about Digital Humanities, but I don't really get DH anyway."

That word "digital" was starting to give me hives.

Stefan went on: "What if he wanted to mess with their grant somehow, or was shutting down the task force and that infuriated them? It might not seem like a big deal but those two can really go ballistic."

Stefan reminded Aldo and Celine about the day-long department retreat at the start of the semester where the twins had gotten into a fist fight over sharing their office. Even though they'd heard the story before, they still looked appalled, mouths open, eyes wide. Aldo said, "I'm glad we weren't invited."

And it hit me that despite the former chair's stated concerns about equality in the department, challenging the hierarchy only extended so far.

Stefan said to Celine, "Can you ask around Humanities and see what the status of the DH task force is?"

"Sure, no problem."

SUM loved the militaristic term "task force" because it suggested energy, strength, action, innovation, direction, and movement when the university was so often reactive, passive, or just blowing smoke.

"What about Ciska?" I asked.

They all turned to me with a "What about her?" look on their faces.

"Well, when she was berating me for...for how I spoke to Boris when I thought he was trying to grab me—" I had to stop, because now that he was dead, I felt even more ashamed for having treated him the way I had. It was so wrong.

"Finish your thought," Stefan prompted.

"Ciska defended him like she really cared about him," I said. "She said he was wonderful and that people adored him, which seems excessive, don't you think?"

Celine nodded. "It does. Well-liked is one thing, but adored?" She grimaced. "That's over the top. So you're thinking *cherchez la femme*?"

"She's a nasty piece of work, you have to admit that. Look at how she's been scheming against me, trying to get me to step down as chair—you saw her emails. It's not sexist to suspect her."

"I wasn't offended," Celine assured me. "I agree with you." She reached across the table to pat my hand.

For a few moments then, we were all silent, eating and drinking, overwhelmed, I think, not just by the murder itself, but by an event that could have terrible repercussions once it became more widely known, and then even more so when the killer was finally discovered.

"So who did it?" Stefan murmured. "Who...killed...Boris?"

There was something a bit heartless, I mused, about surveying people we knew to figure out who might be a murderer—and over a meal, no less—but then I suppose it wasn't remotely as heartless as murder itself.

And it had to be done. I was worried that Valley would frame me somehow. And even though Vanessa was a great defense lawyer, her skill was no guarantee that I was safe from a conviction. If the four of us could somehow identify who really killed Boris, or come close enough to it to take the heat off me, then I would be safe.

Or safer, at least.

Aldo sipped some wine, put down his glass as if it was heavy, and held on to the stem like a judge with his gavel. "What if we're totally off base? What if this isn't really personal, but some kind of hate crime?"

"Because he's Hispanic?" Celine asked. Then she said softly, "*Was* Hispanic."

"Yes. Look at all the white nationalist terrorism right now. The killer could be one of those weird, antisocial dudes who's obsessed with being 'replaced' by people of color and Jews, and posts crazy shit on Facebook. And writes an endless sick manifesto. It happens all the time."

Aldo wasn't exaggerating. According to the FBI, since 9/11, more people had been killed in the U.S. by domestic terrorism directed against minorities like Muslims, Jews, and gays than were killed by foreign terrorists. But so far, violence like that hadn't erupted on our campus.

We were all quiet, almost frozen by the enormity of contemplating the roiling forces of hatred that had become unleashed in our country.

The only sound we could hear was Marco grunting as he scratched first one ear, then the other, and then started to roll around on his back. I felt slightly dizzy, flashing on the gun violence Stefan, Celine, and I had survived only months ago. I thought of lines from a W.S. Merwin poem:

Send me out into another life
lord because this one is growing faint
I do not think it goes all the way

Stefan was looking dubious and shaking his head. "Don't those racists and white nationalist killers go in for big, dramatic events, like shooting people at a mall, or Walmart, a church or synagogue, a music festival? Someplace public and splashy. Killing one person doesn't fit the pattern."

"Unless there's a new pattern emerging," I suggested. "Targeted murders. Assassinations. We don't know what kind of crazy plans people spew online on Reddit." Message boards like that were sites where hatred had free rein and extremists flourished.

Celine pushed her chair back, leaned back, and crossed her arms. "I don't see it. Boris wasn't a well-known figure locally like the provost or the president. But even if this *is* the start of some terror campaign, we're not the FBI here. There's no way we can follow up something like that, and even if we could, I think it would be too dangerous. But we can try to find someone who had a grudge against Boris, someone we probably know at SUM. That seems doable."

We all nodded, and Celine said, "Should we divide up the suspects? I can talk to Heino and Jonas, they like me well enough." She smiled ruefully. "Well, at least they don't despise me."

Aldo said, "I can meet with that new associate dean, say I want to get acquainted or something like that, to keep things running smoothly since our department has another new chair, and then work the conversation around to Boris."

"That leaves Ciska, Lovelace, her husband, and Bullerschmidt."

"We should tackle them together," Stefan suggested. "Safety in numbers, right?"

"Is there coffee?" Celine asked. "I could really use a strong cup of coffee right now."

Through the open windows I could hear crows suddenly cackling and squawking like a coven of witches. It seemed almost too appropriate, and I couldn't help but think of the line from *Macbeth* about "something wicked this way comes."

A moment from a horror movie, or just another day in my bizarre life?

Stefan got up to pour Celine some coffee, and let Marco out into the yard since he loved to chase the crows. They erupted with a cacophony of jeers at his furious barking as they flew off.

I wasn't alone in making macabre associations because Aldo grimaced. "They sound so evil...."

"There's something I don't understand," Celine said, putting her mug down.

I don't think I had ever noticed how fine-boned her hands were, how delicate her fingers. If I were an artist, I would have wanted to sketch them.

Celine continued: "You said that Boris called you and said he had to talk to you, right? But what was so urgent? Why couldn't it wait?"

"He said he knew something about what was going on with admissions."

"But why meet on campus at night? It's not like you guys were doing a drug deal or anything clandestine like that."

"Well, he said he didn't want to meet where people could see us."

"He was paranoid," Aldo suggested.

"Or afraid," I said, "that the twins could be tailing him."

"But why? And why *you*?" Celine asked. "He didn't know you, right? Why reach out to someone who's a stranger instead of a friend or at least a colleague?"

I said, "I don't know. Maybe he didn't trust anyone around him."

"That makes two mysteries," she said. "His murder, and why he contacted you. Are they connected?"

Stefan's face brightened. "Maybe Boris called Nick because he's been involved in solving mysteries before. Maybe he thought Nick was the best person to help him."

The idea of me being able to help anyone seemed pretty far-fetched, but then so was the reality of yet another killing at SUM.

Then I checked myself. Given the rampant gun violence in

America, with thousands killed or wounded last year, why should SUM be exempt?

Celine's chin was down and her eyes looked heavy, so I asked what was troubling her.

"Nick, we don't have enough tools at our disposal. We can't tap phones or read anyone's email to find out what they're hiding, or clone their phones. Will talking to people make a difference?"

The way she had suddenly faded mobilized me. "Listen," I said, "it has to. Agatha Christie wrote that 'in the long run, either through a lie, or through truth, people were bound to give themselves away.'"

"Good quote," Aldo murmured.

I was just getting started. "We don't know what the police are doing or if they're making any progress, if they found the murder weapon or have any clues. But they've targeted me and we can't just sit around and wait for them to decide they want to prosecute me. Well, I can't, anyway. I know that my lawyer would probably warn me to stay out of everything because otherwise I might get charged with interfering in an investigation or obstruction of justice or who knows what—but I have to act."

Stefan was grinning at me, eyes glowing with what I read as pride.

"Celine, Aldo, this isn't your fight," I said. "You do not have to get involved."

"We already *are* involved," Aldo said, holding out his hand to fist-bump me. I did, and then Celine, head high, followed suit with both of us.

"All for one," Stefan said. "Right?" And he raised his glass.

15.

WE MADE SURE that Celine and Aldo had plenty of coffee so they were alert enough to drive home safely, and thanked them profusely for their help. But when they were gone I felt deflated and asked Stefan, "Where do we start?"

He scratched his chin a moment, then said, "Why not do the unexpected? Text Ciska and ask her if she'd like to come over for a nightcap."

Before I could object and say that it was late, his idea was crazy, and I refused to have her in our house again, Stefan said with a sly look, "Tell her that you're considering her suggestion to step down as chair."

"But that's a lie."

"Not really. Haven't you been thinking about it?"

"Yeah—thinking she's a stone cold bitch."

"That's close enough, then." And he grinned, looking absurdly happy.

"She's probably asleep," I said.

"I doubt it. More than likely, she's sitting up imagining how wonderful it'll be to move into the chair's office. I'd bet a hundred bucks she'd be here within half an hour or less."

I texted Ciska what Stefan suggested and expected no reply. But the phone pinged with her one-word text: "Soon."

"That sounds ominous," I said, but Stefan just started cleaning up the kitchen, smiling at having been right. I still didn't understand why anyone would hunger to be department chair the way she seemed to. Unless Ciska really saw it as a stepping stone to a position higher up the soulless SUM food chain. Now, that made sense, because the upper administration was where the money and power were concentrated.

"Put out some scotch," Stefan said.

While he put dishes into the dishwasher and set it for its shortest cycle, I took a bottle of Talisker to the living room, then went back to the kitchen for Glenlivet in case Ciska preferred something less smoky. I set out three of our Galway crystal tumblers because it seemed right and proper even though the idea of entertaining that woman—and under false pretenses—irked me.

Marco was too worn out by the unexpected company that evening to make much of a fuss when Ciska arrived. We didn't hear a car pull up outside so she must have strolled over to our house from her part of the neighborhood.

She did not look like we'd rousted her from bed. If anything, she might have just come from a cocktail party: she wore glittery forest green sandals, a classic little black dress, and three strings of jade beads. Her perfume was something musky and floral.

Ciska seemed unusually cheerful as she sat down opposite me and Stefan and asked for a glass of the Glenlivet. A true aficionado, she inhaled deeply before taking a sip. Marco had come closer and settled down a few feet off to snooze.

"So," she said, holding her glass close, as appreciatively as if it were a gift. "You're ready to let go? I'm not surprised."

I wasn't sure how to proceed, but Stefan must have been planning this in the kitchen because he said, "What's your vision for the department?"

She blinked rapidly. "Is this an interview?"

I picked up Stefan's thread and said gently, "Well, we'd have to know where you want to take the department, to feel it's going to be in good hands. You can see that, can't you?"

She nodded a bit reluctantly, but then took another sip of scotch and seemed to brighten. "Well, I've already told you, Nick, about digital learning. That's not enough. We need a bold new vision. I would definitely push for a more robust interface with other departments and units—not just in Humanities but across the university, especially with Business, Law, the School of Music, Agriculture, Economics. They're all flourishing. It's time we joined them instead of looking on from the sidelines."

Her attitude was much more positive and goal-oriented than when we had spoken about the future of the department just a few days ago. But the idea of linking ourselves to departments like Economics sounded like a pipe dream. We would always be a poor cousin to the wealthy SUM departments and units because their faculty brought in millions of dollars in grants and there was almost nothing like that for us.

"We also need a course in contemporary Trans literature—the whole country is waking up to transsexuals, why are we lagging behind? Look at TV, movies, ad campaigns, fashion magazines— Trans people are *everywhere.*"

She was right about that and I thought the idea made a lot of sense, which was uncomfortable for me because I didn't trust her otherwise.

"Nick, the department should also put pressure on that Michigan Great Reads Foundation to be more inclusive. I've never seen them select a book by a queer Michigan author."

That wasn't at all what I expected her to add, but she was right: twenty books by Michigan authors were honored every year by a nonprofit foundation and in all my years in Michigan there was never anything LGBTQ. Was that ignorance, homophobia, or a bit of both?

This advocacy was a side of Ciska I hadn't seen before, and I found myself wondering if I could have possibly misjudged her. Unless she was just saying it for our benefit. Her arguments gave me that weird sensation you get when you reach for something like a milk carton, thinking it's full, pick it up and it's almost empty so your hand flies into the air.

Ciska wasn't nearly done with her vision for the department.

"Let's make our guest lecture series more diverse, more reflective of how the country is changing, and why don't you think about that in terms of your fellowship?"

She had a point about the department lectures, but the last thing I wanted was someone else telling me how to pick authors for my fellowship.

"I also think we need to encourage faculty to offer more real world learning so we can dethrone the classroom as the nexus of education."

Which meant what? *Alfresco* classes?

"And we should hire an outside publicity firm to boost our image, come up with a logo and slogan. Something really memorable."

Good grief, I thought, more bullshit. Was it a joke? No, it couldn't be because she surveyed me and Stefan as if she were a medieval merchant laying fabulous goods on a rug at our feet. She clearly expected us to be dazzled and enticed by the idea.

"You're thinking of something that would look good on T-shirts?" I asked.

"Of course! We need to promote solidarity in the face of adversity."

Too bad the Poles had already taken the name "Solidarity" or that could have been our slogan. And did adversity mean falling enrollments, my current crisis, or both?

"Why not a theme song?" Stefan asked, deadpan.

"I'd consider it," Ciska said without a trace of irony. "If the music were inspiring enough."

"So what you really want is to rebrand the department," I said, realizing that posing the question probably made me sound like a dinosaur and resistant to change. Some of what she suggested made sense, but some of it seemed ridiculous. And she had clearly not wanted to share any of it when we met the first time in my office, which suggested that she was planning to make a power grab even before I screwed up this past week.

"Absolutely. We need radical change. The department has to

be on the cutting edge, has to be a twenty-first-century department. More diverse, more cross-disciplinary, more relevant, celebrating intersectionality. I myself would love to see us offer a seminar on queer video games. They truly say more about the human condition than anything else in our culture right now. And there's nothing that better penetrates to the heart of the most important question we all face today—what it means to be a citizen of the world."

"Aren't you forgetting climate disruption? There won't be much world left in a few years for all those citizens."

Ciska eyed me speculatively, then she shook her head as if coming out of a dream. "You didn't text me because of the future of the department, did you?" She finished her scotch and poured herself another as if girding her loins for battle. "This is really about Boris, isn't it?"

Our silence said yes. If I expected Ciska to be angry about my deceptive text, I was wrong. She just took it all in stride.

"You want to know if I have any idea who might have killed him, and why. I already told Detective Valley everything I know, which isn't much. Boris was hard-working, smart, well-liked, and really going places. The provost was grooming him to be Dean of Humanities."

It was hard to imagine Bullerschmidt ever retiring, but I supposed that would have to happen someday. Or he could get promoted upstairs.

"I don't know anything compromising about Boris. His private life is a blank to me, but I think he's like a lot of people on campus. He lived for SUM. Oh, and in case you're wondering, I didn't kill him. I was at a recital in Ann Arbor the night he died. The SUM police have already verified my alibi, so don't waste your time trying to investigate that." She smiled with the charm of a B-movie empress about to condemn a disloyal favorite to some arcane torture.

Since we were talking about Boris openly and Ciska had brought up Detective Valley, I said, "So he was perfect and nobody could have wanted to kill him. But somebody did. You have connections at SUM that I don't have. You must suspect somebody."

She shrugged insouciantly.

Stefan helped me out: "Nick didn't do it, but if he's arrested or brought in for questioning, it'll be another black eye for the department. The SUM investigation might not uncover the kind of information we could."

"Which one of you is Sherlock?"

A joke? She actually made a joke. I found that absurdly hopeful. So I asked, "What was his relationship with the dean like?"

Ciska took a long sip of her scotch and I guessed she was weighing how honest she wanted to be, since anything she said could get back to Bullerschmidt.

"The dean is tough. Very tough. And demanding."

We waited for more, and I could sense her feeling like she was in a minefield, dreading where she stood, but determined to make it across.

She pursed her lips, drank some more scotch, set her glass down as carefully as someone laying out tiles on a Scrabble board at a turning point in the game. I imagined that if she were a smoker, this would have been the moment for those little rituals of taking out a cigarette, lighting it, taking a first deep draft, all of that buying herself some time.

"I think the dean was also wary of him. Boris was always watching him, studying him, and was way too attentive. I heard it was rather strange."

This echoed something Celine had said, though without speculating about what it might mean.

I recalled how Boris had been hovering right outside the dean's office when I argued with Bullerschmidt. What if he wanted to talk to me because he had a plan to oust the dean and wanted my help or advice? Lines from *All About Eve*, which I'd seen many times, popped into my head. I was seeing the moment when tough-talking, slangy Thelma Ritter is complaining to Bette Davis about Eve's attention to Davis: "It's like she's studying you, like you was a play or a book or a set of blueprints—how you walk, talk, eat, think, sleep."

Had Boris been that conniving and even sinister despite his reputation as a good guy? And was Bullerschmidt afraid? Of anyone? Was that even possible? And why was Ciska being so forthright with us even though I'd tricked her into coming over? Was it the scotch, fatigue at the end of a long day, or did she have some kind of agenda that I couldn't make out?

"Gentlemen," she said, clapping her hands together, "it's been fun but I need to get to bed. Thanks for the scotch and some very interesting conversation." She sounded as if she was the one who'd been looking for answers, not us. "And Nick, remember that it's not always a good idea to be too curious."

Stefan followed her to the door and let her out while I called a puzzled "Good night!" and Marco barked once in his sleep.

We closed the lights, let Marco out for his last potty run, and headed upstairs to bed, Marco following half-asleep. There was a lot to consider, but both of us were too zonked to think clearly. It would have to wait till breakfast.

• • •

We didn't sleep well or long and the Monday morning news online and on the radio said nothing more about Boris's murder than "SUM police report that the investigation is ongoing."

We had granola with dried cranberries and almond milk for breakfast while Stefan tried to talk me out of asking Celine to clear my schedule for the morning.

"People might complain you're not meeting your responsibilities as chair and Bullerschmidt could get wind of it," he said.

"So what's the worst he could do?"

"He could file a complaint against you for violating the faculty code of conduct. There could be a hearing to consider the complaint. I'm sure department chairs aren't supposed to take time off unless there's an out-of-town conference or an emergency."

"I'd say being targeted by Valley is an emergency. And if the dean wants to file a complaint? Let him. I'll get Vanessa to defend me if I have to. Right now I need time to think and I need to talk to Boris's secretary. I have to find out if anything Ciska told us about him and Bullerschmidt was true."

"Playing devil's advocate for a moment, why would she lie?"

"Why *wouldn't* she lie? She wants my job, she could have been telling us stuff to jam me up somehow. And she threatened me, didn't she?"

"I missed that."

I couldn't see how, so I snapped, "When she warned me against being too curious. On her way out."

He looked at me blankly. "I must have zoned out for a minute."

"Well, she did say it."

"Okay, I believe you!"

I reached for my phone, texted Celine, then pulled up the SUM directory, found the number of Boris's secretary, Olivia Berglund, looked up her phone number and called her.

"Olivia? This is Nick Hoffman, the new chair of English and Creative Writing, and I know it's early, but I wonder if I could buy you coffee before you start your work day? The Starbucks closest to your office?"

There was silence on her end because I'm sure this request was unexpected. I was pulling rank on top of surprising her, but she said, "Sure." Then added with more energy, "That would be lovely. Seven-thirty?"

"Perfect! Thanks so much."

"Well, thank *you*."

I'm not sure why she bothered to thank me, but it wasn't a bad way to start. Stefan wished me good luck and gave me a big hug before I drove off.

Parking off campus was easy at that time of day though traffic was intense at the start of the work week—for Michiganapolis, that is. I've had friends visit from LA and New York and when I complain about having to wait for a traffic light even for a few minutes, they're incredulous. I can't blame them, since Stefan and I live no more than ten minutes from campus and never have to drive very far in town for anything: shopping, movies, cultural events.

The Starbucks where I was meeting Boris's secretary had the typical display case for goodies and a sign cataloguing all the beverages on offer, but it was very cozy and a little quirky, filled with inviting green and brown velvet chairs and sofas, looking like an old-fashioned upscale rec room. It was already packed with bleary-eyed students who looked like they'd gotten dressed in the dark. Though some might not have gotten dressed at all since they wore rumpled T-shirts, colorful flannel pajama bottoms, and fuzzy bedroom slippers, topped by worn cardigans or hoodies. Everyone was fixed on some kind of screen—phone, tablet, laptop—and conversation was muted. The long narrow space smelled mildly rank, sugary, and earthy, coffee aromas mixing with the baked goods and the tang of anxious students.

Olivia waved at me as soon as I entered. She stood out because she was more than twice the age of her java mates—and so was I, of course. She was on the chunky side, a bit like a Russian granny, but dressed very well in a long black-and-white leopard print dress under a black blazer, both of which looked like silk. She was as Scandinavian as her name: pale pink complexion, bright blue eyes, and ash blond hair cut bowl-style.

When we shook hands I tried my Swedish on her: *"God morgon, trevligt att träffas."* Good morning, nice to meet you.

She grinned sheepishly. "I know what you're saying, but I'm third-generation Swedish, just like my husband, and nobody in either family speaks the language."

I sat down on the overstuffed chair that was catty-corner to hers and asked if she'd ever been to Sweden. She shook her head. She already had coffee and I excused myself to get an iced Caffè Mocha. I thought the jolt of sugar and cold might give me the clarity I needed.

Olivia smiled expectantly when I sat back down, and I plunged right in. "It must be hard to lose a boss like Boris."

Her smile dimmed and she nodded sadly, looking down at her coffee as if she could read omens there.

"What kind of boss was he?"

She smiled like a doting grandmother about to open her

walletful of photos. "Oh, he was a very easy man to work with. He knew what he wanted, was clear about his expectations. He was thorough and direct, and he never talked down to me or anyone else in Humanities the way some administrators do."

How people treated their support staff said a lot, and I wondered if she had Bullerschmidt in mind as a bad example.

"He was a good Christian man," she said.

"You mean he went to church?"

She shook her head. "No. I mean that he was decent, compassionate, a pure soul, treating people the way they wanted to be treated and he would do anything he could to help someone in trouble."

Saint Boris, I thought.

Unbidden, Olivia answered a question I had been working toward. "I can't imagine anyone attacking him, let alone...murder." And she sipped some more of what smelled like chai.

"He got along well with everyone in those Humanities offices, even the dean?"

Chin up, she said almost fiercely, "Of course he did! Boris thought of the dean as a father. He called him sir, remembered his birthday, his wedding anniversary, even the anniversary of his appointment as dean, and always sent him cards to help celebrate. Not email cards, *real* greeting cards through the mail, like people used to do."

She seemed proud of Boris, but the card business sounded a little creepy to me, excessive. Celebrating Bullerschmidt's accession to the deanship? Seriously? Was this a case of not speaking ill of the dead? Or loyalty to a boss? Whatever motivated Olivia, her portraits of Boris and Bullerschmidt did not jibe with Ciska's from last night.

"Did you know anything about his family?"

She bit her lip as if she'd been about to say something insulting and her back was suddenly parade-ground straight. "Aside from the weather, we never talked about anything but university matters, and even if we had, it would be none of your business. Boris lived for his job and he loved SUM. He loved leading high school students on campus tours when he could. He had season football and basketball tickets, and he always donated to the yearly fund drive. He was going to put the university in his will. He would have walked through fire to protect SUM!"

As tired and screen-dazed as they were, students around us noticed Olivia's vehemence, but she didn't seem to care and I certainly wasn't going to shush her.

"Protect the university from what?"

"From anything. It would kill him all over again to know he might be the cause of bad publicity."

I studied her face to see if she felt at all awkward about how she had phrased that, but there was no trace of embarrassment.

"You mean bad PR by being murdered?"

"Exactly."

"Was Boris on the Committee of Public Safety?"

Her eyes narrowed and she snatched up her purse and a red Art Institute of Chicago tote bag as if I'd been about to rifle through them for cash. "I don't know anything about that, and you should keep questions like that to yourself. That's all I have to say."

She hurried out of the Starbucks as if I were contagious.

There was a minor stir around me, like that disturbance in the force in *Star Wars*, but it faded. I slowly finished my coffee, pondering what would have made Olivia abruptly flee from me. What nerve did I hit by asking about the mysterious Committee that seemed to operate under the radar at SUM?

I checked my email and was surprised to find mail from the psychologist I'd contacted weeks ago, apologizing for not getting back to me sooner. He said that my email had gone into his SPAM folder for some reason. He'd actually just found my email and someone had canceled his next session at 9:00 if I wanted to come in. He understood it was very short notice. If that didn't work, he had some openings next week.

Why not go today? I thought. I emailed back that I was free and would be there, then texted Stefan to tell him where I was headed from Starbucks, and did the same with Celine. I finished my coffee and went to the counter for some pound cake, and ordered a double espresso, too. I had plenty of time. And I also knew from experiences back in New York and Massachusetts that therapy was serious business. I wanted to be alert, and the more caffeine, the better.

And I wanted to ponder my brief talk with Olivia some more. I found myself suspicious about her rosy portrait of working with Boris, but then I remembered Celine saying there were plenty of good folks at SUM, they just didn't make waves or get attention. But then there was Olivia's reaction when I mentioned that secret committee. What was she hiding or trying to hide?

And then I succumbed to the kind of thinking found in the dark, twisted caverns of conspiracy theories on Twitter. What if Boris knew something about the shadowy committee that had to be exposed for the good of SUM? What if people on it were abusing their power and authority? What if he was in danger of bringing the whole thing down like Samson destroying the temple he was chained to after they cut off his hair and blinded him? I'd been thinking of more personal motives, but what if his death had larger implications?

And once it became widely known that Boris had called *me* the night he was killed and I'd gone to meet him on campus so late, would I be the next target?

16.

MICHIGANAPOLIS has lots of pretty, green neighborhoods, but it's also marred by nondescript and often shabby strip malls like many other cities across the country. Visiting one of those little malls in town, you could be anywhere and nowhere. They smell of asphalt, car exhaust, and slush in the fall and winter, and too much air conditioning in the summer that grabs you with every opening door.

Dr. Eric Martini's office was in one of the dozens of Michiganapolis strip malls that was on the newer side but still squat and ugly. His office was flanked on one side by a dry cleaner's, a sandwich shop, a tattoo parlor, and on the other by a small aerobics studio, a bakery, and a de-cluttering consultancy called Joy Joy Sparks. I think the name was meant to evoke that *Star Wars* character Jar Jar Binks, but it seemed like an odd blend, especially since so many fans of the franchise hated that character.

Martini's small outer office was utilitarian and bland, more like an artist's first sketch than a finished drawing. The chairs were functional and bland. Each little side table was piled high with a wild variety of magazines: everything from *People* and *Us* to *The New Yorker* and *Men's Health* to *Elle*, *Psychology Today*, and *Vanity Fair*. There was a labeled wall button with instructions to flick it to indicate I had arrived—I guess it flashed a light inside his office.

When he emerged a few minutes later and led me into his office, it was nothing like his waiting room. The walls were painted black and everything else—desk, chairs, sofa, curtains—was crimson. It looked like a stage set for a play about the Devil. The only thing missing was the smell of sulfur. The glossy black walls were bare except for an array of degrees and certificates.

Martini himself seemed out of place there. Looking to be about sixty, he was short, pudgy, with salt-and-pepper hair and a close-trimmed beard to match. He wore dark jeans, a blue blazer, a blue buttoned-down shirt, penny loafers, and seemed vaguely professorial. Nothing fiendish in how he presented himself.

I sat on the stiff red leather couch opposite his red plastic chair which didn't look remotely comfortable, trying to picture being in this hellish environment on a weekly basis. I wasn't sure I could stand it and the thought crossed my mind to just try someone else and make some excuse for leaving before we began. Could I say I had changed my mind about therapy?

Martini crossed his legs and positioned an open black leather portfolio with yellow notepad in his lap and started writing before I'd spoken a word beyond "Hello."

I decided to try working with him, or at least talking to him. What did I have to lose? So I said, "You were recommended to me after the mass shooting I survived." I didn't think I needed to explain which one. If he lived in or near Michiganapolis, he couldn't have missed the coverage of that singular event.

He glared at me, forehead creased with annoyance. "Could you let me finish this?"

"I've had trouble sleeping since then and—"

"—You are interrupting me," he snapped.

Chastened, I said nothing. I'd done therapy in college and read a little about various schools, so I speculated that maybe this was all part of some therapeutic technique I wasn't familiar with. But his attitude made him seem less like a listening ear and more like a cop who'd pulled you over for speeding and was wondering how drunk you were.

He finished whatever notes he was making. "And you need to stop talking about the past because that's a dead end. Where you are now, *that's* what matters." He went on to tell me a long, involved anecdote about something some Buddhist monk had shared with him in Nepal, but I couldn't follow it because I was distracted by his having cut me off, and I didn't understand why he was doing so much talking. Wasn't the session supposed to be about me and my issues? This moment reminded me of being trapped at a party and blared at by a half-drunk bore.

When he was done, he grinned as if I'd just been granted great wisdom, but I asked, "How can I talk about *now* if I don't talk about someone trying to kill me last spring, and what it feels like to have seen him die just a few feet away? It could have been me."

"It's that kind of thinking that's gotten you into the mess you're in at the university."

I could feel my chest tightening. There was something odd in the way he spoke those words, as if continuing a conversation from a previous session, or speaking from a script. What was going on here?

"Let me tell you something, Professor Hoffman, and forgive me if I'm being too blunt. That's the kind of man I am, and if you're smart, you'll appreciate it. I've only known you a few minutes but I have to share my assessment of you. You are obviously someone whose mental life is all out of balance, someone who worries far too much, someone who is much too curious about others when you should be cultivating your inner self. I can help you become less curious and direct your attention more profitably and peacefully for all concerned."

I was about to say that after someone tries to kill you, cultivating your inner life might not be the answer, but then I asked, "Why did you bring up my being too curious? What do you mean by that? How could you possibly know anything about me?"

Ciska had just told me not to be "too curious." Was this just a coincidence?

Martini shrugged as if to say, "That's my job."

"Has somebody on campus been talking to you about me?"

It sounded half-crazy when I said it, but the expression on

his face seemed like the twinge of someone who's been exposed. That's when I focused in on the elaborately framed degree certificates hanging on the wall closest to us: all three were from SUM. My hands suddenly started to feel cold.

Had he been instructed to contact me after not having responded to my initial query? Was he working with Bullerschmidt or someone else in the administration to manipulate me in some way or to find out what I knew about Boris? Could he be in league with Ciska?

Quickly regaining his composure, he said, "People know about you. You've been in the news quite a lot, too much in fact." His tone was somewhere between prim and censorious, as if I'd offended him personally.

Get out, I thought, this guy's acting suspicious. But I didn't even like walking out on a movie I wasn't enjoying, so I hesitated. I felt briefly paralyzed. Even if I was being paranoid, he didn't remotely seem like the right choice for me to do therapy with. Before Martini could tell me more about myself based on our too-brief acquaintance or share another convoluted story, I stood up and said, "You know what? I don't think this will work for me."

Now he looked even angrier than when I'd interrupted him before. "You can't leave now, we're not finished. Besides, I need your insurance information."

"For ten minutes of bullshit? Don't make me laugh."

I walked out feeling better than I had in days. So I guess meeting with this so-called therapist hadn't been a total waste of time.

But when I got to my SUV, the feelings of lightness and liberation had already begun to evaporate. I sat inside for a while, hands on the steering wheel, unable to start the engine, shaken by the man's hostility and by the weird possibility that he might actually be working for or with someone at SUM. Because his sudden availability had come right on the heels of my recent interactions with the dean and Ciska, and he seemed so damned untrustworthy—something felt wrong about him.

And those words kept reverberating for me: "too curious."

Even if he had nothing to do with SUM, Martini was unbeliev-
ably critical *and* a blabbermouth to boot. Years ago, a friend had
joked about doing therapy in a loose riff on *Fight Club*: "The first
rule of Psych Club is this: the shrink does only ten percent of the
talking and you do ninety percent." How did someone like Martini
maintain a practice and make a living? Why would people want
to keep seeing him? You'd have to be a masochist.

But somehow I'd ended up in his bizarre office. I seemed to
be a magnet for dangerous people at the moment, and that was
truly unnerving.

I pulled myself together and did a quick check of email and
texts, which reduced the list of possible suspects. Aldo reported
that the other associate dean in Humanities had been in Berlin at
a conference when Boris was murdered. He was going to double-
check Facebook for photos, just to be sure.

I finally drove off thinking that now was the time to check in
on Dawn Lovelace because the chaos of the last week had begun
with her visit to recruit me for the summer program in Sweden. I
texted her at the first stop sign that I wanted to talk about Sweden,
because I was sure she'd make time for me in her schedule, and I
was right. Dishonest, but right. She texted back a few minutes later
that she was currently free as I drove onto campus.

I parked in the faculty lot opposite the Study Abroad building, which looked like a nineteenth-century mansion more than
a home to administrative offices. Georgian-style, it was three stories of red brick with casement windows and black shutters, and
a sharply peaked roof covered in black slate tiles. There were
even dormer windows where you could imagine servants living
cramped little lives—the only things missing were chimneys, a
curved gravel driveway, and potted topiaries flanking the pillared
entrance.

The terrazzo marble–floored lobby was filled with posters of
China, Nigeria, France, Argentina, and easily a dozen other countries where SUM had summer programs. It was quite impressive,
if a bit like a travel agent's office, and slightly old-fashioned. The

more I looked around, the more charming it seemed, each poster a doorway to adventure, and a reminder of how easy it was to be culture-bound, and how easy to expand your horizons.

Lovelace's secretary's office was stark and modern, with a white drop ceiling, white-on-white furniture and nothing more than a framed poster of Van Gogh's sunflowers on the wall. The work table held a printer, shredder, and a gleaming Gaggia espresso machine.

I was ushered right in to see Lovelace, who came out from behind her glass-topped desk to shake my hand and guide me into a chair as if I were visiting royalty. She beamed at me, and it struck me as odd that she was still wearing the same clothes she had on when she burst into my office a few days before, and they looked rumpled. Her smile was a bit masklike and she seemed frazzled.

"Can I get you some coffee?" she asked. When I declined she said she'd get some for herself if I didn't mind, and she nipped out to her secretary's office.

Her own office was mildly chaotic. Bookcases bulged with disorganized travel guides and jammed-in foreign knickknacks of indeterminate origin, while thick file folders and open ring-binders lay scattered across almost every surface, with some piled on the floor by her desk, and even underneath. It reminded me of how years ago so many of us had bought the myth of the "paperless office."

A cork bulletin board on the wall to the left of her desk chair was covered with pinned photos and thank-you cards. I thought one of the pictures might be of Boris, looking dashing in a black turtleneck and puffy jacket, with mountains behind him, but it was in a corner furthest from my chair. Maybe the rumors about her and Boris that Aldo had shared were true—but if that were so, would she risk putting up his photo?

"Before we talk about Sweden," she said, returning and sitting down, "I just want to say how sorry I am about the kind of negative attention you've been getting right now. It happens to everyone sooner or later. Social media is like a meat grinder."

Her remarks left me stupefied. Lovelace was already so much

friendlier than when she first came to recruit me for the summer program, not at all dictatorial. There was even a look of compassion in her eyes. Or was it pain?

"And my God," she said, "finding Boris dead? I can't imagine how horrible that was." Her eyes glistened and she looked like she might cry. She breathed in deeply and took a long sip of coffee from a mug with a Canadian flag on it.

"Thank you, Dawn. That means a lot." Sympathy for other people's problems was typically in short supply at SUM. "I was really surprised that Boris called me and wanted to meet me on campus so late at night." I sighed. Then I added, "I didn't really know him." It was an opening gambit I had planned on the way over, hoping that would get her talking. It worked.

"Oh he was a gem, you missed knowing someone special. Boris was so smart, so funny! He could do imitations of—" She lowered her voice and said, "Of everyone on campus. He was a true comedian. And so campy. When he was out of the office and away from SUM, of course."

"Campy? Was Boris gay?"

She nodded. "In the closet, but yes—very, very gay. His favorite show was *The Golden Girls*. He could quote whole scenes."

"You saw him socially?"

"Yes. We got together so often, people started gossiping about us, saying we were having an affair." She shrugged. "I didn't mind. My husband knew the score, and it helped Boris. I know everyone talks about diversity and inclusion and all the other buzzwords, but there's a lot of homophobia in the administration. It's subtle, but it's there. He didn't feel safe being out."

"Did he have a spouse or lover? A boyfriend?"

"He was seeing somebody and I think it was rocky. Someone who wasn't out, either." She shook her head and I marveled at how our conversation wasn't just civilized, but collegial, human.

And she went on to dolefully answer the question that was most on my mind. "I have no idea who would have wanted to kill him, Nick. He was popular with staff and colleagues, students he interacted with. I never heard complaints about him. In fact, they loved him. He was kind, he was funny, and he treated them like adults."

"Wow."

"Seriously, he was amazing. He really helped out Study Abroad when we needed him. One of our program leaders had an accident twenty-four hours before he had to leave for six weeks in Amsterdam. Boris was part-Dutch, I think, knew the city really well because he spent a year abroad there in college, went there a lot on vacation and had plenty of Dutch friends, too. He said that was where he would retire someday. So he was able to step into the program like he'd designed it himself. He got up to speed on the flight over there and his evaluations were through the roof."

I suddenly felt myself in a version of the classic noir movie *Laura*, where Dana Andrews interviews people about the murdered fashion editor played by Gene Tierney, discovering more and more about who she was and how she lived.

"So who kills a paragon?" I asked.

She shrugged helplessly and I had a surprising desire to comfort her.

"Nobody's said it yet, Nick, but his death could have been a hate crime."

I felt as chilled right then as if someone incredibly stealthy had been following me and I could suddenly feel hot breath on the back of my neck.

"Our financial officer, Aldo, said the same thing, because Boris was part-Hispanic. Did Boris speak Spanish?"

She nodded.

"Okay...what if someone heard him speaking Spanish in town and decided to target him." It wasn't any more unlikely than customers going berserk at fast food joints when they heard personnel speaking Spanish, but if that was the case here, unless the killer bragged about the murder or posted something on social media, this case would go unsolved.

"But how would a stalker, if that's who it was, get access to the Humanities building at night?" she asked, and then answered it herself. "Stalkers are determined and relentless."

"Right. Following him around wouldn't be hard, and if the doors downstairs had been locked, it would have happened somewhere else."

Lovelace met my eyes now with an uncompromising stare. It wasn't aggressive but it *was* fierce, and she leaned forward to say, "I know your reputation and I just hope you can find the monster who took Boris away from us. I don't have much confidence in the SUM police."

I was having doubts about Boris being stalked by a bigot, but the revelation that he was gay as well as Hispanic opened up whole new avenues of inquiry. He could have been killed by someone who had no connection at all with SUM. A lover in town or somewhere nearby who was jealous, or wanted to break free, or who was afraid their relationship would somehow become public. I wished then that I was better hooked into the local LGBTQ community. Stefan and I went to fund-raisers and even the Gay Pride marches, but having grown up in a city as diverse and cosmopolitan as New York, we'd never chosen our friends for their sexual identity.

I saw now how that disadvantaged me in exploring whatever gay network Boris might have had.

Dawn shifted gear. "I owe you an apology."

I must have looked startled because she chuckled. "An apology for pressuring you about the program in Sweden. I think it was partly a response to Victor Dahlberg retiring unexpectedly, and I'm under a lot of pressure myself to make SUM look good."

"Through the summer programs? Really? How does that work?"

"The administration considers our students to be good-will ambassadors."

Except when they got drunk and rowdy in countries where the legal drinking age was lower than twenty-one. I knew that was an enticing side of foreign cultures for many of our students.

"So Nick, I hope you'll forgive me."

"Uh, sure."

"Do you know much about Lund and the south of Sweden?"

"Not really. Most of what I've read is about Stockholm."

"But you speak Swedish," she said.

"*Jag pratar lite svenska.* I speak a little."

She smiled. "You may be the only person on campus who does. I don't think we even have exchange students from Sweden. So where are you in thinking about Victor's program? You'd have to move quickly." She reached for an accordion file on the windowsill behind her and handed it across to me. It was heavier than I expected. "This is all the correspondence Victor collected, info about sites, tours, restaurants and schedules for how he did the program in the past. Would you at least look at it?"

"Okay, I will, on one condition."

Her eyes narrowed. "And what would that be?"

"Tell me about the Committee of Public Safety. What do you know?"

She rose and closed her door, sat back down, and suddenly became very businesslike. "I'm not on it," she said. "But I hear things."

"So it's real, it's not just a paranoid fantasy."

"It's too real, in my opinion."

"Do you know who *is* on it?"

She nodded soberly. "The president, the provost, someone from Criminal Justice, someone from the campus police, a professor from Communications, and faculty from the Law School. Maybe others. Oh, and a bunch of IT specialists or engineers or techies or whatever you call them, they're off campus."

"Where do they meet?"

"It may sound crazy, but this is what I heard: They have a secure room underneath the basement of the Administration Building. It's apparently a bomb shelter left over from the Cold War that's been retrofitted to shield them from eavesdropping and whatever. And it's supposed to withstand a direct hit."

"From what? A nuclear bomb?"

She shrugged. "I guess so."

I was finding that hard to assimilate, but had to press on. "I know there are cameras all over campus. Are they tapping desk phones and bugging offices, too?"

"Phones for sure, offices on a case-by-case basis. And they can track anyone they want through their phones. That's what people tell me, and I believe them."

"How about monitoring email?"

"Absolutely. I never use campus email for anything I wouldn't want to see go public. For privacy, I use a burner phone. I don't think their surveillance is that sophisticated yet, but maybe I'm wrong. They don't have a link to Homeland Security or the FBI or anyone else in the federal government. But it's being talked about."

"But where does the funding come from?"

She shrugged. "Administrators can always find money for pet projects if they want to."

"Was Boris on the committee?"

The question did not surprise her. "I think he was, and it troubled him. I think something was going on that he didn't like."

"You mean more than spying on everyone?"

"Yes, something *specific*," she said. Then her eyes widened. "My God, it must have been about you. Why else would he want to talk to you when you didn't really know each other?"

Of course, I thought, it made total sense, or as much sense as anything could at SUM in the current climate. He wanted to warn me.

"Aren't you worried about this office?" I asked.

She shook her head. "I hired someone to do a sweep for listening devices. My husband said I was crazy, but the guy I brought in found one underneath a desk drawer."

17.

"I HAVE TO GO." I grabbed Viktor's file about Lund and said, "Talk to you later!" I hurried from her office out to my car.

But driving to my office and parking wasn't easy. It was ten minutes to eleven, classes were changing. The streets, sidewalks, and crosswalks on campus teemed with thousands of students walking, biking, or skateboarding to their next class while they checked their smart phones or listened to music on headphones, oblivious to each other and to cars like mine.

It looked like the chaos of a beehive or Fifth Avenue at Christmastime, but it was all purposeful, everyone heading somewhere specific. Maddening, but fascinating at the same time, even though I was rushed. When I finally managed to edge into a parking space, I left the file in my car, ran into the building and bolted up the stairs, unwilling to wait for an elevator which would be packed at this time of day and equally slow to empty. Leaving the stairwell on my floor, I could see that Celine's door was open and I heard conversation in her office, but not in English.

I found the German twins there arguing sotto voce in front of her desk.

"What are you doing here? Where's Celine?"

I had clearly startled them because they threw up their hands in surprise and then checked the gesture, perhaps aware of how cartoonish it made them look. "We are waiting for her," they said in ragged unison, and it sounded like a complete fabrication.

Today they were in identical black from head to toe, missing only berets and masks to complete their cat burglar outfits.

My door was closed and I didn't see anything disarranged on Celine's desk or in her office, no open desk or file cabinet drawers, but looking at me, both of them seemed defensive. Their hands were also twitching as if something important was just out of reach. I couldn't imagine why they would be there—what could Celine have in her office that would interest them, or anyone else for that matter?

"If I'm not in and she has to step out, she never leaves the door open," I said, wondering if they could have possibly picked the lock. Why not? This was an old building and the doors were not very secure. But wouldn't someone have seen them? Was I crazy to be thinking along these lines?

"We were already here and she asked us to wait," one of them said. "She will be back momentarily."

I didn't believe that for a minute. "Well she's not here now and I'm very busy, so how about you come back another time?"

My tone was way too harsh, but Dawn Lovelace's report about her office had me spooked, and I was pissed off at them for lying to the dean and saying I'd called them Nazis.

They glanced at each other, communicating something unreadable to me, and started to leave.

"We are going back to our office," one of them said.

"Yes, the office you tried to take away from us," his brother added.

They smirked and left. It was a total misrepresentation of what had happened last week, but that seemed like old news. I was convinced that they had been spying on me, on Celine, or on both of us. Trying to, anyway. The dean had probably enlisted them as his minions when they complained to him about their office re-assignment. It would have been a quick trade: they stayed where they were, he got spies inside the department.

I closed Celine's door and unlocked mine. If my office was bugged, it could have happened overnight, any night, but it seemed more likely that the Committee of Public Safety, through the dean, had compromised my privacy when the furniture was upgraded. I shut the door behind me quietly, determined to make as little noise as possible. I did not need anyone in the department thinking I was tearing my office apart in some kind of frenzy, but I had to be thorough.

One by one, I first upended each chair, surveyed it carefully, and ran my hands across every surface, poking fingers into notches and corners. Nothing. I searched my desk, carefully pulling out each drawer and feeling under it, then checking behind them, too. I rifled the contents of every drawer but found nothing suspicious. I looked behind every book on my shelves, then I took off each framed poster from the walls and checked the frames. Again nothing. I kept a powerful little flashlight in my office just in case of a power failure, so I used it to look behind the bookcases, but there was nothing but dust. I even scanned the boxes of the previous department chair's paper files that I hadn't unpacked yet. Nothing out of the ordinary.

There was no point in checking the desk phone since they listened in on our calls. That left the lamp. Hadn't the dean said I needed a new one in addition to the furniture that Celine had ordered?

I sat down and pulled the lamp closer, tilted it a bit to look under the heavy glass shade, but found nothing there. Maybe I'd seen one too many spy movies.

But as I set the lamp back down I noticed what might be hinges in the bottom of the base, sticking out through a thin green felt protective pad. I set the lamp carefully on its side with the shade hanging over the edge of the desk, then pulled the felt pad loose. What I saw staring back at me was a small square door which I was able to pry open with a fingernail.

Inside was a black box with rounded edges, a little over an inch square. I had read about devices like this online. It was likely battery-operated, voice-activated, and probably had the capacity for several hundred hours of audio.

I didn't know if it had a transmitter function and could be monitored remotely or not. Maybe some janitor was working for the Committee and checking it every night. Maybe Heino and Jonas had been given a key to my office and they were the ones responsible for checking. It didn't really matter. What did matter was that I was, like Dawn Lovelace, a target, and SUM had clearly escalated its war on campus privacy.

For a moment I thought of calling Fabian Flick to come see what I'd uncovered, but I realized the university would claim I was the one who put it there in an attempt to make the administration look bad, and I wouldn't gain a thing. Photographing the device and splashing it across Twitter or Instagram would only have the same effect. I knew I had to be smarter about this.

The listening device was just plastic and metal with some sort of memory chip, no doubt, but it felt enormous and poisonous. SUM was becoming a mini–police state, and I was caught in its insidious web of surveillance and scrutiny. Feeling violated was too inflammatory a word to use in this context, and not even earned, but I did feel betrayed, and that old-fashioned word, besmirched.

If I yanked the tiny gizmo out and stomped on it, or went to the men's room and tried flushing it down a toilet, whoever was listening would know I'd discovered it. And if this one had been purposely planted in my office, there was nothing to stop the Committee—who else could it be?—from doing it again.

Trying to catch my breath, I closed the lamp's little door, smoothed back the felt and stood the lamp up, wondering what my next move should be.

I thought I heard the sound of heels echoing down the hallway and then there was a knock and Celine walked into my office. She was looking unusually corporate in a flared mauve dress and matching jacket.

"Where did they go?" she asked. "The twins were here and I asked them to wait for me because I forgot to leave something in the mail room."

"Oh." I could feel my face growing hot. "I thought they broke into the office and were spying on you—or something."

Celine's eyes widened and she shook her head. "No...I knew they were here. Well, whatever they wanted, they'll come back, I guess. You know, Nick, just because—"

I had the feeling she was about to advise me not to be completely paranoid and assume everyone around me had a secret agenda or was leagued against me. I held up my hand to keep her from saying anything more, pointed to the lamp and then my ear. She comprehended instantly what I meant and stepped back a moment in surprise. Then she crossed her arms and frowned.

Before I could write something down for Celine, there was a knock on her outer office door and Peter DeVries appeared behind her with a backpack. He was dressed in a red polo shirt and distressed jeans shredded at the knees.

My mind went blank, and then as if someone had nudged me, I said, "You're here for your independent study." How had the week gone by so quickly? Then I checked my desk calendar. "Wait—I thought we were meeting on Tuesdays this semester?"

"Shit. I got the day wrong. I can come back tomorrow."

But he didn't take a step out of the office, and I said, "Since you're here, why not?" After all, I could be arrested the next day for Boris's murder.

"I'll leave you to it," Celine said cheerfully, but she gave Peter the side eye as if she suspected something. "Door open or closed?"

"Open is fine," Peter said, looking at me for confirmation. "I have nothing to hide."

That was certainly ironic.

"Yes, open," I said, and I heard the creak of Celine's desk chair and her punching in a number and speaking to someone softly enough not to disturb us.

Peter sat down and brought out a notebook and a Penguin paperback of Henry James short stories. It bristled with blue Post-it tabs.

My brain kicked right into teacher mode, thanks to over twenty years of classroom experience. I quickly cleared my mind of the fraudulent circumstances surrounding his admission to SUM. For as long as he was enrolled as a student here, I would work with him. And he *was* here, he hadn't decided to drop out in the days since we'd last talked.

"Okay," I said, "let's get right to the heart of 'The Middle Years.' What do you think James meant by 'the madness of art'?" I recited the whole passage: "We work in the dark—we do what we can—we give what we have. Our doubt is our passion, and our passion is our task. The rest is the madness of art."

It was probably the most famous James quotation in a story about a dying author, Dencombe, for whom awareness dawns that he won't get to write the books he feels he really could write. The tragedy is that he sees this now as he's approaching the peak of his talent. But he finds solace in the praise and attentions of a young doctor who idolizes him, because he realizes that he hasn't just touched someone, his work resonates completely, it's understood in all its depth. And more than that, he understands what everyone must grasp when faced with mortality: we only have one chance at life.

Peter leafed through his paperback and I didn't rush him.

"You know," he said, "when I toured the van Gogh Museum in Amsterdam, I thought about crazy artists. I don't think that's exactly what James meant, though, that all artists are nuts." He closed his eyes as if to concentrate better.

"That's a popular stereotype of creative people in general," I offered. "But of artists and writers especially. Crazy or depressed or alcoholic."

"They're intense, but that's not the same thing as crazy." Peter seemed a bit edgy as he checked some of the pages he'd flagged with those sticky tabs, so I changed the subject to give him time to marshal his thoughts, and asked him if he'd enjoyed Amsterdam.

His eyes flashed. "Totally! I fell in love." Then he stammered out, "With the food and the canals and the museums and the people—they were amazing. So friendly, especially when they knew the city well. I could totally live there. Jeez, just for the beer alone…" He grinned. "That was the first time I had Belgian beer and when the glass came and there was a slice of lemon in the bottom, I just felt a million miles from home." He shrugged. "The river cruise to get there was sucky, all these rich Michigan assholes drooling over the wine, and talking about their boats and their second homes in Charlevoix. They were like my parents' friends, well most of them. There wasn't anybody I could really hang out with. Well, one of them was cool—" He shook his head as if surprised he'd said that, and I had no idea what was wrong, but then he smoothly continued: "Amsterdam, it rocked, so I forgot about the Charlevoix crowd."

Charlevoix is one of the wealthier and more scenic Lake Michigan resort towns, with a gorgeous harbor. I'd heard people refer to their mammoth Victorian-style homes there as cottages and I imagined his parents had a Charlevoix cottage, too.

Peter seemed much more relaxed now, probably thanks to basking in pleasant memories. His enthusiasm made me think of another line in the James story we were discussing, where the author's fan is described as "this gushing modern youth."

"So," I said, "what about that madness of art?"

He looked down at a page and ran his finger across some lines. "I think this means more, this is what James was getting at." He read slowly, sonorously, as if the text were biblical or historic: "The thing is to have made somebody care." Peter paused and something shadowed his face. He looked haunted.

I thought that the admissions bribery was on his mind—how could it not be? But I didn't bring it up. Flick hadn't published a story yet, so he was probably still investigating. Maybe there wasn't much of a story anyway, maybe Peter's case was an isolated one, and SUM wasn't as corrupt as all that.

"Tell me more," I said. "About caring."

He closed the book and held it to his chest. "It's like what

E.M. Forster wrote, 'Only connect.' The writer can see that he's touched somebody, his work makes the doctor feel alive even while *he's* dying. The madness? Those are the things that don't matter. Art is passion, but it's also—what does he call it?—*diligence*. You need both things to go deep enough to change someone's life, make it richer, more real."

I grinned and he asked defensively, "Am I wrong?"

"Not at all, that's a viable reading of the story."

He frowned. "Viable?" He started to breathe as fast as if he were about to have a panic attack, and his face suddenly tightened.

"Peter, whoa! I wasn't being critical. Everything you said makes sense."

He gulped some air. "Sorry. Sorry. I've been under a lot of stress. And I love this story. I love James as much as Wharton and Sinclair Lewis. They all speak to me."

"That's great." I wished I had more students like Peter. As far as his enthusiasm went, of course. Not the bribery.

He was looking at me eagerly for another question, I suppose. I saw myself at his age, reading James and being bowled over by his vision, his prose, but that was well before my crazy life at SUM and being middle-aged.

Being older was probably why my own favorite lines were about the passage of time: "He sat and stared at the sea, which appeared all surface and twinkle, far shallower than the spirit of man. It was the abyss of human illusion that was the real, the tideless deep." I hadn't understood those lines in college, though I admired their sonority. In middle age, I found them painfully true.

"I have a question," he said. "Is the relationship between the two guys like a fan thing, hero worship, or is there something more going on?"

"What do you think?"

He shrugged. "I found a book in the library of his letters to a young man and they're kind of seductive, romantic in a flowery way. And some of the biographies I've looked at make him sound gay. So I wondered."

"Would it change the story?"

"It gives it another layer, I guess, but that's not the point."

"I agree. You know, Wharton wrote about artists, too, like her novella *The Touchstone*, which we didn't get to read last year. Why don't you take a look at that and see if there's a paper topic in there for you somewhere? We can talk about that next week, no, in two weeks so you have more time to read and reflect. We can also discuss Wharton's relationship with James—it was fascinating." I'd assigned him a number of James biographies for supplemental reading.

"Are we done?" he asked, checking what looked like a very new Rolex. I hadn't seen him wear it before and didn't think kids his age were even into wristwatches.

I smiled. "This is an independent study. Some days we go long, some days we don't. It's up to us." Well, it was up to me, really, and I thought he was on the edge and could use the break. More than that, though, I needed to check in with Celine.

"Okay, thanks, Professor Hoffman!" He bounded out of his chair and left my office as if on a mission. This was definitely one very mercurial young man.

I heard Celine's printer going and she soon walked in and sat down where Peter had been. She handed me one of two sheets of paper she was holding, and it read *I'm only going to talk about department business here so we're cool.* And she pointed to the lamp.

"Tell me what's up?" I asked.

"Two pressing things. You need to have a department meeting soon to discuss the change in leadership since you weren't most people's first choice."

"I don't think I was anyone's first choice, except the dean. They weren't even offered a choice...." Could that be used against me somehow? "But anyway, can you start looking at tentative dates?"

"Sure. And diversity is going to be on the agenda, too."

This was a longstanding problem in our department. Though

we had achieved gender parity, we were unable to retain faculty of color. They found SUM too bland, too stodgy, too white, too provincial, and moved on to universities on either coast, or to historically black colleges and universities. Whenever the issue came up at meetings, the discussion quickly devolved into a rhetorical dumpster fire. Charges of racism were as hot as the coffee was cold and nothing got accomplished.

Celine must have read the dread on my face, because she said, "But before that I think we need for you to host a department party."

"At my house?"

She nodded. "It would ease the tension. Raise morale. Maybe even be fun."

Right. I had images of Valley staging an arrest in the middle of it all, and media he'd contacted in advance waiting outside to witness my humiliation. That would be loads of fun. But I kept my fears to myself and said, "Do I organize it?"

"You could, but you've got a lot to handle right now. Let me take care of the catering arrangements. There's a budget line for this kind of thing. I think we move quickly, do it this weekend, even, to show how we're on top of things. Saturday afternoon is usually a good time."

She passed me another sheet of paper with this message:

I don't believe our cell phones are safe. What if someone put malware on them and they can even read our texts? My husband has a cousin who works for the FBI and he said it's not hard to do and it happens all the time. Let's arrange to meet with Aldo somewhere without cameras and with our phones off.

Celine clearly knew more about how someone could use your smart phone against you than I did, and I was grateful. I scrawled a quick *Where?* on the sheet of paper and handed it back to her. But before she could reply, a student appeared in the doorway between our offices. "Dr. Hoffman, can I speak to you?" Her voice was soft and a little shaky, as if I scared her, and I wondered what I could do to make her feel more relaxed. She was thin, very pale, with jet black hair in a pageboy, and was dressed a bit like Madonna in her early years on MTV: lace, leather bangles, and multiple crucifixes. It looked like a costume she had rented for Halloween more than her own clothes.

"Come on in, dear," Celine said. "He's a pussycat."

The three of us laughed and whatever tension had entered the room with this student immediately dissipated. Celine yielded her chair and went back to her desk while the student, who told me her name was Janine Wu, sat down and crossed her legs. I didn't hear an accent, so I assumed she was Chinese American, not Chinese.

"How can I help you?" I asked.

She coughed and I asked if she wanted something to drink but she waved the suggestion away.

"I'm here on behalf of students in Dr. Balanchine's class," she said.

"Which one?"

"Literary Rebels. We've been reading Kerouac and Salinger to start."

"Is there a problem?" The most common complaint among our students was being assigned too much reading, which seemed bizarre, given that they were English majors.

"The readings are great," she said. "It's class discussion that sucks. Dr. Balanchine cuts you off if she doesn't agree with what you're saying, and she rolls her eyes like she thinks you're an idiot. But her favorite students, they always get compliments."

I waited to hear if it was the male or female students, but Janine went elsewhere: "And you can say something she kind of ignores, then when someone she likes says the exact same thing, she goes, 'That's great!' or whatever. It's frustrating. It makes you want to skip class."

"Does this happen a lot?"

She hesitated. "Pretty much every class."

"Can I ask why you've come forward?"

"Because I'm one of her favorite students. We decided that if anyone else talked to you, it wouldn't sound the same."

That was a smart move. And before I could ask Janine what she wanted me to do, she said, "Could you, like, talk to her?"

"Yes, I can. I will. But I think I'd like to hear from a few more students. I believe you, but I want more context."

She smiled and stood up. "No problem! I'll get on it. Thanks."

"Thank you for sharing this." I hoped that was enough. But then she startled me when she stepped up to the edge of my desk, lowered her voice to a whisper and said, "I think there are spies on campus."

"What do you mean?"

"I think some of the Chinese students are being paid to listen for anyone saying anything hostile about the Communist party there, or their president. Be careful." And she hurried out before I could respond.

Well, I had read in *The New York Times* about students spying on professors or each other at Chinese universities to report "disloyalty" to President Xi Jinping, but never imagined that kind of foreign surveillance would be at work at SUM. And if it was true, what could I do about that? Even if I made inquiries, wasn't it an issue for the State Department? If Janine Wu was correct, could Chinese intelligence be somehow linked to the Committee of Public Safety? I made a mental note to quietly ask around if other professors had heard anything similar and tried to let it go, even though it was deeply disturbing.

What I could focus on in the short term, though, was the report about Ciska. I felt sorry for the students who were unhappy in her classroom, but this complaint wasn't entirely surprising. I'd heard similar gripes from students about other professors in the department, and even worse, heard indirectly that some professors had used their graduate students' research without attribution when publishing articles and books of their own.

If what Janine had told me was accurate, raising it with Ciska could go sideways. She could deny it and claim that I was persecuting her because she wanted my position. But it would put her on the defensive no matter what, and that was a good place for her to be right now.

18.

BRIEFLY WONDERING how secure the system was, I checked Ciska's password-protected digital personnel file. These faculty files were supposed to be only accessible to the department chair and the individual professors, at least that's what we were all told. The password was changed by the IT division on campus each time someone new became chair. I had the password saved in my Inbox and so I had no problem accessing her file, though it felt a little creepy around the edges.

Clicking through the pages, I looked for a record of student complaints, but there hadn't been any thus far. So if Ciska was playing favorites in her class and students were feeling ignored or hassled, was this behavior of hers new, or was the absence of complaints a product of student apathy? Maybe even fear of retribution? Or just plain fear. Students could find even easy-going professors intimidating, which was one reason they avoided office hours.

Perhaps something had changed recently in Ciska's life. Perhaps that was why her file was free of student complaints until now. Could it be connected to Boris? What if they were lovers and he broke up with her, and she killed him out of rage? That would certainly spill over into her classroom—how could it not?

It wasn't inconceivable for personal stress to poison your classroom: Years ago at SUM, a graduate student who'd behaved erratically with his students had ended up shooting his wife dead on campus when their marriage collapsed. And I heard stories about professors' mood swings all across campus. From the out-side, academia looks like an easy life given that none of us works forty-hour weeks, but the competition, the pressure to publish and rise in your field, and the demands from students wear some of us out and make others anywhere from cranky to disruptive to explosive.

I exited Ciska's file, cleared my head, and then did a quick Google search and moved on to scan Facebook, Twitter, and Insta-gram. The continuing social media silence about the Admissions scandal and Boris's murder was eerie and disorienting. Was there truly no news about either story? Not even filler stories to say that there were no new developments?

That's when I heard Celine shout, "Oh my God," and she rushed into my office.

"Nick, I just got a text—Ciska is being arrested for killing Boris. Right now! *Here!*"

I hurried after her out into the hallway and sure enough, Ciska, handcuffed, was being led to the elevator bank by Detective Valley. Chin high, she looked quietly regal in a brocade navy blue suit. Though the black-and-white Alexander McQueen scarf draped around her neck was, under the circumstances, a bit morbid with its signature pattern of skulls.

The hallways that converged on the elevator bank were filling up with several dozen faculty and students, and her arrest was being filmed on numerous phones and sent out to the world as it was happening. I could imagine how the upper level administra-tors would be thinking in terms of PR: Murder was bad, a killer professor much worse than that.

A phalanx of campus cops surrounded Valley and Ciska as if she were extremely dangerous—unless they were afraid of some attempt to stop them from taking her away. Did anyone really think English professors or students could turn violent, become a mob? After all his years at SUM, Valley had absolutely no idea who we were. Riots occurred at SUM only when one of our teams won a big game, or lost one. Nothing else seemed to generate that much passion among our students, and faculty often made a show of being above every fray.

Watching her erect, dignified figure, I flashed on some play or movie about Joan of Arc I'd seen years ago even though Ciska was hardly a martyr. Or was it Mary, Queen of Scots I was remembering?

Valley was reading Ciska her Miranda rights, but her eyes were closed as if she were willing herself (or him) to disappear.

When he was done, it was her turn to speak: "I'm innocent," she said with as much force and clarity as if speaking to a filled auditorium. "This is bollocks, it's a travesty of justice. I haven't killed anyone." Then turning to all of us, she added, "And if they can arrest me for no reason, you're all vulnerable." She raked the bystanders with a bitter glare but sounded amazingly calm.

A murmur spread through the crowd.

"Does one woman really need eight cops to guard her?" I muttered to Celine.

I felt surprisingly upset to see her treated this way. It felt so demeaning, brutal even. While I did not want to sympathize with Ciska, this spectacle was retriggering how violated I had felt when that SWAT team was sent to our house last spring after a false anonymous tip and I stood helplessly by as Stefan was being dragged off in the night by the police.

"It could be worse," Celine whispered. "They could have arrested her while she was teaching a class."

Had they found a murder weapon? Was it connected to Ciska somehow?

The cluster of cops radiated hostility and there was a tang of testosterone in the air as strong—but nowhere near as refreshing—as the smell of ozone after a spring thunderstorm. I'm sure they hated being filmed by lowly students, but they couldn't stop anyone from doing so, and for all their weapons, muscles, and power, they were trapped until the elevator doors opened, offering them escape.

Valley noticed where I was standing with Celine but disdainfully looked away.

One of the three elevators finally arrived, its bell rang, and the doors whooshed open. The cluster of cops tightened around Valley and his prisoner, then all of them moved into the elevator, filling almost every square inch of the car before the doors closed. One of the cops tried to turn Ciska around to face the crowd of onlookers, but she held her ground and the doors closed on this bizarre *Still Life with Cops.*

I had expected some kind of shout of defiance or outrage from Ciska at that moment. Her silence was unnerving. Maybe she was even regretting having said she was innocent—didn't lawyers advise you not to say anything at all when you were arrested? That's what Vanessa had told me and Stefan.

The gawkers dispersed and Aldo joined us as we headed back to my office. I should have been jubilant that my rival and critic had been arrested for murder, but it seemed like a very hollow victory.

Aldo and Celine followed me into my office and they looked as troubled as I felt.

I sat down heavily in my desk chair, Celine paced slowly back and forth, and Aldo perched on the windowsill. He said "Wow," a few times.

Celine shook her head. "It's one thing to talk about who murdered Boris, and try to investigate because you seemed to be Valley's prime suspect, but being right there when she was arrested, well, that was disturbing."

"There's a bright side," Aldo said gravely. "You're in the clear, Nick."

I shrugged, not feeling especially liberated. It was always possible that Ciska's arrest was some kind of ruse—I'd seen it happen often enough on TV. Valley might be trying to lure me into making some mistake he thought would expose me as the real murderer. Me, or someone else...

Celine stopped pacing and frowned. "How do you think they figured out it was Ciska?"

Aldo was about to speak when Celine caught herself, held a finger to her lips, pointed to the lamp and then her ear. His eyes widened and he clearly got it right away. There was a heavy silence in the room, then all three of us jumped when my office phone rang. I half expected whoever was surveilling my office to be at the other end, gloating.

It was Fabian Flick.

"Professor Hoffman, what can you tell me about the arrest of Ciska Balanchine?"

"The reporter," I mouthed for Celine and Aldo, then said to Flick, "Nothing."

"Does that mean 'No comment'?"

"It means that I know she's been arrested, nothing else." How had the news spread so damned quickly? I wanted to hang up, but realized that doing so could easily become part of the story, however small, and make me look bad. I decided not to tell him I had witnessed her arrest, or part of it, anyway.

"What was her relation to the deceased?" he continued.

"I have no idea."

"Can you guess at a motive?" he asked.

"If you want information about Ciska, you should try talking to someone who really knew her."

"She's your colleague and your associate chair—and you're saying that you don't know her?" His tone was tinged with sarcasm.

"Exactly."

There was silence on his end. Flick was apparently waiting for me to elaborate, but that's the last thing I wanted to do. There was always the chance that anything I said right now in this explosive situation could be taken out of context.

"Why not talk to her students?" I asked.

He laughed. "Interviewing students is really tricky right now. Lots of them think calling or emailing is an invasion of privacy, and God forbid we take photos of a demonstration where there's any kind of violence, even a little scuffle. That's 'trauma porn.' Doesn't matter that they're out in public trying to call attention to a cause."

I waited from him to trot out the word "snowflake," but he

didn't use it. All the same, what he was reporting struck me as weird and sad.

"Well, thanks for your time," he said at last and ended the call. I could just imagine him spinning the little that I'd offered into something damning, but I had no control over what he wrote. I didn't seem to have control of much right now.

When I glanced up, both Celine and Aldo were apparently musing about Ciska's dramatic arrest, and me, I felt surprisingly flooded with pity for her plight.

Valley had made a spectacle of the arrest to humiliate and intimidate her, and even though I had been thinking dark thoughts about her for days, I was still angry about how she was being treated. Valley could have taken her into custody at home, without an audience. It would have been the civilized thing to do. Even if she *was* guilty, it's not as if she was a serial killer or a terrorist. And it was unlikely she had a criminal record, because she wouldn't have been hired at SUM with that kind of past. At least I didn't think so.

Celine emerged from her silence to ask, "Should we postpone the department party, or just cancel it altogether?"

Aldo pointed to the lamp and cocked his head, clearly asking if we should avoid the subject given the surveillance.

"I'm happy to talk about that," I said, maybe too emphatically, and he nodded okay. "No," I said. "Go ahead with planning and send out the e-invites. We need a party more than ever now."

I should have offered buzz words about solidarity and team spirit, but I felt hollowed out by all the trauma of the last week, the arguments, the accusations, and the craziness. And maybe a party wasn't the best idea, but as department chair, I felt it incumbent on me to make some kind of stand. A department meeting could turn rancorous, but I doubted that would happen at a party, where people would be better behaved and less likely to turn on one another.

Though there was of course the X-factor of alcohol to consider....

I followed Celine and Aldo as they walked back into her office so they could make preparations for the faculty party.

Suddenly Roberto Robustelli burst into Celine's office with a strange smile on his face. "Nick, you need to know people are really pissed at you." He looked hip in dark jeans, white shirt, and black-and-blue checked blazer, but he seemed very agitated.

What now? What the hell was *he* doing here? Was he addicted to SUM? Couldn't he stay away?

I beckoned him to follow me into my office, hoping to calm him down or at least not add more fuel to his fire, but even though I sat behind my desk, he remained standing. His burly arms were crossed and he swayed a bit from side to side pugnaciously. He must have been a wrestler in college or high school, I thought.

"Nick, you let them drag your associate chair off to jail and you didn't say squat."

"What do you mean *let them*? What was I supposed to do? What are you *talking* about?" Then I remembered his own recent arrest by Detective Valley, one that I had also witnessed. Maybe this little diatribe was all about him and had nothing to do with Ciska.

He shook his head as if I were an idiot. "Nicky, Nicky, Nicky, you weren't supposed to act like a pussy, that's for sure. Now, that's not me talking, of course, that's the word in the department—on the street, if you get my meaning."

How had a consensus built so quickly, and was it even real, or was Robustelli just here to harass me? He was a pariah; were people really confiding in him?

I looked at the lamp and wondered about inviting him downstairs to the coffee shop where we wouldn't be overheard—or at least spied on—since this was already feeling embarrassing, but what guarantee did I have that SUM's minions weren't listening everywhere? And that would only have prolonged our time together.

"Roberto, what would *you* have done in my place?" I asked, hoping to placate him.

He grinned and seemed surprisingly buoyant. "*Told* Ciska that we supported her. *Warned* the cops not to mistreat her. *Alerted* the media to these Gestapo tactics."

"Gestapo? Are you kidding? They weren't rough with her at all, at least as far as I could tell." Certainly not as rough as they had been when they arrested Roberto just a few short weeks ago.

Robustelli groaned. "You don't get it, do you? You trash the cops and it puts them on the defensive, it guarantees they won't cross the line."

"And do what? Ship her off to a black site in Poland? Waterboard her in some Middle East basement?" I was being deliberately outrageous for my unseen listeners.

"You never know. Just don't say I didn't warn you. You did not score any fucking points just now, you made yourself look really bad. You might want to think about hiring a consultant to help polish your image—because frankly, it sucks."

I did not point out that Roberto was facing a murder trial and could end up with life in prison, so he was hardly in a position to be giving me advice. But then I wondered if with all the stress of his arrest he was starting to become unhinged. Why was Roberto even here? Why was he inserting himself into this moment? You'd think he'd want to keep a low profile at a time like this—surely his lawyer had warned him not to make waves or bother me.

"Listen, I have work to do," I said, trying to get him to leave, but Roberto wasn't going anywhere just yet. Out of the blue, I found myself asking quietly, "Do you think she did it?"

That seemed to stump him for a moment. His eyes blinked rapidly and his face went blank. Then he looked as if he had just tasted something gross and wanted to spit it out. "How the fuck should I know? It's not like Boris was an angel." He grimaced.

What did he mean by that? But before I could ask, he said, "My opinion isn't worth shit. What counts is that this is still America. You're fucking innocent until those cunts prove you guilty. Don't you get that? I mean what is wrong with you? What fucking planet do you live on? The cops are your enemy and you need to get off your butt and take a stand."

I was done being badgered.

"Roberto, I don't get involved with the police. You know what they can be like and you know what I've been through. If I'd said something when they arrested Ciska, they could have accused me of obstruction or something like that and they would have arrested me too."

"Fucking awesome! Then that would prove they have a vendetta against the department and we could nail them to the wall."

Was that what he wanted? Would it help his case?

"I really do not want to talk about this anymore, Roberto."

He uncrossed his powerful arms and sneered. "You're really too fucking weak to be chair. You're gonna get crushed and you know it. Your attitude is for shit."

I didn't know if he was trying to goad me because he needed someone to argue with or was just blowing off steam in advance of his trial and didn't care who said what. Honestly, facing a long prison sentence like he was, I don't know how I would behave.

Celine saved the day. Without knocking, she surged into the room and said, "You have an urgent phone call."

The tension in her voice seemed to propel Robustelli from my office into Celine's. But at her door to the hallway, he turned and shouted, "Don't be a jerk! Don't be an asshole! History's gonna kiss your ass if you do the right thing!"

The air seemed to echo with his declamations and I wondered where he was headed next and who else he planned to hector. Was he deliberately trying to call more attention to himself and get mired in even more trouble? What else could explain his perverse behavior?

"Thanks, Celine," I said. "I assume there wasn't any call."

She nodded. "I just thought it was time to intervene before it got worse. That man is five kinds of crazy. He should be lying low right now, not making a spectacle of himself."

Aldo walked in and said, "If that dude gets acquitted, we'll all have to deal with him all the time. The university won't be able to get rid of him."

"Cross your fingers," I said.

Aldo was now reading from his phone. "Local news says that Ciska sent Boris threatening texts."

"How would anyone know that?" I asked, and then answered it myself. "The cops are leaking information to make Ciska look bad. By tomorrow we'll have the texts themselves."

I spent the rest of the day in a fog of digital busywork, fielding myriad requests from faculty, replying to former students who wanted letters of recommendation for graduate school, ignoring media requests for comments or even whole interviews, and doing a hundred other things that almost distracted me from Ciska's arrest and Roberto's visit.

Aldo stopped by at one point, held a finger to his lips and pointed to the door. I followed him down the hall to the men's room. My tension grew with every step because he was acting so strangely. He ducked inside and I followed. It was as sterile a place as anywhere else in that building, which I guess made sense, but there was way too much fluorescent lighting and whatever the janitors used to clean in there was cloying and borderline disgusting, like a vase of flowers whose water hadn't been changed.

"I don't think they'd be bugging the johns," he said, after checking the three stalls to make sure they were empty.

"What's going on?"

"I found something out of place in my office."

I had to smile despite his somber tone, because there was almost nothing in his office, nothing visible that is, or loose—it was all filed away or in drawers. The room was like some kind of science fiction white void, and I assumed there wasn't roiling chaos behind the scenes but that everything was placed with mathematical precision.

He took out his phone and pulled up a website selling recording devices that looked like pens and handed me the phone. They *were* pens, in fact, when I scrolled down the page and read about what they did. "That one," he said.

It was listed as a VA30 Voice Activated Recorder Pen, and according to the ad copy, it was "one of the most powerful voice activated recorders on the market." Better still, the pen was easy to use—all you had to do was twist the top and that started the recording. Even better than that, you could plug it right into a USB to transfer files. There wasn't even any need for special software.

"Somebody left it in one of my desk drawers like they thought I wouldn't notice." He snorted derisively.

"But it looks just like a pen," I said. "What made you think it was different?"

He blushed so dramatically I felt my own face might turn red since blushing could be contagious. "Because I spied on my girlfriend before we broke up because I thought she was cheating on me. And she was."

Everybody had secrets, I thought sadly.

"It's got to be the Committee," he said. "And I bet I'm not the only office manager they're spying on."

That made sense, but what were we supposed to do? Going public would evoke a fierce response from the administration, claiming it was fake news, that he had planted it himself.

I said, "Leave it where it is and just watch what you say. Unless you want to throw it out?"

"No, they'll try something else. This way, I'm on guard."

"Who was in your office today? Did it happen today?"

He frowned. "I leave my door open because there's nothing to steal, really. It could have been anyone." His thoughts were following the same track as mine, because he said, "You should check with Celine about her office."

Why hadn't I thought of that myself after discovering the bug in my lamp? I'd been suspicious when I found the German twins there, but hadn't taken it further.

"Send me the website," I said, "and let's leave separately or it'll look weird."

Well, nobody was in the hallway, so it didn't really matter.

Back at Celine's office, I showed her the website on my phone and said casually, "This looks interesting, what do you think about it for yourself?"

I then watched Celine quietly, swiftly, and methodically search her office. She paid particular attention to the hourglass that Jasmine Aminejad had given me, but it didn't seem to be hiding any listening device. She shrugged apologetically when she put it down, as if embarrassed to be so suspicious, but I said, "You're fine." After all, why couldn't Jasmine be working for the administration—her hostility would be a perfect cover.

After half an hour, Celine came up empty, but I didn't know if we should have been relieved or not.

And not much later, I got a call from Vanessa.

"Nick, your colleague Ciska Balanchine wants to hire me for her defense. Because the police were looking at you at one point as a suspect, I need a conflict of interest waiver from you in order to represent her. It's totally up to you whether you'll sign one. Ciska's already signed a waiver, but I need one from you, too."

"What does that mean? What's the waiver about?"

"It's so that I can represent her in this case even though I represented you during the investigation. I can't share any information that you shared with me and, of course, I never would. It means both of you acknowledge you've spoken to me about any potential conflicts of interest, you absolve me and my firm of any risks that might arise from my representing her, and also that you can both revoke the waiver at any time, which would mean ending my representation."

"Okay," I said. "Is this typical?"

"For sure. Waivers are standard in a situation like this, and I can answer any questions that you have. I don't really see any conflict now or in the future, but I want to make sure that everyone is covered, just in case. Now, if you don't want to sign it because you work together, then I certainly understand."

Working together wasn't how I thought of Ciska, but technically, I suppose, that did describe our situation, even though she was aggressively after my position. But all that was beside the point. I trusted Vanessa completely, so I said, "Of course. She deserves the best lawyer she can get, and I don't see any conflict."

"Super. This will count as a verbal waiver and I'll have my assistant follow up with a written one for you to date and sign."

I have to admit that I felt a strange little twinge of jealousy at the thought of "sharing" Vanessa. It was as if I was a little kid in a sandbox not wanting to let go of a pail. Not a great way to feel, but then what had been lately?

19.

I WAS WRONG about Ciska's texts. We didn't have to wait until the next day. By the time I got home at the end of yet another very bizarre Monday on campus, her threatening texts were on the Internet for everyone to see and were even featured on the evening news in town and probably all across Michigan. *BuzzFeed*, *The Daily Beast*, *The Huffington Post* were playing up the story even more dramatically than legacy news sources like *The New York Times*. It made for great clickbait.

What would be next? Pages from her diary? A sex tape? Anything was possible.

And in a development that shouldn't have surprised me, the news about Boris's murder and Ciska's arrest was eclipsing the nascent admissions scandal. Local media and even state media were devoting much more space and time to the "sexier" story, and my Inbox was blowing up with requests for comments, requests I just deleted.

Ciska's texts were widely being called "threatening." But I wasn't convinced they were indisputable evidence of murderous intent. The texts, recently sent on different days, were ambiguous enough to mean lots of things:

Do you really want a life-long enemy?
What you're doing is crazy.
Somebody has to stop you.

Stefan agreed with me that they weren't truly incriminating, and he was angry about the invasion of her privacy, despite how he felt about her personally.

I knew from experience what he should have remembered: when it comes to murder, privacy is always under siege as reporters and bloggers scramble for information.

Ciska wasn't saying anything in public, but as her lawyer, Vanessa issued a short, strong statement: "My client has tremendous empathy for the victim's family, and she has great confidence in our criminal justice system."

Family? I wondered who and where Boris's family was.

Stefan wasn't as angry or surprised as I might have expected, though, when I told him about Robustelli's tirade and that my office and Aldo's were being bugged. The problem solver in him took over: "Nick, you have to make sure that if you want to talk about something, and be certain it stays private, you have to physically leave the building—you don't even know that the bathrooms there are one hundred percent safe. I mean it. From now on, if it's got to be private, meet in one of the campus parking structures. No, better still, pick a parking lot in town. Michiganapolis isn't London, we don't have CCTV cameras on every street."

The image of meeting in a parking garage or parking lot made me feel that I'd truly entered an alternate universe. Or a crime drama involving a drug deal or a whistle blower like Deep Throat.

"Uh...I guess I can do that," I said, feeling a new level of anxiety rising in me. But once again, cooking served to settle us both down, and setting the table slowly was like creating a small refuge.

Over a dinner of sausages roasted with Spanish onions and red seedless grapes, I tried to shift gear. We talked about his novel, dire climate change reports from around the world, and the political mess in D.C., but Stefan kept coming back to his outrage about the texts being out in public.

"Texting is worse than Twitter," he said. "It's way too easy to vent without thinking, and any text or tweet can look terrible read the wrong way, read without context. I know it's probably bizarre to defend Ciska, given what she's been trying to do to you, but—"

"—No it's not. You were shafted by the cops, too." And then for some reason I said, "But you're white and privileged so nobody shot you and claimed they thought you had a gun."

He didn't seem to follow me, so I quickly added, "I mean, of course it was bad enough, but who knows how much worse Ciska would have been treated if she were Black or Latina."

He cocked his head at me the way Marco does when we say something he doesn't understand.

"I'm not making much sense, am I? I didn't think so. This whole situation is unnerving." My thoughts were way too jumbled right then.

Stefan nodded and closed his eyes tightly, either starting to relive the events of that horrendous night of his arrest last May or else trying to exorcise them. Me, I took a sip of the smooth Sonoma Zinfandel we were drinking, and reached down with my free hand to scratch the back of Marco's neck. I'm sure he would have preferred a piece of sausage, but physical contact was a close second to food for him.

Stefan had slumped in his chair, ignoring dinner, me, even Marco. To shake him out of his reverie, I asked for the second time that evening, "What do you think Roberto meant when he said Boris wasn't an angel?"

That worked: he sat up straighter and lifted his chin higher. "I don't think he meant anything. Everyone liked Boris, apparently, so Roberto has to slime him, because he obviously knows better than the rest of us, he has the scoop on everything, and he loves disparaging people. He's a true narcissist."

"So you think it was just him mouthing off?"

"I do. You can't trust anything that Robustelli says. He's crazed. And jealous, I guess. He collects grievances."

"So...did Ciska kill Boris?"

Stefan shrugged. "I don't trust the police leaking her texts—because who else could have?—but yes, maybe she did kill him. Why not? It didn't have to be planned. A jealous rage would do it."

I remembered lines from another Joseph Kanon thriller, "Who knows what goes on between people? Not even them sometimes."

My cell phone rang and it was Vanessa: "Nick, you're off the hook, officially. You are no longer a person of interest."

"Is this for real?"

"It is."

"Okay, then."

"You don't sound pleased."

I hesitated. "It's hard to feel happy with everything still so chaotic."

"I get that. It'll sink in after a while, trust me."

When she ended the call, I asked Stefan, "Do you think those texts are *really* Ciska's?"

He shrugged. "Why wouldn't they be?"

"Someone could have hacked her phone, right?" It did indeed feel strange to be defending Ciska, if that's what I was doing, but I think I had become poisoned by the miasma of suspicion and paranoia pervading our campus. I had no idea anymore what was true, what made sense, or even whom to believe.

I needed a gigantic psychic cleanse. Was that available on Amazon, I wonder?

"Nick, they could have been lovers and Boris dumped her, or he was sleeping around and she found out and got angry and dumped him. Lots of things can go wrong in an affair. Maybe it wasn't anything more than just a hook-up and he wanted out or she did. Who the hell knows what anyone might do under extreme stress or rage?"

I flushed because years ago, not long after we came to SUM, I had briefly wondered if Stefan might have done away with an ex-lover who had been hired to teach in our department and was keen to make trouble for the two of us. And somehow that brought me back to Roberto's assertion that Boris was no angel. He'd sounded so sure, so definite, as if he knew something personally, not via rumors or gossip.

"Oh, shit," I said. "I forgot to tell you! We're having a department party this Saturday afternoon. *Here*."

Stefan breathed in deeply, then out again as if preparing himself for an ordeal, but all he said was, "Your idea?"

"Celine's."

"Okay. New chair. Unhappy faculty. Scandal. I guess it adds up, I guess she's right. Let the healing begin. I assume she'll get everything set up, caterer, whatever?"

I nodded. "She and Aldo are making all the arrangements. You know they'll get it all done right."

"We'll have to keep Marco on a leash so he doesn't slip out onto the street with all those people coming in and out."

"No problem." He was a very social dog and would love the hubbub.

Dinner over, we loaded the dishwasher and I said, "My intuition tells me that Roberto wasn't bullshitting. He *knows* something." I remembered a line from an Agatha Christie novel I had taught one semester, though the book's title escaped me, "Very few of us are what we seem."

"It's easy to find out if you're right," Stefan said, adding a soap pod, pressing the button for the long cycle and shutting the dishwasher door. The heavy lemony scent wafted up at me as soon as the water started flowing.

"How's that?" I asked.

He grinned. "Roberto will be at the party Saturday, right? The invitation went to the whole department and he's clearly not being a hermit."

"And?"

"We have to get his phone away from him and see if there's anything revealing or incriminating on there."

"Right—like ambiguous text messages?"

"No. If he's got something to hide himself, it's on his phone. That's *my* intuition talking."

"And we'll do this how? Hire a pickpocket?"

Almost jaunty, Stefan said, "We'll figure it out."

The opportunity will present itself, I mused, but then I asked, "Wouldn't the police have confiscated his phone when he was arrested?"

"I thought the same thing. If they did, he'd have a new one and could have downloaded emails, photos, whatever from the Cloud. And if he didn't have his phone on him when he was arrested, or if the cops couldn't find it, then we're okay, too."

"How do you know all that?"

He shrugged. "I saw it on some crime show you slept through."

We picked something familiar and escapist to watch that night, *The Bourne Identity*. We'd seen it so often we knew all the dialogue from most of the scenes, but as the titles were coming up, I got a call from my cousin Sharon in New York and we paused the film.

"Nick," she said softly, "I should have reached out sooner but, well…"

Sharon was a former fashion model-turned-librarian who had gone on disability after brain surgery and a stroke, and I was the one who owed *her* a call. When she was out of touch it was usually because she was depressed or had some new health issue. But not this time.

"I've been completely absorbed in writing a memoir," she said brightly, her voice as rich and smooth as a late night radio DJ's. "About everything that's happened to me, to my health in the last fifteen years." Until her surgery for an acoustic neuroma she had been an active jogger, hot yoga enthusiast, and used to swim three times a week. All that faded from her life, and it reminded me every time we spoke how precarious health is. Luckily she now lived in the same Upper West Side apartment building in Manhattan as my parents, so I knew she was only as alone as she wanted to be, and there was always someone able to check on her.

"A memoir? That's great!"

"I think I've learned so much about hospitals and doctors,

what to say and do, what to beware of, how things can go wrong, who to rely on, when you might need private nursing. It's a whole different world and I can give people a kind of road map. I just don't have a title yet. Maybe Stefan will have some ideas. But tell me about SUM first. The news sounds dreadful."

I filled her in on everything that had happened in the last week. It took quite a while, and she prompted me now and then when I lost steam with "And then?" or "Seriously?" or "Unbelievable!"

"So you don't think the woman they arrested really did it?" she asked when I was finished, and I felt like the Ancient Mariner in Coleridge's poem having unreeled a long and half-mad narrative. "But what about the kid who keeps lying to you? What if he's the murderer? Isn't there some kind of connection there somehow? Doesn't he have a Dutch name and isn't the dead guy Dutch, the one with a Spanish surname? Maybe it's my chemo brain, but I feel like you said some things that fit together."

"Huh. I hadn't thought about that." Peter had lied to me, that was for sure, and he had a somewhat violent past. Could he have been Boris's lover? Could they have met on that boat cruise? Was the watch Peter wore a gift Boris gave him? The questions made me dizzy.

"Well, you know how it sometimes plays out in mysteries, right? The person who couldn't have done it *is* the killer, or it's someone who's the least likely. If this woman, Ciska, was having a fling with your victim, it's almost too obvious that she did it. Too much 'Hell hath no fury like a woman scorned.'"

"Maybe there's DNA evidence."

"And maybe not. She wouldn't be the first person being railroaded by the police."

We chewed that over a little, and even though I was intrigued by the idea of who might be most unlikely to have murdered Boris, it demanded a total shift away from how I'd been thinking about his death. I didn't feel flexible or sharp enough at the moment to suddenly change course.

I passed Stefan the phone and for a few minutes they talked about memoirs and publishing, and he said he'd send her some reading recommendations, and yes, he would be happy to read her book when she was done and suggest agents if he didn't think his agent was right for her.

When he handed the phone back, Sharon said, "Even if that Ciska person didn't kill—what's his name again?—Boris, those texts you told me about might still be a clue to who did. Why was she warning him? Don't assume it was just rage-texting or that she was drunk. She could have been stone-cold sober and calm and really worried about him as a friend."

"That actually makes a lot of sense." But then Sharon always did, even when she was down or worried about some new threat to her health.

"Sweetie," she said gently, "have you ever thought about leaving that madhouse and living in New York again? Think about the museums, the concerts, the plays, the recitals. Stefan could see his agent and his publisher whenever he wanted to, and I know your parents would love to have you visit more often. So would I."

I told her we'd actually considered retiring early and living in our condo in Ludington. Thought about it *a lot*.

"Okay, then you could find a pied-à-terre here. Or you could look for something bigger in New Jersey, like in North Bergen. The views of Manhattan are fantastic and rents are super affordable—compared to Manhattan or Brooklyn—if you didn't want to buy a place."

I was old enough to remember when "Jersey" was a general laugh line for native New Yorkers, but I had been following the explosion of great housing there, and what she said was sorely tempting.

"How did all this start for you, Nick? All the chaos at SUM?" She added after a pause, "The new stuff, I mean." She already knew my whole gory history on campus.

"I guess it's been about a week." I told her how Dawn Love-

lace's invitation-cum-order to take on the Swedish program
seemed to have set the juggernaut in motion.

"Oh, no, don't go to Sweden as a job. Go for fun. The last thing
you need is supervising students and troubleshooting. When I
was in college and did a summer program in Rome we drove the
professors crazy. We skipped classes, got drunk and high, and had
sex constantly. I picked up some Italian and saw a lot of ruins and
art, but that was way at the bottom of my list."

I laughed, remembering a phrase from Byron: "In my hot
youth."

"Okay, I have to go, sweetie, want to get back to my book. Call
me this weekend and let me know how you're doing."

Even though we'd been discussing very dark things, I felt
refreshed by her call.

Before I could share her insights with Stefan, Roberto Robustelli's caller ID came through. Was this guy ever going to leave
me alone? I could see him writing me letters from prison. I didn't
take his call and he left a message which I thought about eras-
ing without listening to, but Stefan said, "No, put it on speaker
phone—he's a trip."

The message was short and loud: "Dude! The party idea is
fucking brilliant. They all hate you and there you'll be, lording it
over everybody. I can't wait to see those motherfuckers squirm!"

Stefan chuckled.

"It's not funny! We've got an accused murderer who's awaiting
trial coming to our party."

"Hey—even if Celine thought about taking him off the mailing
list, he would have heard about the party and showed up anyway.
Roberto is irrepressible."

"I can think of some other things to call him."

"Text him," Stefan said. "Not to insult him, but to say you're
glad he's coming. Soften him up."

"Why?"

"It'll put him off his guard, and who knows, maybe he'll let
something slip about Boris."

"There's something else going on," I mused as I sent off the text. "You want to see him in action, don't you? So you can put him in a book? You think he's...*material.*"

Stefan grinned. "Maybe. Is that so wrong? You have to admit he's colorful, one hundred percent unique."

"He's so over-the-top, wouldn't you have to tone him down? "

"Yes, in a book. But right now, in real life, I'm beginning to think he holds the key to Boris's murder."

I found myself wishing I could read minds, but then I remembered words of Hercule Poirot: "Unless you are good at guessing, it is not much use being a detective." Guesswork would have to do for now. The tension was obviously getting to me, and my thoughts were crowded with all the crime fiction I'd read over the years. Val McDermid and Walter Mosley were probably next.

"Listen," Stefan said, "it's getting late, why don't we turn off our phones and watch the movie?"

We did, after pouring ourselves a few fingers each of Glenlivet. *The Bourne Identity* was a perfect escape, familiar but exciting. We were swept away by the propulsive action, the driving music, and Jason Bourne's relentless search to find out who he was and escape whoever was after him.

Perhaps perversely, I felt sorry for the assassin sent to kill Bourne in the French countryside, the one whose last words were "Look at what they make you give."

Stefan fell asleep easily that night when we went to bed, was soon breathing as peacefully as if he were in a commercial about the ideal mattress. Me, I was unable to unwind, unable to stop sorting through the grotesque events of the day. Surveying the pile of fiction, histories, and biographies on my bedside table—some of which Sharon had sent me—I picked a short novel by Somerset Maugham, *Up at the Villa,* and tried to lose myself in it.

The book was set in Florence and the distraction started to work as I imagined myself on the heroine's terrace "from which she could see the domes and towers of Florence." I could picture moonlight on her cypress trees and hear her fountain. And

I remembered being with Stefan there after listening to Gregorian chant in ancient San Miniato with its green-and-white marble façade, and emerging into the sunlight to gaze in unvarnished wonder at the city far below. Maugham's book was flooding me with memories. Stefan and I stayed at a hotel on the quiet side of the Arno River, and one wall of the terrace where we took our breakfast was covered with flowering jasmine. I could almost smell it all over again as I fell asleep with the book in my hands.

20.

THE DAYS BEFORE the party flew past in a blur as Ciska's arrest and Boris's murder completely swamped SUM's admissions scandal. I felt as if I had been sucked through a black hole into a world ruled by tabloid headlines. Fox News was especially brutal, variously calling for SUM to be shut down, privatized, turned into an Army base, sold to the Chinese, and burned to the ground. The only thing they did not call for was salting the earth the way the Romans did to Carthage. "Nest of Killers" was one of their mildest chyrons.

Amid the furor, I began to suspect the university administration of manipulating the media, doing damage control by feeding the press incendiary information about Boris and Ciska, stoking suspicion about one story in order to hide another, one that was much more damaging. But if that was indeed the case, it didn't last. *The Washington Post* published a report quoting anonymous sources who revealed a deeply entrenched system of bribery at SUM. No names were mentioned specifically, but the bare outlines were damning enough. The Admissions Office released a statement denying the report, but within a day, SUM's Public Relations Office announced an internal investigation.

If the official stance changed in twenty-four hours, the truth had to be dire. Otherwise, the denials would have gone on much longer in spite of the media maelstrom. And why else would two members of the Board of Trustees resign "to pursue other opportunities" and have no comment about the timing of their departure? Were their resignations due to the guilt of complicity, or a protest? In either case, they were eviscerated on Twitter by SUM alumni because even though they were Michiganders, they had committed the sacrilegious act, years ago, of earning advanced degrees out of state. "Traitors," "Human Scum," "Enemies of SUM" were just a few of the digital hand grenades being thrown at them.

It didn't end there: Fabian Flick's paper ran a story whose headline read MICHIGAN PARENTS CHARGED WITH BRIBERY AND FRAUD. It was all about Peter's parents and though I should have known something like this was likely, I was still shocked. Even SUM administrators were being rounded up and questioned in connection with those bribery charges.

But that was only the beginning of the storm. The U.S. Department of Education announced that it would be conducting its own independent investigation about under-reporting of sexual assault at SUM as well as other crimes like burglary and assault. Now there was the threat of massive fines along with the promise that SUM would be even more under the microscope than ever before.

How I longed to escape to a far-away isle.

Back at home, Stefan kept saying things like, "We're living in the shadow of a volcano that's slowly erupting" and "I think I should rewrite my book and work all this into it." It was getting harder to tell with him where disgust and disillusionment ended and a writer's lust for juicy material began.

Given the feverish media scrutiny, I was surprised that none of the reporters was writing about the Committee of Public Safety, but maybe that, too, was coming.

Then Fabian Flick called once more to request another interview.

"Given the latest developments at SUM, I want to profile you," he said. "It would be sympathetic. You know, charting a course through rocky seas."

His metaphor was all wrong. We were more like those poor

Russian sailors trapped in a sunken submarine, in the Barents Sea way back in 2000, but I neither agreed nor disagreed, simply said that I would consider it. Which seemed to satisfy him, for now.

"What do you think this will do to our students?" Stefan wondered. "Some kids are triggered simply by the hint of anything violent in assigned readings."

"It's probably smart to not talk about it, and if anyone brings it up, just say it's an ongoing criminal investigation."

"Isn't that censorship?"

"Of course it is, but I'd prefer that to being raked over the coals by other faculty."

Sharon called me as soon as the bad press went nuclear and said, "Nick, if you can quit, get out now or as soon as you're able. That place is a cesspool. You'll always be tainted if you stay there."

"But I *live* here, it's my home!" Somehow it felt cowardly to throw up my hands and quit because of the chaos and adverse publicity swirling about us.

"Think of it this way: you're like a victim of climate change, like all those people out here on the East Coast whose beaches have washed away or had their homes totaled by a hurricane, or over in California where the wildfires are raging out of control and turning paradise into a living hell. Life at SUM isn't sustainable. That place is a disaster."

"I can't just cut and run."

"Oh yes you can. Talk to a financial advisor, talk to whoever's at the university who can explain early retirement. Make plans."

"But I love teaching, you know that."

"Will how much you enjoy being in a classroom be enough to counter-balance the insanity?"

It was a good question, and I told her so. But Sharon was a loving friend even more than a close relative, so she knew when to stop pushing, and immediately switched the subject to something seemingly more pleasant: the faculty party. I assured her that everything was under control thanks to Celine and Aldo and

Chuck's Restaurant, which had catered other gatherings at our house previously.

"I wish I could be there!" But I knew Sharon's health problems prevented her from flying on airplanes.

"I know, it would be great. And Marco would be thrilled."

"Tell me about the food."

I did. But I did not tell her about how Stefan and I were planning to get hold of Robustelli's cell phone at the party. She would have said we were utterly crazy, and who could blame her? Roberto was combustible, and a murder suspect awaiting trial, so there was no predicting how he would react if he caught us.

Don't get caught was my mantra for the fateful afternoon of the party.

• • •

The news was beginning to disturb our department in ever-more weird ways. On the day of the party, I received an email signed by all the graduate students and copied to the rest of the department that slammed me personally:

> Professor Hoffman, at a time of grief, mourning, and controversy, we believe that holding any sort of festive event is not only inappropriate but insulting. We cannot be diverted by bread and circuses! Parties that bring together graduate students and professors are a sham since they pretend the hierarchy doesn't exist and we are all equal members of a community of knowledge and inquiry. Furthermore, we believe that your appointment as chair of this department is illegitimate, an administrative coup, and we demand that you step down and we the graduate students be allowed to veto any candidate who does not respect our needs.

This was the first rumbling of discontent I had heard from that quarter, and I was too worn out to be upset or angry, so I decided to wait awhile until I could consider what needed to be done. Luckily, neither Stefan nor I taught graduate students, who seemed to be turning as fractious as the faculty. It was undoubtedly a displacement: there were hardly any jobs in English and it had to dawn on them that all they were good for was a source of cheap labor to teach undergraduates. But I felt guilty for not having met with them before this to introduce myself. I hadn't even thought about trying to find someone to take the position of associate chair for graduate studies. No wonder they felt ignored, outraged, out for blood.

Stefan didn't care what might be driving them. "They think *you're* illegitimate? What about the ridiculous research *they're* doing? One of those geniuses is writing a dissertation about Madonna! What the hell does that have to do with English, with literary studies?"

"She did publish a book, once."

"Yes! A book of nude photographs. And if they have problems with your appointment, why didn't they raise them with the dean? What are you supposed to do, march yourself off to the guillotine?"

"I guess they're locavores. They want to chew someone up, so they reach for whoever's nearest."

"I wish that were funnier."

"I know. It should be, but it's not."

Stefan was so angry he changed and went out for a run to burn off his feelings. I was just feeling burnt out, which was okay at the moment, but how long would it last? How long would *I* last as department chair?

• • •

By the time Chuck's catering truck pulled up that Saturday afternoon, I had been so bombarded by all the negative press—which when it focused on me personally, called me everything from a raving queen to a pillar of the white supremacist hierarchy—that I was ready to call the whole thing off, get in the car, and just drive as far away as I could manage. Argentina was sounding pretty good.

Of course escape was impossible, and when Peter jumped out of the van, dressed in his waiter's garb, I briefly thought that perhaps the party would go some small way toward healing the various wounds among our faculty and perhaps even create a bit of good feeling. But I was worried about him. Was he going to be charged along with his parents, and if he wasn't, how would he deal with their crimes?

"Professor Hoffman, when I heard it was your party," he said, "I asked for the assignment." He seemed completely unruffled.

"That's great," I said, feeling a twinge of discomfort about him inserting himself in a more intimate setting than the classroom, my office, or even the restaurant. But that feeling passed by the time Peter was finished efficiently and quickly setting everything up, after many trips to the van plus consulting with me and Stefan about what would go where. He was cool and professional, and anyone who didn't know would never have guessed that his parents were in the news and that he was my student.

"Grace under pressure" was Stefan's only comment.

Our living room was a dramatic setting: brushed black slate tile floor, a wall of windows looking out at the small backyard's towering hemlocks and under-story of holly shrubs. The walls were all white, and for contrast we'd hung framed Mark Rothko posters in orange and yellow.

For the party, we'd moved the dining room chairs out to the garage so people could have freer access to the food. At the center of the mahogany table loomed a large baked *Brie en croute* with bowls of fig spread. It was surrounded by colorful platters of crab cakes, coconut shrimp, vegetable spring rolls, Swedish meatballs, empanadas, and tandoori chicken on skewers. The dessert tray laid out neat circles of baklava, miniature blondie brownies, and Russian teacakes.

The wine from Michigan's Chateau Chantal winery on Old Mission Peninsula was a Cabernet Franc and a late-harvest Riesling. Peter set all that up on the sideboard along with the plates, glassware, cutlery, and serviettes supplied by Chuck's. At the center was a huge vase of flowers that Sharon had sent us with a "Good Luck!" card: yellow roses, orange Peruvian lilies, and baby's breath.

Peter showed no signs of stress or apprehension about the burgeoning admissions scandal. He told us to call when the party was over and he would return to handle the cleanup and help us package leftovers.

When he was gone, Stefan said, "I guess he's resigned to whatever's going to happen to his parents, and to him." He put some classic Ella Fitzgerald on the CD player and her mellow, upbeat voice was Valium for my troubled soul.

• • •

As the first cars pulled up outside, I realized that given the recent turnover in faculty, I hardly knew anyone well and I should have studied the department website to familiarize myself with people's research and publications. Better still, I should have arranged one-on-one get-acquainted meetings with all the faculty. I expressed my misgivings to Stefan who pointed out that I'd been just a little too busy these past two weeks for planning anything like that.

"Don't worry about today. Just ask what people are working on now," Stefan advised. "That's my plan. It'll sound like you know what they've already published."

He was right. As the first faculty members arrived, some of them with spouses and partners, but many of them solo, I was embarrassed that so few of them looked especially familiar. But when I welcomed them and asked about their current projects, everyone seemed happy to launch into a monologue, helped by occasional interjections of "Really?" "Wow." "I did not know that."

Celine and Aldo arrived together and took it upon themselves to steer people to the food and wine, while Stefan schmoozed every new arrival comfortably, as if he were at one of his book signings. Soon after he got there, Aldo sidled up to me and asked softly, "Did you see the story about Peter's parents? I bet this is

244. 244.

just the beginning. They can't be the only ones involved. It's just going to get worse and worse." He looked disconsolate—working at a scandal-ridden university would be bad for anyone's morale.

Within half an hour, the house was buzzing, guests were clustered around the food and wine, also chatting in the living room and the kitchen, and circulating through those connected rooms. A few were even stationed in the hallway, either waiting to greet newcomers or else ready to make a quick exit. Nobody seemed to be having an especially good time: there was no laughter and barely any smiling, despite the lively music playing. But then Ciska had just been arrested, so what should I have expected?

I tried to keep track of the names of people's partners and spouses as they introduced themselves, but it all blurred very quickly.

Carson Karageorgevich walked in looking like death eating a sandwich, nodded at us and headed straight for the wine, followed by Jasmine Aminejad, who actually ignored us in our own home, sallied up to the food, surveyed it with disdain, and then stalked out to the kitchen. To complain? To mock us? To scrawl graffiti on a wall?

Marco, to his credit, growled at her. Otherwise he was quiet and we needn't have worried about him slipping out the front door. He was too intent on keeping the food company in the obvious hope that some scrap, some crumb would fall onto the floor.

Roberto Robustelli showed up as we had expected and he bounced around the room like a cruise ship activity director who was frantic to keep people busy and entertained. Every now and then, like most of the faculty, he'd check his phone and sometimes put it down on the nearest table or shelf, to leave his hands free for eating.

Having made the rounds, he swept over to me and Stefan and pumped our hands as if we'd won some kind of award or he was a glad-handing politician. "You guys are the fucking best!" he said, and I wondered if he had gotten high before the party because I hadn't seen him drink anything yet, though he seemed way too enthusiastic to be sober. "Everyone's talking about what a great house you have and how terrific the food is."

We'd barely had any compliments on either yet—or even neutral comments—so I assumed he was just bullshitting us, though why he would was beyond me. I watched him, and so did Stefan. Like almost everyone there, he was either on his phone with someone or checking Twitter and email. They were all as phone-crazed and as easily distracted as any of my students in class.

Stefan shadowed him discreetly, though I still didn't see how he was going to snatch Roberto's phone without him noticing—or if it would even matter.

But then I saw him stop at the sideboard, set his phone down as he poured himself some of the Riesling, down a whole glass at once, then head right toward me to ask where he could take a leak. I told him he'd find the powder room straight through the kitchen and my eyes went wide as he headed that way without picking up his phone. Stefan drifted up to where the phone lay, palmed it, and hurried over.

I prayed that the phone wasn't password-protected and my prayers were answered. Stefan was busily working the iPhone's photo app, with images whizzing past.

"What are you doing?" I whispered. I confess I'm old-fashioned and preferred a real camera over my phone, especially since trying to figure out the photo app on my phone always left me frustrated.

"I'm in Years and going to Months—I'm looking for something incriminating."

"You better be quick."

Stefan said a quiet "Wow" and pointed Roberto's phone at me. On screen was a selfie of Boris and Roberto in bed, both fully nude. There were more selfies and they were grinning like they were stoned or stupid. In some of the photos they were as tangled as the snakes on Medusa's head. But there were also photos of Ciska and Boris just as frantically enmeshed.

There weren't any of the three of them together.

"But wasn't she sleeping with Carson?" Stefan asked. "And Viktor?"

"Hey, no slut-shaming! She can sleep with anyone she wants to." Maybe that was the only thing keeping her sane in our madhouse of a department. And if I weren't married, who knows what I'd be doing, and with whom.

But why take photos? I knew that sexting, nude selfies, and sex tapes were epidemic in our culture, yet I had never understood why anyone would bother with that homemade porn. Was an affair or even a simple hook-up unreal until it was photographed? And who else in the department was busy foolishly documenting their sexcapades?

"That's why Ciska sent Boris those texts warning him to stop," Stefan said as quietly as he could. "She was furious that he was cheating on her."

Could you really be jealous when you had more than one lover? Well, why not?

"So you're saying that Ciska *did* kill Boris? Or was she warning Boris about Roberto, telling him to break it off because Roberto is dangerous and should be in prison?" I asked.

"I think she was warning him," Stefan said. "Roberto isn't playing with a full deck, he's not just inappropriate, he's combustible, he's nuts, and for God's sake, he's going to be tried for murder already. What if Boris tried to break it off with him and Roberto just lost it and killed him? And he thought he could get away with it because who would suspect him?"

It made total sense. He was the classic murderer who instead of hiding, kept showing up and showing up as if to parade his innocence. No wonder he hadn't been holed up in his apartment—he was as conspicuously present as he could be, to "prove" that he had nothing to do with Boris's murder. I'd seen it in enough cop shows—why hadn't I recognized what he was up to?

Stefan shuffled out of the photo file quicker than I could have done and stealthily returned the phone to where Roberto had left it. When Roberto came back through the kitchen, he beelined for his phone, grabbed it, and waded back into the crowded living room.

I kept my voice low because I was so shocked and I could see Aldo and Celine staring at us, aware that something was up. "But we still don't know why Boris called and wanted to talk to me. Why not you? You knew him from the gym."

"Maybe that's why. It would have felt awkward. But he met you at the restaurant and—I don't know—you're out, he felt comfortable and he needed to talk to someone about what was going on in his life, but someone who wasn't close. Friends aren't always the best person to confide in."

"Really?"

"And he could have admired the way you stood up to Bullerschmidt. Just because Boris worked with him so closely doesn't mean it was a comfortable place to be."

I chewed that over for a moment. "Okay, so what happens now?"

"We have to tell Detective Valley about the photos."

"Tell him that we took someone's phone and invaded their privacy? Isn't that illegal? It's probably a felony!"

"If it is, who cares? If Roberto killed Boris, that's a hell of a lot more important. Vanessa would help us if we were charged and it came to trial, and what jury wouldn't be sympathetic?"

I couldn't get my mind around this newest revelation. While Roberto was awaiting trial for one murder, he went ahead and murdered someone else? Unbelievable. But par for the course at SUM's Department of Death.

Before we could hash out what exactly to do next, Stefan didn't wait: he got out his phone and shot off a quick text to Detective Valley. "It's up to Valley to sort things out now," he said with the gravity of a climatologist pronouncing global doom. Valley texted him right back, and Stefan whispered, "He said they're on their way and to keep an eye on Roberto and let him know if he tries to leave."

"Are we supposed to stop him?"

Stefan shrugged.

I thought our lives couldn't get any crazier and I was wrong.

Because that's when the twins arrived, a double vision in purple, armed with what looked like flyers, but turned out to be something very different. They ignored the food and wine and stood side-by-side in the living room in front of the fireplace after handing two small stacks of paper to whoever was standing closest. "Please pass those along," they said in unison, but began speaking before everyone had a copy, alternating between them as if following a script they'd practiced.

Heino, I think, started and as he continued, more and more people filtered into the living room. "We are here under protest," he said and there was a ripple of sotto voce comments.

Stefan frowned. "What the hell is he talking about?"

"Maybe this is about the graduate students."

"And he came to say he doesn't want to be here? That's bizarre." I thought of the old Groucho Marx song lines, "I cannot stay/I came to say/I must be going."

But what followed was way more bizarre than that. Sweeping the room with an angry gaze, Heino continued: "This department has a long history of endemic xenophobia—consider what happened after a scholar of French origin was recently appointed chair."

Well, the previous chair had indeed been murdered, but nobody claimed that it was due to his being French. Where was this stunt going?

The flyers or whatever they were finally reached me and Stefan in the dining room but neither of us took one. Whatever it was, I sure didn't want to touch it because I felt certain it spelled trouble.

"We have learned from our esteemed Dean Bullerschmidt that like Yale, SUM is planning to revise its mission statement to focus on the promotion of diversity, inclusion, leadership, social justice, and action."

That was news to me. What about the pursuit of knowledge?

"So then, we inform you that German Americans are making up a full fifth of Michigan's population," Heino said, raising his voice to be heard over Ella Fitzgerald who was singing "When I Get Low I Get High."

"Therefore, in recognition of German-American contributions to Michigan, the Midwest, and the esteemed United States, we demand more representation of German Americans on the faculty of this department, and we demand active recruiting of German-American students for our graduate program."

His brother, Jonas, continued from there: "To balance courses on the Holocaust offered in various departments and programs, we demand that German history seminars, workshops, and other educational opportunities be offered on a regular basis campus-wide, but excluding the 1933—1945 period, and that the university set up a German Cultural Center as a safe space."

Now Heino picked up, his small voice steady. "Because faculty and students freely apply terms of denigration like 'jack-booted thugs' and 'brown shirts' and 'Nazis' that rightly offend all German-American students, we demand that the department issue a clear statement disavowing these terms and forbidding faculty and students from using them in their classes. Faculty will be required to sign a statement avowing their abhorrence of these terms and pledging never to use them under any circumstances whatsoever."

My head was spinning. Didn't the department, and the university, already have hate speech policies in place? And these guys wanted more than that, some kind of oath? Sealed in blood, perhaps?

Now Jonas took the torch. "Given the vast ignorance of both German and German-American culture, along with the equally vast ignorance of German cultural sensitivities, we demand mandatory diversity training for all faculty including adjuncts and graduate students, to alert them to the special issues of *this* population. We also demand access to all classes at any time whatsoever to monitor content that might be anti-German."

"This sounds Stalinist," Stefan whispered to me. "They want to be commissars." Someone we couldn't see shushed him as if we were at a chamber music recital.

Jonas went on: "And at the end of every semester, German-American students as well as faculty shall be given the opportunity to air their grievances and confront perpetrators of anti-German stereotypes in a public forum."

"Errant faculty who refuse diversity training to combat this xenophobia," Heino intoned, "or whose behavior is egregious and offensive should be denied travel funding, denied the ability to serve on dissertation committees, and their assignment to graduate courses should be immediately curtailed, pending review by a joint board of German-American faculty and students which will have final say over all such matters."

If my hair wasn't standing on end at that point, it should have been. Working with graduate students was considered a plum by many professors, since the classes were smaller and pitched at a higher level. And this new board being proposed—how could that possibly function? Could it even be allowed under university by-laws?

Red in the face now, Jonas finished the job: "Any attempts to deny the toxic reality of institutional and systemic anti-German xenophobia will ipso facto be an effort to derail our vital discussion of diversity. The perpetrators of this outrage against community standards should be called out for their bigotry and automatically banned from the classroom. Any other decisions made by this Board of Review in regards to disciplinary action will be final and irrevocable."

Except for Ella singing a song whose title I couldn't recall, there was eerie quiet when the twins stopped speaking. And then to my dismay, well over half of the faculty present applauded, whooping and yelling their approval. Robustelli was one of the loudest, his devilish eyes sparkling with mischief. Was he behind this somehow, on top of likely being a double murderer?

Carson was doing that celebratory ululating as if he was at

a wedding or some other Third World celebration and my first thought was that someone in the department would soon be calling him out for "cultural appropriation" since he was white. For all I knew, though, maybe they did celebrate like that in Serbia.

Everyone else was silent. That's when I remembered a Latin phrase that my European-educated mother often quoted from her school days: *Cum tacent, clament.*

Loosely translated, it meant, "They screamed in silence."

And so did I.

. . .

ACKNOWLEDGMENTS

ONE OF the best parts of writing crime fiction is interviewing professionals about the work they love. My thanks go to Linda Cornish for explaining her jobs as financial officer and office manager; David Stowe for sharing experiences as a new department chair; Michael Koppisch for his insights into the world of administrators; Marty Vander Vliet for his expertise on surveillance technology; Owen Deatrick for information about surveillance and police procedure; and Mary Chartier for explaining complicated legal issues. I also owe a great debt of thanks to GK Consulting, Inc. for timely and inspiring input.

ABOUT THE AUTHOR

Lev Raphael is the author of twenty-six books in genres from memoir to mystery. His work has been translated into over a dozen languages and he's also the author of hundreds of short stories, essays, and blogs. He was born and raised in Manhattan but has lived more than half his life in Michigan and reviewed crime fiction at the *Detroit Free Press* for over a decade.

More Traditional Mysteries from Perseverance Press
For the New Golden Age

K.K. Beck
WORKPLACE SERIES
Tipping the Valet
ISBN 978-1-56474-563-7

Albert A. Bell, Jr.
PLINY THE YOUNGER SERIES
Death in the Ashes
ISBN 978-1-56474-532-3

The Eyes of Aurora
ISBN 978-1-56474-549-1

Fortune's Fool
ISBN 978-1-56474-587-3

The Gods Help Those
ISBN 978-1-56474-608-5

Hiding from the Past
ISBN 978-1-56474-610-8

Taffy Cannon
ROXANNE PRESCOTT SERIES
Guns and Roses
Agatha and Macavity awards nominee, Best Novel
ISBN 978-1-880284-34-6

Blood Matters
ISBN 978-1-880284-86-5

Open Season on Lawyers
ISBN 978-1-880284-51-3

Paradise Lost
ISBN 978-1-880284-80-3

Laura Crum
GAIL MCCARTHY SERIES
Moonblind
ISBN 978-1-880284-90-2

Chasing Cans
ISBN 978-1-880284-94-0

Going, Gone
ISBN 978-1-880284-98-8

Barnstorming
ISBN 978-1-56474-508-8

Jeanne M. Dams
HILDA JOHANSSON SERIES
Crimson Snow
ISBN 978-1-880284-79-7

Indigo Christmas
ISBN 978-1-880284-95-7

Murder in Burnt Orange
ISBN 978-1-56474-503-3

Janet Dawson
JERI HOWARD SERIES
Bit Player
Golden Nugget Award nominee
ISBN 978-1-56474-494-4

Cold Trail
ISBN 978-1-56474-555-2

Water Signs
ISBN 978-1-56474-586-6

The Devil Close Behind
ISBN 978-1-56474-606-1

What You Wish For
ISBN 978-1-56474-518-7

TRAIN SERIES
Death Rides the Zephyr
ISBN 978-1-56474-530-9

Death Deals a Hand
ISBN 978-1-56474-569-9

The Ghost in Roomette Four
ISBN 978-1-56474-598-9

Death Above the Line
ISBN 978-1-56474-618-4

Kathy Lynn Emerson
LADY APPLETON SERIES
Face Down Below the Banqueting House
ISBN 978-1-880284-71-1

Face Down Beside St. Anne's Well
ISBN 978-1-880284-82-7

Face Down O'er the Border
ISBN 978-1-880284-91-9

Margaret Grace
MINIATURE SERIES
Mix-up in Miniature
ISBN 978-1-56474-510-1

Madness in Miniature
ISBN 978-1-56474-543-9

Manhattan in Miniature
ISBN 978-1-56474-562-0

Matrimony in Miniature
ISBN 978-1-56474-575-0

Tony Hays
Shakespeare No More
ISBN 978-1-56474-566-8

Wendy Hornsby
MAGGIE MACGOWEN SERIES
In the Guise of Mercy
ISBN 978-1-56474-482-1

The Paramour's Daughter
ISBN 978-1-56474-496-8

The Hanging
ISBN 978-1-56474-526-2

The Color of Light
ISBN 978-1-56474-542-2

Disturbing the Dark
ISBN 978-1-56474-576-7

Number 7, Rue Jacob
ISBN 978-1-56474-599-6

A Bouquet of Rue
ISBN 978-1-56474-607-8

Janet LaPierre
PORT SILVA SERIES
Baby Mine
ISBN 978-1-880284-32-2

Keepers
Shamus Award nominee, Best Paperback Original
ISBN 978-1-880284-44-5

Death Duties
ISBN 978-1-880284-74-2

Family Business
ISBN 978-1-880284-85-8

Run a Crooked Mile
ISBN 978-1-880284-88-9

Lev Raphael
NICK HOFFMAN SERIES
Tropic of Murder
ISBN 978-1-880284-68-1

Hot Rocks
ISBN 978-1-880284-83-4

State University of Murder
ISBN 978-1-56474-609-2

Department of Death
ISBN 978-1-56474-619-1

Lora Roberts
BRIDGET MONTROSE SERIES
Another Fine Mess
ISBN 978-1-880284-54-4

SHERLOCK HOLMES SERIES
The Affair of the Incognito Tenant
ISBN 978-1-880284-67-4

Rebecca Rothenberg
BOTANICAL SERIES
The Tumbleweed Murders
(completed by Taffy Cannon)
ISBN 978-1-880284-43-8

Sheila Simonson
LATOUCHE COUNTY SERIES
Buffalo Bill's Defunct
WILLA Award, Best Softcover Fiction
ISBN 978-1-880284-96-4

An Old Chaos
ISBN 978-1-880284-99-5

Beyond Confusion
ISBN 978-1-56474-519-4

Call Down the Hawk
ISBN 978-1-56474-597-2

Lea Wait
SHADOWS ANTIQUES SERIES
Shadows of a Down East Summer
ISBN 978-1-56474-497-5

Shadows on a Cape Cod Wedding
ISBN 1-978-56474-531-6

Shadows on a Maine Christmas
ISBN 978-1-56474-531-6

Shadows on a Morning in Maine
ISBN 978-1-56474-577-4

Eric Wright
JOE BARLEY SERIES
The Kidnapping of Rosie Dawn
Barry Award, Best Paperback Original. Edgar,
Ellis, and Anthony awards nominee
ISBN 978-1-880284-40-7

Nancy Means Wright
MARY WOLLSTONECRAFT SERIES
Midnight Fires
ISBN 978-1-56474-488-3

The Nightmare
ISBN 978-1-56474-509-5

REFERENCE/MYSTERY WRITING

Kathy Lynn Emerson
*How To Write Killer Historical
Mysteries: The Art and Adventure of
Sleuthing Through the Past*
Agatha Award, Best Nonfiction. Anthony and
Macavity awards nominee
ISBN 978-1-880284-92-6

Carolyn Wheat
*How To Write Killer Fiction:
The Funhouse of Mystery & the Roller
Coaster of Suspense*
ISBN 978-1-880284-62-9

**Available from your local bookstore
or from Perseverance Press/John Daniel & Company
(800) 662–8351 or www.danielpublishing.com/perseverance**